N.P. MARTIN

INFERNAL JUSTICE

ETHAN DRAKE SERIES: BOOK ONE

This is a work of fiction. Names, characters, businesses, places, events and incidents are either the products of the author's imagination or used in a fictitious manner. Any resemblance to actual persons, living or dead, or actual events is purely coincidental

N.P. Martin

Infernal Justice

Ethan Drake Series Book 1

info@npmarin.com

Cover design by Original Book Cover Designs

FREE BOOK

DON'T FORGET! VIP'S get advance notice of all future releases and projects. AND A FREE ETHAN DRAKE NOVELLA! Click the image or join here: www.npmartin.com

FOLLOW and LIKE:
Neal's FACEBOOK PAGE and INSTAGRAM ACCOUNT.
I love interacting with my readers so join me on social media and say hi!

"If these guys are the good guys, I don't want to know the bad. "

— Bruce Hornsby, "Defenders of the Flag"

1

"I *love you, Daddy…*"

I awoke to the sound of my dead daughter's voice echoing in my head, a remnant of the dream—or rather nightmare—I'd been having. Bathed in a cold sweat, I sat up on the couch and groaned at the tightness in my skull before staring into the empty living room, half expecting to see her there, my angel, smiling at me.

Callie…

God, her voice sounded so real…but it wasn't. She was gone, and there was no bringing her back. Not even her ghost remained. Closing my eyes, I waited in vain for the pain to pass, even though I knew it wouldn't. Only the Mud could dull things enough for me to function, and that was locked up in the bedroom, which meant I would have to get up and get it. But only after I'd had a cigarette.

The TV was on and *Apocalypse Now* was still showing. I barely remembered putting the movie on before falling asleep, which meant I hadn't slept for very long. Willard was on his way to kill Kurtz in the final scene. As I stared at the screen, smoking my first cigarette of the day—the first draw like sandpaper against my throat—my phone rang on the table beside me, next to an empty bottle of whiskey and my badge and gun. Picking up the phone, I saw it was Hannah Walker calling. Rather, the celestial being who now occupied Hannah's body, who I still didn't fully trust and probably never will. "Yeah?" I answered, my throat hoarse as I took another drag.

"Ethan. Are you awake?" Walker asked.

"What do you think?"

"There's been another disturbance at Cave Hill Cemetery. More serious this time."

"More serious than the dead dog we took away yesterday?" Walker used to work Vice until she overdosed on a speedball and died. That's when the demon took over her body. Only no one else knows that but me. We became partners a few weeks ago after the police commissioner reassigned me to the station sub-basement to handle the "special cases". It takes one to know one, I suppose.

"A grave was dug up."

"Whose grave?"

Walker paused before answering. "Barbara Keane's."

"Shit, seriously?"

"The press is already all over it. The ones called Stokes and Routman are on the scene now."

"What'd I tell you about talking like that? You wanna blend in here or not?"

"Yes, sorry. I mean Stokes and Routman."

"Better," I said. "Isn't their shift over? What's this have to do with Homicide anyway?"

"Nothing, but they were near the cemetery when the call came in."

"Is the body still there, or was it taken?"

"It was taken," she said. "You think the two incidents are linked?"

"It would be a hell of a coincidence if they weren't," I said, taking a drag on my cigarette.

"There must be some occult connection. Why steal a body, especially one as infamous as Barbara Keane's?"

"Because some fuckwit probably thinks it has special properties." I stabbed my cigarette in a glass ashtray that was overflowing with old butts. "Or maybe they just want to have sex with her corpse."

"Sex with a corpse?"

"What, you think demons have all the fun?" I said. "I know plenty of humans who'd turn even your stomach, Walker, the things they do."

There was a moment's silence, before she said, "Should I pick you up or meet you there?"

I thought for a second. "I'll meet you there shortly."

"Should I bring coffee?"

"I don't know, you tell me."

"Yes?"

"There you go. You're learning. Black, two sugars."

I put the phone back on the table and stared at the TV as Kurtz gave his final speech, moments before he would meet his end at the hands of Willard. "I've *seen horrors…*" he began.

"Yeah?" I turned the TV off. "So have I, pal."

Pulling myself up off the couch, I walked to the tiniest bathroom—for me anyway—in Washington County so I could splash cold water on my face, which did a harsh job of severing any tendrils of sleep that still clung to me. Still in yesterday's shirt and pants, I went into the bedroom that didn't have a bed, but which functioned instead as a storeroom for all my shit. Inside I kept an extensive collection of weapons, stacks of old books and shelves filled with ingredients, some medicinal, some not. Taking a medium-sized glass jar down, I shook the purple liquid inside and stared at its murk for a second or two. Despite being used to the smell, I still recoiled when the acrid scent of the liquid inside the jar hit my nostrils. I placed the open jar on a narrow table that had used containers and spilled ingredients all over it. I took a small dropper bottle out of my pocket and used the dropper inside to suck up the purple liquid. This I did about six times, enough to fill the glass bottle. The last dropper-full I squeezed into my mouth, wincing as usual at the taste—like licorice mixed with blood, with just a hint of absinthe for good measure. Instantly, the effects of the home-brewed substance hit me, soothing my nervous system, smoothing over the turmoil already raging like a motherfucker inside me, pushing it into the background so it no longer interfered with my thinking. Now I could focus on the job without the darkness doing its best to fuck me up.

In the living room, I found my scruffy tan trench coat lying on the floor behind the couch. I gave it a quick shake before putting it on over my shirt and tie, noticing as I did that it was drizzling rain outside. Grim-faced, I acknowledged the Fairview weather for being as predictable as ever before clipping my badge and holster to my belt. I stood for a moment, my muscles relaxing under the influence of the Mud.

Another day ahead without my angel in it.

Another day ahead chasing the darkness, sifting through the detritus it leaves behind like black scum. Someday I won't have to do it anymore. Someday I'll be dead, and I can leave this world to its shit once and for all.

I can only dream…

The sarcasm behind the thought wasn't lost on me as I reached into my coat pocket and took out the small gold locket that I bought Callie for her sixth birthday, two days before she died. It hung around her neck as I held her in my arms, her guts spilling from her belly as her precious life drained away. Blood spilled from her mouth as she tried to mouth the word *Daddy*, the last word she ever spoke before her sad eyes glazed over and she was gone, leaving me holding her limp body. She wasn't the first person to ever die in my arms, though you'd think it was to hear me screaming at the time.

"Boss," a raspy voice said behind me. "I feel your pain…"

I didn't turn around to see the source of the voice. I didn't need to. "Fuck off, Scroteface," I growled. "Shouldn't you be out with the other malefactors terrorizing the neighborhood pets or something?"

The Hellbastard made a familiar hissing noise, a sign of frustration. "We grow bored waiting in the shadows."

"Nothing I can do about that." I kissed the locket before putting it back in my coat pocket. "When I need you, you'll be the first to know. In the meantime, fuck off and try to stay outta trouble, would you?"

Scroteface—full name Scrotum Face—gave a dramatic sigh from behind me. "You're the boss."

"That's right, you little shit, I am. And Scroteface?"

"Yes?" he hissed.

I looked over my shoulder slightly, but not far enough to see the diminutive demon standing behind me. "Don't ever tell me you feel my pain again, you got that? If you do, I'll teach you the real meaning of the word."

"Of course."

"I'm going out now. If I need you, I'll summon you. Until then—"

"Yes?"

"Try not to kill anything or any*one*, especially homeless bums. The people I work with think there's a fucking serial killer targeting the homeless."

Scroteface sniggered. "There is. Us!"

"Just keep your fucking crew in check…and yourself." I turned to look at the Hellbastard for the first time, who was perched on the edge of the couch. His long ears twitched, and his pointed tail swished lazily behind him as he focused on me with bulbous red eyes, which as ever, were full of mischievousness. "Remember, Hell is just a few words away."

The demon flinched at the mention of his birthplace. "Understood. We hanker for the old days…the blood, the violence…we wants it again."

I knew full well the days he was talking about, despite trying to forget them. "Those days are over," I said, my thoughts drifting for a second. "I'm going to work now. Make yourself useful and clean this shit hole of an apartment up when I'm gone. And tell Snot Skull to stop leaving puddles of snot all over the fucking floor, it's disgusting. There's also a mutilated cat on the fire escape. Get rid of it."

Scoteface stretched his wide mouth into something approximating a smile, revealing his yellowed, pointed teeth. "Consider it done, boss."

I stared at him a second longer, then asked, "Why do I even keep you fuckers around?"

"Because you love us?"

"Yeah, sure, because I love your ugly asses so much." My face twisted up as I stared at him, at his scarred, greenish-black face. "I'm going now. Bye, you little bastard."

"Love you too, boss," Scroteface called out as I walked out the door. "Have a good day at work."

I headed down the hallway toward the stairs. The Hellbastards could be a real pain in the ass, but they were also useful in my line of work, which these days, was more than just regular police work. Back in the day when I worked for Blackstar, the Hellbastards used to assist on many of the missions we went on. When I left and joined the police department, I had little need for bastard demons to do my dirty work, except on rare occasions. As a cop, the only monsters I dealt with were the human variety, and after the madness of Blackstar, that's how I liked it. But in the last few weeks, things had changed a great deal, so I summoned the Hellbastards back into service again, figuring I would need their assistance once more. I was also trying to find out who killed my daughter and my ex-wife only two weeks before. Blood would be spilt by the time I was done, and the Hellbastards liked nothing better than to spill it with me.

I slowed my pace as I came to the end of the hallway,

spotting the girl sitting on the landing. Her name was Daisy, and she was twelve years old. I'd come across her a few times as she sat reading a book. This time she was reading *Abarat* by Clive Barker. She had mousey brown hair cut into a rough bob and her skin, what I could see of it under her tatty dressing gown, was pale, her body a little too slender like she was undernourished. There were also dark circles under her eyes as if sleep was something she only got occasionally. Usually when I met her sitting out there, it was because she wanted to get away from her alcoholic mother or one of her mother's boyfriends. "Hey," I said, stopping to talk to her.

"Hi, Detective." She looked up at me with deep brown eyes that didn't hold much in the way of joy and had probably witnessed too much in her short lifetime. "You going to work?"

"I am. Why are you sitting out here this early in the morning? Your mother again?"

"Her new boyfriend just crashed into our apartment drunk. They threw me out to get some privacy."

I set my jaw at the thought of a parent throwing their kid out at this time of the morning just so they could have sex in peace. "I'm sorry," was all I could think to say.

"Don't be," she said. "I don't want to hear their rutting, anyway."

"Here." I took a ten-spot out of my pocket and gave it to her. "Go to the cafe around the corner and get yourself some breakfast. At least you can stay warm there. It's freezing out here."

She hesitated for a second before taking the money. "Thanks. You're a real gentleman, you know that?"

"Am I? Don't tell anyone."

She smiled and winked at me. "Your secret's safe with me."

"You coming then? I'll walk you down."

"I'm going to finish this chapter first. Things are just starting to get interesting."

"Okay, I'll see you later."

"Catch some bad guys, Detective."

Smiling to myself at the irony of her comment, I walked out of the apartment building to the street outside, pausing for a moment to look up at the gunmetal gray sky, turning my collar up against the persistent rain before glancing around the street. I lived in Longford—though most just called it Old Town—south of the river, in an area that was not only a shit hole but had a well-earned reputation for violence and every other crime you could think of. The row houses across from me were dilapidated, some of them boarded up, and nearly every streetlight had been smashed by the dealers who stalked this place. After Angela kicked me out two years ago, this is where I ended up, in the asshole of the city with the rest of the shit stains who live around here: the junkies, pimps, gang-bangers, dealers, and every other kind of lowlife in between. And that's not even including the supernatural elements that regularly haunt this place, most of them in search of human meat.

"What's up, copper?" a raspy voice said as I walked to my car.

I turned around to see a bearded face among a pile of dirty rags bundled inside the doorway of what used to be a pharmacy before it closed due to being robbed so many times. The man in the doorway was called Jed, an old homeless guy who I'd pumped for information on a few occasions. Very little happened here without him knowing about it. "Morning, Jed," I said as I opened the driver's side door of a black Dodge Charger, the front half of which was covered in a dark gray primer. "Anything interesting happen last night?"

"I saw some dealer get stabbed, right over there." He pointed to the corner across the street. "Screamed like a bitch he did."

"Did he die?"

"Not as far as I know."

"Pity. Catch you later, Jed."

I started the Dodge's engine and let it idle for a moment as I lit a cigarette, taking a few drags before pulling off with the window cracked an inch to let the smoke out. On the radio, the news had already picked up on the body-snatching at Cave Hill. "In a strange turn of events," the female broadcaster said, "the body of convicted murderer, Barbara Keane, has gone missing from the cemetery where she was interred just two days ago after her state execution. Local police have yet to give any statement regarding the incident. Although the priest who conducted Keane's burial ceremony, Father Mike Brown, was earlier asked what the reason might be for the body-snatching, to which he replied it was the Devil's work. More news on that as it comes in…"

The Devil's work, I thought as I drove across town toward Cave Hill. *Everything is the Devil's work in this damn city. People don't know the half of it.*

When I pulled up at the cemetery twenty minutes later, I had to park behind all the news vans, squad cars, and forensics vans that were blocking the gates, tutting because I knew I would have to run the gauntlet to get inside the graveyard. And as if on cue, half a dozen reporters came running at me like dogs as soon as I got out of the car, pointing their microphones and recording devices at me, all of them talking at once, firing questions at me that I had no intention of answering. Most of them knew me, calling me by name as they barked their questions at me. "Detective Drake," the loudest of them said, a man named Gordon Jenkins who worked for the city's biggest TV news station. "Do you have any leads yet?"

"No comment," I said.

"Who do you think stole the body?" he asked back straight away.

"No comment."

"Is this connected to the Satanic ritual that took place yesterday in the cemetery?"

I was about to say no comment again when I paused to look at the reporter who was in his late thirties and dressed in a flashy dark suit. At six foot four, I towered over them all as they stared up at me, waiting on scraps of information that I had no intention of giving them. "What Satanic ritual is that?" I growled. "We found a dead dog. I wasn't aware of any Satanic ritual."

"But we know about the pentagram carved into the dog's head," a female reporter said. "That's a Satanic symbol. Do you think Devil worshippers stole Barbara Keane's body?"

"I wouldn't know anything about that," I said. "Now get the hell away from me before I dump you all into Keane's empty grave for a closer look." I finished my statement with a smile as I took some satisfaction from seeing the disappointment on their faces. No doubt the captain would be pissed if my brief non-statement ever made it on air, but then what did I care? I didn't answer to the captain anymore. I only answered to the commissioner, and Commissioner Lewellyn didn't give much of a shit about what I did if I got the job done. The job he had outlined for me, and which didn't include talking to the press.

Two uniforms manned the gates of the cemetery, both of whom I nodded to as I walked inside to make my way up the hill and across to the scene of the crime. The rain had now turned from a drizzle to a steady downpour, and I saw that the crime scene technicians had already erected a tent over the open grave to maintain the integrity of the scene. Detectives Jim Routman and Russell Stokes stood outside the tent; their hands dug into their coat pockets as they hunched their shoulders against the rain. Turning to look at me, I sensed their displeasure at my presence, something I was well used too. I enjoyed being the source of their discomfort anyway. Walker broke away from them and came to meet me with two styrofoam cups in her hands, one of which she handed to me. "Black, two sugars."

"Thanks." I took the cup, just as everything shifted out of focus, turning the falling rain into a single wall of water in which we were both momentarily suspended. A side effect of the Mud in my system. It would pass.

"Are you alright?" She was staring at me, as she often did, though she didn't know I was on anything. A lot of things just confounded Walker.

"Why wouldn't I be?"

"Should I answer that?"

"No, just tell me what happened here."

Walker stared at me for another few seconds with her dark eyes. Her Visage—the shadow of her demon form—hovered barely visible above and behind her, unseen unless you knew what you were looking for. And even if you saw it, you'd probably dismiss it as a trick of the mind. People have an inbuilt knack for explaining away the strange things they see every day. "The grounds-keeper, one Jack Kemper, came across the open grave this morning," Walker said as she moved a lock of dark, wet hair away from her face. "The coffin had been forced open, and the body was gone."

"He see anything?" I stabbed a cigarette into my mouth and lit it with a silver zippo, which had been a gift from my ex-wife before she started hating me. Before she was killed. "Like who did it?"

Walker shook her head. "He gave a statement to one of the uniforms. He didn't see anything."

"Forensics turn anything up yet?"

"At least four sets of footprints, not including the grounds-keeper's. Possibly teens due to at least one small-sized tennis shoe print. We'll know more later, I'd say."

"Anything else?"

"An empty cigarette packet that might give us fingerprints."

I nodded with approval. "You know, you might actually pull this off."

"Pull what off?"

"Passing as human."

She didn't know whether to be pleased or angry at my comment. Not that I cared either way. Demons are creatures that were forged in the asshole of the universe, thus becoming the greatest assholes in the universe by default. A simple theory, but one I've rarely had disproved. I hoped Walker would prove me wrong, but I doubted it. So what if she turned out to be a total demon asshole like all the rest? As long as she does her job with this asshole right here.

So far, I had to say the demon in Walker's body wasn't the worst I'd met. It seemed to have maintained most of Walker's personality traits and general disposition, picking up where Walker had left off before she overdosed herself into oblivion. It was early days, however, and it would take a while longer for the demon to settle in and regain its memories and former self. If it overstepped after that, I would just put it down, as I had done to plenty of others of its kind. The demon inhabiting Walker's body seemed to sense this, so it trod carefully around me.

Walker fell into another one of her confounded silences. Routman and Stokes trudged over, looking like they couldn't wait to get home, or at least off the job for a while.

"Ethan," said Routman by way of greeting.

"Drake," said Stokes, barely looking at me.

"Shouldn't you two be at home?" I asked them.

"We're heading there now," Routman said, his lined face as implacable as ever. For a veteran cop in his sixties he still looked fit, with broad shoulders and a full head of steel-gray hair. "I'm surprised to see you here. I thought you'd be on compassionate leave." He called me by my first name because

I used to be partners with him, back when I first joined Homicide. Our partnership had been strained—mostly because of how he did things—but we got on okay. Mostly.

"You know me better than that, Jim," I said. "I can't sit around while there are people stealing corpses from graves, now can I?"

"Jesus, Drake," Stokes said. "You lost your fucking family. Take some time, will ya?" I stared hard at him for a moment until he looked away and shrugged. "I'm just saying."

Stokes was a rakish weasel of a man in his early forties—a few years older than me—though he looked more worse for wear than Routman thanks to his alcoholism, which everybody pretended not to notice. He had a gambling problem, and I was pretty sure he was dirty as well, taking kickbacks from dealers in exchange for information. Something else the department pretended not to know about, except IAB, which had already been on to him once, though they never brought him up on any charges. Stokes was on borrowed time. Sooner or later, he would eat his own gun, or someone would make him eat theirs. "Worry about your own problems," I told him with a glare.

"So, Ethan," Routman said, changing the subject, as diplomatic as ever. "Word is you're working directly for the commissioner now, and that you and Walker here are handling the more…weirder cases. What the fuck's that all about?"

"Like fucking Mulder and Scully." Stokes laughed to himself until I stared at him once again.

"Hey, we're not judging," Routman said. "We know how much weird shit goes down in this city. Lord knows I've seen enough myself over the years."

Yeah, and turned a blind eye to it like all the rest.

"Well," Stokes said, pushing his luck. "I can't think of a better man than you to be investigating shit like this. What are you thinking, Drake? Devil worshippers like the news is saying? Or maybe graveyard ghouls or a hungry werewolf?" He laughed to himself as if the whole thing was ridiculous.

Taking the last drag on my cigarette, I crushed the butt under my boot and stepped up to Stokes, looking down at him as I considered how easy it would be to crush his skull with my bare hands. "Do yourself a favor and get the fuck away from my crime scene before I bury your broken body in this graveyard. I'm sure your wife'll not miss you."

Stokes' jaw hardened in anger, and he tensed up as if he wanted to hit me. His own fear and insecurity soon betrayed him, however, and he backed down. "You're a real asshole, Drake," he muttered before walking away.

"Good luck with the case, Ethan," Routman said. "I'm going home to my family." As he went to walk away, he stopped. "I didn't mean—"

"I know what you meant," I said.

Routman gave a small sigh before heading after Stokes, who had almost reached the front gates, the media crew outside getting ready to descend upon him, which at least gave me some satisfaction.

"According to Hannah's memories, you used to be partners with those two," Walker said. "They don't seem to like you very much."

"I'm not in this life to be liked by anyone." I turned toward the crime scene, thoughts of my dead daughter going through my head. "Come on. Let's make like Mulder and Scully and see if we can't solve this thing."

"Okay," Walker said. "But who are Mulder and Scully?"

"The truth is out there, Walker," I said as I trudged on ahead to the crime scene.

2

As the rain got heavier, I ducked inside the tent to get a look at the open grave, while Walker remained outside to speak with Father John Brown, who had conducted Barbara Keane's funeral ceremony two days before. No doubt the priest had plenty to say about the "Devil's work" again, as he did the day before when the dead dog had been discovered.

Gordon Mackey, one of the crime scene technicians from the Analysis Bureau, was still working in the tent when I ducked inside. Mackey is a bald Polynesian guy in his early thirties. Tattoos cover most of his body, and he has several piercings in various places, including his cock. I only know this, not because I spy on him in the showers at work, but because a few years ago I came across him in an S&M club while I was there looking for a suspect who'd given me the slip inside. In an effort to find the suspect, I ended up at the basement level of the club where most of the hardcore freaks were doing their thing. I came across Mackey as he was spread-eagled on a cross-shaped rack, naked, his skin punctured in various strategic places by fishing hooks as someone in a PVC gimp suit lashed Mackey's body with a cat-o'-nine-tails. With every swish of the whip, Mackey would issue a cry that was less pain and more pleasure as the leather left scarlet welts on his skin. When his wild eyes focused on me, they widened in recognition before he froze. I didn't know what was going through his head right then. Once I realized my suspect wasn't in the room, I closed the door and resumed my search, eventually finding the guy I was looking for two rooms down, looking freaked out as two men—one wearing a gas mask, the other poured into a leather suit with bunny ears—took turns hitting each other with foot long black dildos. My suspect practically put the cuffs on himself just to get out of that room.

"Gordon," I said. "Doing any fishing lately?"

"Very funny." Mackey threw me a look as he held a digital camera in his hands. "That never gets old, seriously."

I smiled. "It doesn't, does it? Anything here I should know about?"

Mackey stood by the mouth of the open grave and gestured down at the cheap coffin inside, the lid of which had been pried off, the body it once contained now gone. "It seems they used a crowbar to open it. I'm sure it wasn't easy getting the corpse out of the grave. We found four sets of footprints, so I'm assuming it was a team effort. Do you think the same people who did this also left the dead dog hanging on the tree the day before?"

"Pretty certain the two are connected." I scanned the gravesite for any signs that a ritual had taken place, but the scene seemed clean.

"Connected how?"

"The dead dog had a pentagram carved into its head. I wasn't sure why at the time, but I have an idea why now."

"And what's that?" Mackey asked.

"I think the purpose of leaving the dog was to deconsecrate the ground here."

"Meaning?"

"Meaning Barbara Keane was buried in unholy ground yesterday."

"Okay." Mackey slung the camera over his shoulder and removed his latex gloves, pushing them into the pocket of his white lab coat. "And why would someone want a murderer buried in unholy ground?"

"We've still to find that out," I said, before sipping on my coffee. "Let me know what you get from the footprints and the fingerprints on the cigarette packet."

"We should process the evidence by this afternoon. I'll let you know if we find anything useful."

By the time I stepped out of the tent and into the rain again, I was convinced Barbara Keane's corpse had been stolen for the purpose of being used in some occult ritual, hence why the ground had been secretly deconsecrated before she was buried. I just needed to find out by whom and why.

"Detective Drake." Father Brown came walking over as soon as he saw me emerge from the tent. He was a tall man in his late fifties, who wore a black overcoat and a black hat on his small head to keep the rain off. "I told you yesterday something was going on here, didn't I?"

"Are you accusing me of something, Father?" I said to him. "I don't much like your tone."

The priest stopped in front of me and adjusted his white collar like he was getting ready for an argument, his blue eyes full of self-righteousness. "I asked you yesterday to post some officers here overnight, just in case something happened. I knew that poor dead dog was just the start of it. Now Barbara, God rest her soul, has not only been buried in unholy ground, but her body has also been stolen. This wouldn't have happened if you'd done as I asked."

I let him have his rant then lit a cigarette while Walker stood behind him, looking on as if she was trying to understand why the priest acted this way. Walker did that a lot.

Xaglath, the demon in her, was still getting to grips with the human condition it seemed. "You finished, Father?"

Father Brown shook his head and sighed in exasperation. "Barbara didn't deserve this. She should never have been executed in the first place. That poor woman was no murderer, no way—"

"The evidence says otherwise," Walker chipped in, coming to stand to our side now. "She killed her husband and two children."

"She did not," the priest shouted. "I don't care what your evidence says. I've met plenty of murderers in my time, counseled them on death row, and I'm telling you, Barbara did not do that to her husband and two children. She loved her kids more than anything. Their deaths destroyed her inside. Her soul was in turmoil at the end, as I'm sure it still is."

The priest seemed convinced of Keane's innocence, though that wasn't my concern at that point. Routman had caught the Keane case fourteen years ago, and it was he who sealed her fate by compiling all the evidence. As far as anyone but the priest was concerned, it was an open and shut case. Barbara Keane had poisoned her husband and two kids, though I have to admit, she did protest her innocence right to the end. Her last words before her lethal injection were, "I loved my kids and my husband. I didn't kill them. I could never do that. *Never.*"

"Listen, Father," I said as the rain continued to pour down on us, though less heavily now. "I'm not here to discuss Barbara Keane's innocence. I'm here to find out who stole her corpse, and why."

"You already know who," the priest half growled. "Devil worshippers—agents of Satan—stole her corpse."

"You may be right, but we still have to find them. Have you seen anybody suspicious hanging around here lately, anyone that stands out? A group of teenagers, maybe?"

"Teenagers?" Father Brown screwed his face up and shook

his head. "Are you thinking this might be down to some teenage prank? Really, Detective, I can't believe you would—"

"I'm not saying anything at this point." I cut him off, having had enough of his attitude. "Neither am I ruling anything out. So, I ask you again, have you noticed any suspicious individuals of late?"

The priest dropped his gaze. "I have not."

"Okay. If you'd excuse us, then. We'll contact you if we need you."

Father Brown shook his head. "I hope you get that poor woman's body back," he said. "It's the least she deserves, to have a proper burial so her soul can rest in peace."

"Her soul is most likely in the afterlife now," Walker said. "That's if she hasn't remained here as a ghost. Either way, I doubt she cares about what happens to her rotting corpse."

The priest stared in shock at Walker as I tried not to laugh. Then he blessed himself as if for protection. "Satan is everywhere," he half-whispered in near despair.

"Actually, it's been a long time since anyone has even seen Luc—"

"Thanks, Father." I cut Walker off before she could say anything else. "We'll keep you informed."

Father Brown took one last look at Walker like he was only now seeing her for what she was, even though I knew he couldn't. If he could, he would've looked a lot more scared than he did. "Lord have mercy on you both," he said before hurrying off toward the nearby chapel.

"What was that?" I asked Walker when the priest had gone. "I told you before you can't be talking like that to people who don't know shit about the way things are."

"Sorry," Walker said as raindrops ran down her olive-skinned face. "I keep forgetting about human ignorance. Once upon a time, such matters were not a mystery to them."

"Well, it's all a giant mystery to most now, and for a good reason--their minds can't handle it."

"Yours can, it seems."

"Yeah, don't be so sure. Come on." I ducked under the yellow police tape surrounding the scene. "We got work to do."

THE DEAD DOG THAT WAS FOUND HANGING FROM A TREE yesterday at the graveyard was a purebred Labrador, and upon examination, I noticed it was well-groomed, indicating it was most likely someone's pet. It was also sufficiently well-bred to be a show dog and was therefore expensive. The dog's belly had been slit open, so its intestines hung out, the cut rushed and ragged. The pentagram carved into its head seemed shoddy, almost like an afterthought by my reckoning. Serious occultists tend not to fuck about when it comes to marking out symbols, even in flesh. They know how important it is to get the symbols as perfect as possible, so they take their time in doing them. Whoever carved the symbol into the dog didn't take their time with it to get it right, which told me whoever did it was an amateur at best. That, coupled with the footprints found at the scene of the open grave, made me think both incidents were down to teenagers who were dabbling in things they knew nothing about. The incidents were no prank, but neither were they the work of those who had done such things before.

But even ignorant amateurs can cause trouble. The dark, supernatural forces of this world—MURKs: Monsters, Unnaturals, Reapers, and Killers/Kunts—didn't much care about the expertize of those who tried to reach out to them by whatever means. In fact, the less people know, the better it is for the fiendish MURKs that live in the dark waiting for the ignorant to open the door so they can insinuate their eldritch forms into this world. An expert in occult practices could likely have some control over the MURKs that are summoned. Amateurs, on the other hand, nearly always find out to their detriment that they have no control whatsoever over what they summon, usually when it's too late to do anything about. If the suspects who stole Barbara Keane's body were intending to reach out to some MURK, I needed to find them before they got themselves or others killed. Although I could care less about a bunch of stupid idiots getting themselves killed. But it's my job to clean up these messes, so…

Yesterday, I had Walker make some inquiries with local animal shelters, which led to her finding out a purebred Labrador had been reported missing recently by a local family, the Hawthorns. After phoning them up, John Hawthorn said it was okay to call at his home so we could ask him some questions, which is where Walker and I were heading now. She left her blue sedan parked outside the graveyard and rode with me in the Dodge as I negotiated the early morning commuter traffic that congested the gloomy streets of Old Town.

"So," Walker said as water still dripped from her hair on to the shoulders of her black leather jacket. "What do you think's going on here? Should we be worried?"

"Worried?" I stared across at her after stopping for a red light. "Why do you even care?"

Mild consternation registered on her fine-boned face as she seemed to consider the question for a second. "I'm not sure what you mean by that."

"You know what I mean."

She nodded. "I see. You think because I am not human I am incapable of caring. If that's the case, why did you make me your partner after you found out who and what I am?"

"I still don't know who you are," I said as I pulled off from the light. "I don't think you do either. And I already told you, there was no one else. Every other cop in this city turns a blind eye to the MURKs or pretend they don't exist at all."

"But you thought I was still Hannah when you found me

that night. If she was still here, would you have kept her on as your partner?"

"I don't know, maybe. Hannah was pretty screwed up. I think you need to be screwed up to face what we face every damn day."

"She's still here."

I gave her a look. "Just because you have her memories and residual feelings inside that body, doesn't mean Hannah Walker is still here. We both know there's only room for one soul in there."

"Humans never used to be this cynical," she said, almost to herself as she looked out the window at the rain running down the glass. "Before my kind were cast down, we lived among the humans when they were bastions of light, touched by the grace of the Maker. Their souls were beautiful, and we loved them all. Even after the Fall, we still fought for them, but..."

"But what?"

"We lost. We lost everything."

"And I guess we lost too then, because here we are, bastions of everything but fucking light."

"This world makes me sad, but—" She turned to focus her dark brown eyes on me, and in them I saw a distant glow, a faint echo of the Elohim within. "I can't help loving it."

"I guess anything's better than Hell, right?" We were on the freeway now, heading for Riverside Hills and the suburb where the Hawthorns resided.

"I don't want to talk about that place. My memories of it are...sketchy, yet terrifying. I try not to think about it."

"You ever think maybe you just substituted one Hell for another?" She wasn't sure what to say to that and lapsed into silence for a time as I hit play on the CD in the car stereo, and the first bars of *Me and The Devil Blues* started playing. "Never mind." A slight smile crossed my face for no reason. "Robert Johnson feels your pain. He sold his soul to one of you."

We reached Riverside Hills just as the song was ending. I cut the engine outside the Hawthorn residence, a white-painted Four-Square house with a perfect lawn and a black Tesla parked in the driveway. Queasiness overcame me as I stared at the house through the window. It was nearly identical to the house I used to live in with my ex-wife and daughter, both of whom got pulled into my orbit, a place where no one else should be, which they found out to their detriment.

"Ethan?" Walker's eyes seemed to look right through me.

"Let's go see if these people can give us a lead," I said, ignoring her probing stare.

It had stopped raining when I got out of the car, though the sky was still full of dark gray clouds that were getting ready to burst again. I waited a moment for Walker to catch up, and we both walked up the driveway to the front door, which I knocked three times with my knuckles.

"It's quiet around here," Walker said. The only sounds came from the birds singing in the rain's aftermath, and the distant sound of traffic from the nearby expressway.

"Dead more like," I said.

"Dead." Walker pondered this as if it was of great philosophical significance. She did that a lot. "This entire world seems dead, or half-dead anyway. I never imagined the great garden would end up like this."

"I guess this is what happens when the Creator of that garden fucks off somewhere and leaves his creations to it."

"You think the Maker has abandoned this world?"

"Don't you?" I paused when I saw the look on her face. "Stupid question."

A second later, the white front door of the house was opened to reveal a man in his early thirties, dressed in dark slacks and light jersey, looking like he was about to hit the golf course. "Yes?" he said, the tension increasing in his face as he took us both in.

I flashed my badge at him, and he flinched from it as if it

was offensive to him. "Mr. Hawthorn, I'm Detective Drake from Fairview PD. This is Detective Walker. We're here to discuss your missing dog."

Hawthorn stepped out under the porch and closed the door behind him as if he didn't want his son hearing anything, who was chattering away inside to his mother. "I hope you haven't come to tell me she's dead," he said. "I already know she is. As soon as I saw the body on the news, I knew it was Teela. As did my son. He's been traumatized by that image of his beloved pet hanging from a tree with its innards hanging out. How could they even show such a thing on the TV?"

"We're sorry you had to find out that way," I said. "Have you identified the body yet?"

"Yes, yesterday. It was definitely Teela." He stopped and shook his head as if the memory of seeing the dog so mutilated was too much to bear. "The news is saying she was killed for some Satanic ritual, is that right?"

"We can't really comment on that," I said.

"Then what are you doing here?"

"We'd just like to know if you saw anything," Walker said. "Did you see any suspicious characters hanging around the street before your dog was taken?"

"We didn't see anyone. We came home from the movies three nights ago to find Teela missing. Her collar had been cut away and left in the backyard. That's all I can tell you. Are you any closer to catching the bastards who did this?"

"We're still working on it," I said.

Hawthorn gave a tight nod, the same nod I'd seen countless times after the person realizes I'm not going to give them concrete guarantees about anything. They all want to hear the bad guys will get caught and brought to justice, and when I don't tell them exactly that, they turn on the resentment and the cynicism and do their little nod that says, *Fine, whatever.* "I hope you catch these people and punish them accordingly. My son will have nightmares about this for the rest of his life. He loved that dog."

Just then the kid came around the side of the house with a basketball in his hands, clutched to his chest as he stood staring at us, especially at me. He didn't look any older than seven or eight. Small for his age, with his father's soft features. He had dark circles under his eyes as if he hadn't been sleeping right the last few nights. "Are you here to bring my dog back to me?" he asked in a voice that was barely a note above flat.

"Jimmy, we talked about this," the father said, looking at me and Walker like he was about to explain why his son thought their dog was still alive. Not that he needed to, and nor did he get the chance to anyway, for Walker suddenly stepped past him and crouched down in front of the kid as he continued clutching the basketball like it was cold comfort.

"Hi, Jimmy." Walker smiled, passing for human in a way I hadn't observed in her since finding out she was a demon. That unnerved me, for it didn't feel right. Something was off, though I wasn't sure what, so I just let it play out. Only afterward did I think I shouldn't have.

"Hi," Jimmy replied in a small voice as he looked into Walker's eyes, almost like he couldn't help it.

"My name's Detective Walker." Her smile was warm, yet somehow sinister, and the shadow of her demon Visage hung over her, its arms seeming to reach for the kid. "Teela is in a different place now. Do you know where that is?"

I became more uncomfortable as the kid stared back at Walker, the father looking on, seeing only a cop trying to comfort his kid, not seeing the demon shadow get darker as long, smoke-like fingers caressed the boy's head. "Where did we say Teela is now?" the boy's father said to him.

The kid looked at his father and then back to Walker "Doggie Heaven," he replied in a small voice.

Walker shook her head. "That's not true, Jimmy. Teela

resides in a place called Hell, where her little doggie soul will burn forever in the Eternal Fires as it writhes in torment knowing nothing but pain and torture forever and ever."

"What the fuck?" Hawthorn rushed forward to grab his son just as the kid dropped the basketball and burst out crying, wailing the dog's name over and over again.

Walker stood up with a sly smile on her face, the eyes of her demon Visage burning bright as if to say *fuck you*. Then, as quickly as it appeared, Walker's smile vanished, and her expression became one of consternation. "I—I'm sorry."

My jaw set hard as I struggled to contain my anger, not only at Walker for what she just did, but at myself for allowing it to happen. I knew where she was going, and I let her go there anyway because some twisted part of me wanted to see it play out.

The kid was bawling his eyes out now, his head buried in his father's shoulder, whose face was now red with fury. "Get off my property," he snarled, clutching his kid and stepping away from Walker, who merely stood like she didn't know how to react. "You'll both be hearing from my lawyer; I guarantee you that." He stared at Walker then, afraid of her despite his anger. "You're finished."

"We're very sorry, Mr. Hawthorn." I grabbed Walker by the arm and started leading her away. "We'll be on our way now. Thank you for your time."

As I gripped Walker by the arm and led her down the driveway toward the car, Hawthorn called out, "You're sick the both of you!"

3

I got into the car and slammed the door behind me. A second later, Walker got in, and I leaned across and grabbed her by the throat, doing it so fast she barely had time to cry out in surprise. Not that she could speak, given the pressure I was putting on her larynx. "You ever do anything like that again," I snarled. "I'll fucking kill you. I'll banish your soul back to Hell so fast you won't know what hit you."

For a moment, a fire burned deep in Walker's eyes as she stared back at me. I felt her body tense, and for a second, I thought she was going to fight me, maybe even use her powers against me. But she soon relaxed knowing she wasn't strong enough. Not yet, anyway. All I would have to do was snap her neck, and the demon would have to vacate the body it had moved into. With a snarl, I let go of her throat and sat back in my seat. Walker struggled to take in air again, gasping as she rubbed her throat. "I'm sorry," she choked. "I don't know what came over me. I—I wanted to see that little boy suffer." She shook her head as if the idea disgusted her. "A part of me took pleasure in it."

"You're not in Hell anymore. You'd do well to remember that."

"I still struggle with the torment I faced there, with the demon I was."

"That you *are*, you mean."

"No. I left that monster behind. I came here to atone, to regain the good graces of my Maker once more. I am a being of light, a—"

"Shut the fuck up, will you? Deal with your existential crisis in your own time. When you're with me, you're a goddamned cop, got it?"

She nodded, her large eyes dark and wet. "I fucked up. I will lose my badge now, won't I?"

I said nothing as I stared straight ahead. She wasn't wrong. If Hawthorn went to the media about Walker, there would be a shit storm, especially with all the attention on the Keane case already. I doubt even the commissioner could save her. The 13th precinct was under constant scrutiny thanks to a corruption scandal a few years ago involving dirty cops. One whiff of misconduct and the mayor would demand Walker's head on a silver platter to be shown to the media. But Walker was my partner, and the only one I had. Given the lines of investigation I was following these days, there weren't any other cops out there I could trust, and none who would have the stomach to work the kind of cases that were sure to come my way. Walker may be mixed up in the head, but that was mainly because the demon was still adjusting to its new life here. It would settle down soon enough, leaving me with a juiced-up partner to back me up against the MURKs.

"Alright," I said, my anger subdued. "Get out and start canvassing the street. Talk to the neighbors, see if they saw anything the night the dog was taken."

"What are you going to do?"

I looked toward the Hawthorn house. "Fix the mess you made."

"How?"

"Leave that to me. Just go and knock on doors and try to keep your more sinister urges in check."

We both got out at the same time, she heading off to the neighbors' houses up the street. I walked back down the Hawthorn driveway and knocked on the door, not liking what I was about to do, but knowing it had to be done. Hopefully Hawthorn hadn't lifted the phone yet. Even if he had, what I was about to do would make him forget all about it.

His eyes widened in disbelief when he opened the door to see me standing there again, having had the nerve to darken his door with my presence once more. From inside the house, I could hear the kid crying, calling out the dead dog's name. "I told you—" he said, but then stopped when I held my hand up in front of his face. As expected, his eyes went to the palm of my hand and the swirling mass of black tattoo ink that had, moments ago, made its way down my right arm. As more of the ink gathered, it moved in mesmeric patterns around my palm, causing warmth and a mild tingling sensation to spread up my arm. Hawthorn's eyes had already glazed over, his attention taken by the swirling ink. After I uttered a few syllables of power, his mind was mine to manipulate in whatever way that I pleased.

"You never saw me or my partner here," I said in a steady voice. "There've been no cops at your door today. Understand?"

Hawthorn, with a faraway look in his glassy eyes, nodded. "I understand."

As the ink continued to work its magic, I told him to turn around and go back inside the house. "You won't remember any of this. Goodbye, Mr. Hawthorn."

I walked away from the house as Hawthorn did as I told him and closed the door. The kid would still remember everything, but there was nothing I could do about that. It wasn't like the kid was going to call his lawyer. Walking back up the driveway, I felt the ink leave my palm and work its way back up my arm, settling back into the pattern it was originally drawn in. My time with Blackstar may have become a living nightmare by the end, but at least I walked away with some things that were useful, the tattoos being just one.

When I got back into the car, I drove it slowly up the street until I spotted Walker standing in the driveway of another house, talking to some old guy. I pulled the car up and got out, joining them in the driveway as spots of rain began to fall.

"This is Mr. Dent," Walker said, still wary of me. "He says he saw some suspicious characters the night the Hawthorn's dog was taken."

"Is that right?" I said to the old guy, who must have been in his mid-seventies, most of his hair gone apart from a few gray wisps, his deeply lined skin sagging on his shrinking bones.

"That's right," he said, his voice still strong even if his body wasn't. "There were four kids hanging around across the street there."

"Kids?" I said. "What age?"

"I don't know." He shook his head. "They all look the damn same to me. Teenagers, maybe sixteen or so."

"Can you describe them?"

"I already did, to your partner here. Best I could anyway."

"Two white males," Walker said, reading from her notebook. "One tall with dark hair, wearing jeans and a black T-shirt. The other smaller, dressed all in black, with longer hair. Plus another male and someone Mr. Dent thinks might be a female."

"They all looked the damn same," he said. "I knew they were up to no good soon as I saw 'em. Lil' bastards stole that dog from down the street, didn't they? The one on the news?"

I nodded. "Seems that way."

"Kids these days. Ain't they got nothing better to do? What the hell's wrong with them, killing dogs? What's wrong with their parents for letting 'em. I tell you, back in my day—"

"You've been very helpful, Mr. Dent," I said, cutting him off.

"Yes," Walker said. "Thank you, sir."

"If you catch the lil' fuckers, throw 'em in jail," he said as we were walking away, then said louder, "Better yet, fucking shoot 'em! Make an example of the bastards!"

"We'll bear that in mind," I said.

On the way back from Riverside Hills, I got a call from Captain Edwards, who asked if I could come to the precinct so he could discuss the Keane case with me.

To be honest, it surprised me to hear from Edwards at all. When Commissioner Jack Lewellyn asked me to head up the semi-clandestine investigative unit, named only Unit X, it was understood that the unit be autonomous with no interference from anyone. We would report directly to him. Whatever reports we wrote about the cases we worked were also to be sent straight to Lewellyn and were for his eyes only until they were suitably redacted.

Anyone who knew about the unit didn't have a problem with it as far as I knew, since we were dealing with stuff that most of the other detectives didn't want to deal with, stuff other cops knew about but didn't openly admit to. Things that turned their blood cold and made them falsify reports just so they wouldn't seem crazy to their fellow officers and superiors. Often these cases were just dropped because no one wanted to explain how a killer could run up the side of a building while being chased or take three bullets to the chest and smile before disappearing in the blink of an eye.

Thus, criminals of the MURK variety often got away with everything, because no one knew how to deal with them.

Even me, when I worked Narcotics and Homicide, I took part in this unspoken cover-up like everyone else, even though I was more clued in than most. A few times I may have taken justice into my own hands and dealt with the MURK criminals myself, but that was a rare occasion. Fact is, I had enough *human* criminals to deal with, and since chasing down MURKs wasn't my job anymore, I toed the line like everyone else and pretended the MURKs didn't exist.

When Lewellyn made commissioner after a long career as a serving police officer (one of the few commissioners to have come through the ranks), one of the first things he did was to formulate a plan to deal with the stuff that he saw covered up and ignored for so many years, at the cost of many human lives. He thought it was time to do something about this continuous loss of human life, and that I was the man to help him.

Somehow, he knew about Blackstar and the fact that I used to work for the company, even though that information was highly classified. Regardless of how he found out about me, he thought I was the man for the job.

"For as long as I can help it," he told me, "your unit will remain active, Ethan, and you will answer only to me."

Which is why I was annoyed, though not surprised, to hear from Captain Edwards. He wanted updates on the Keane case, and when I told him to see the commissioner about that, he said he would have my badge if I weren't in his damn office inside the hour.

Lewellyn would never allow Edwards to take my badge, but I told the captain I would be there anyway. No sense rocking the boat too much and causing undue hassle. He just wanted to know that the case was being handled.

I drove to Cave Hill Cemetery first, to drop Walker off at her car. "Start looking into those descriptions," I told her. "And see if Mackey got anything from the gravesite. We might get lucky with the fingerprints."

Walker remained silent for most of the drive back. There

was still a red mark on her neck where I had grabbed her earlier. "What are you going to do?"

"Tell Edwards what he wants to hear."

"Then what?"

"What are you, my fucking boss now? I'm going to my ex-wife's house to look over the scene again."

"I see."

"Something on your mind, Walker?"

"Yes, actually. Can we meet later for a drink?"

"I don't think I've ever seen you drink."

"After expelling the junk from Hannah's system, I didn't think it needed any more poison in it. But I keep getting these urges…"

"For more junk?"

"Not that stuff, just for a mild relaxant."

"Fine. I'll call you later. We'll get a drink."

She smiled somewhat awkwardly, as if she was still getting used to doing so. "Good. There's something I'd like to discuss with you. It concerns Hannah."

"What is it?"

She opened the car door. "Later," she said.

Bloody demons, I thought as I sped away again. *They'll be the death of me someday.*

Twenty minutes later, I drove through the electronic gate that gave me access to the precinct parking lot. After parking the car, I had to sit for a moment. As often happens, thoughts of Callie entered my mind, a random memory from a few weeks ago when I took her to the movies. Grief built up in me, seeping in until it felt like a fist clenched my guts. Almost instinctively at this point, I reached into my coat pocket and took out the dropper bottle containing the Mud. After filling the dropper all the way up, I squirted the contents into my mouth, wincing at the sour taste. After that, I reached into the inside pocket of my trench coat and took out a small hip flask filled with Jack Daniels. I swilled a mouthful of Jack to clear the taste of the other stuff, and then took another mouthful for good measure. Moments later, the pain in my gut began to ease up, and the world became less jagged as my nerves smoothed out. Shades of gray outside were replaced by brighter tones as the sun shone its morning light down from a clearing sky. Snorting, I managed to clear any further thoughts of Callie from my mind. Then I was ready to go.

I crossed the parking lot and went in through the door at the east entrance of the precinct which opened directly into the booking area. To the left was a side corridor leading to three interrogation rooms and four holding cells that were affectionately known as The Tombs, as much for the rank smell as the gloomy interior. I climbed the west staircase to the second floor where I passed the main conference room and the large circular window that looked down on Miller Avenue below. When I passed the bullpen at the southwest corner, I glanced inside and saw the usual faces, a few of which nodded a curt hello. As much as I despised the place sometimes, a certain camaraderie existed in the bullpen that I missed, because we were all doing the same job, which inevitably led to much piss-taking and sarcasm that would often lead to scorn and derision if tensions were high, which they often were. Homicide detectives are always under pressure to close cases, especially if said cases are high profile.

Speaking of which, I had a feeling this is exactly why Captain Edwards wanted to see me. The Keane case was attracting a lot of media attention, and Edwards—always the politician—was no doubt acutely aware of this, and the fact that the department would be made to look bad if no progress was being made on the case. As I walked down the corridor to his office, I wondered if he'd already spoken to Lewellyn, or was this meeting going to be about how he couldn't understand why my unit had landed the case instead of some other bureau.

I sat in Edwards' secretary's office for five minutes while I waited on him calling me in. When Rosie McCardle—the plump secretary in her mid-fifties—said it was okay for me to go in, I got up and entered the captain's office. He didn't acknowledge me at first, except to gesture for me to sit down as he continued with whatever paperwork he was doing. Much like his personality, the captain's office was neat and well organized, with a bookshelf on the south wall filled with books that reflected his eclectic tastes in reading, ranging from Lee Child's Jack Reacher novels to the complete works of Edgar Allen Poe, who I was familiar with myself, having read Poe and Lovecraft obsessively as a kid. On top of the bookshelf were several photo frames containing pictures of the captain's family, and one of him shaking hands with the mayor. Hanging on the wall above the photos was a large expressionist painting, which I knew was done by the captain's wife, who is quite a big deal in the Fairview art scene and the greater Washington County area. The captain himself is a tall black man with a smooth bald head and a tight muscular frame. For a man in his fifties, he looked good. His inscrutable countenance, as always, gave little away as he finally finished with his paperwork and sat back in his leather chair to consider me for a moment.

"You asked to see me, sir?" I said, the Mud making me slump into my chair like I didn't give a fuck.

"Yes." Edwards leaned back in his chair and interlocked his fingers across his stomach. "What's happening with the Keane case?"

"We're looking into it, sir. Detective Walker and I."

"Any leads yet?"

"Yes." I told him about the descriptions we got from the old guy in Riverside Hills, and about the evidence collected at the gravesite. "Hopefully forensics will turn something up."

"I don't have to tell you, Drake, that there's a lot of press attention on this one."

"I know, sir."

"Find out whoever took that body and get this case cleared."

"Will do. Is that all, sir?"

"No." He leaned on his desk; his dark eyes focused hard on me. "I don't like being kept out of the loop, Drake."

"I report directly to Commissioner Lewellyn now, sir. You know that."

"What is this unit he has you running? A unit that only has you and Walker in it? Walker, who was suspended from duty for drug abuse, by the way."

"You would need to discuss that with the commissioner, sir," I said, shifting slightly in my chair.

"I already have. He's about as unforthcoming as you are, and I don't like it."

"With respect, sir, no one is asking you to like it."

His eyes widened and his nostrils flared slightly for a moment, though I didn't care about his anger. We both knew he had no authority over me anymore. I was just there out of courtesy. "Screw you. Homicide is a man down now so you can run around investigating stuff we all know should be left alone."

"Do we, sir? Should the Keane case be left alone too?"

"If it weren't for all the damn media attention, then I would say yes, it should. No one cares about a dead woman who poisoned her husband and two kids."

"If that's what happened."

Edwards raised his eyebrows. "You're disputing the facts of the case now?"

"I'm just saying. She protested her innocence to the very end."

"Don't they all?"

"No, sir, they don't."

Edwards sighed as he stared past me for a moment. "Look, I don't want you stirring up any shit in my precinct, you hear me? While you're out there looking for stuff that doesn't exist—"

"Doesn't exist, sir?"

"—My men are solving real crimes. Just don't get in the fucking way. Are we clear?"

"Crystal, sir."

"Get the fuck out of my office."

I stood up and walked to the door, pausing to look back at him. "You know, Captain, you and the rest of this precinct can bury your heads in the sand all you like, but things are getting worse out there. Soon enough, you won't be able to deny the real truth."

"The real truth?" he said scathingly. "And what's that?"

"That Hell has moved here, and it's here to stay."

4

Once I left the precinct, I drove to Crown Point to my ex-wife's house, a sizable four-bedroom overlooking the river that divided the city in two. Angela had chosen the house shortly after we were married about eight years ago. The place was a fortune in rent each month, and I'd protested it was too much, but she was adamant she wanted a view of the river. She was a surgeon at Salem Hospital over in Bedford, the more affluent—though no less dark and seedy—side of the river, so between us she said we could afford it.

I never liked the place. The neighbors were all wealthy white-collar workers who would look down their nose at me as I left for work every day in my scruffy trench coat and crumpled suit. As a cop, they saw me as the enemy, someone to be feared and despised. But the reality was, unless they killed someone, I was no threat to them whatsoever.

By the time Angela kicked me out of the house over two years ago, I was glad to get away from Crown Point and its overwhelming stench of money and aspiration. I remember walking up to the house the day after Angela and Callie were killed. Quite a few of the neighbors were out rubbernecking, and the looks they gave me said it all:

This is your fault.

And they weren't wrong.

~

THE RED BRICK COLONIAL REVIVAL STYLE HOUSE WAS STILL cordoned off with yellow police tape. I ducked underneath it and walked up the driveway toward the white front door. All I could think about was that night I got here to find the two of them, Angela and Callie, bleeding out in separate rooms…

I was out tailing a suspect in Little Italy that night when I got a call from Angela. I knew straight away something was wrong, for she rarely called me, and never that late at night. She'd moved on, and had little need to talk to me any longer except about Callie. She probably felt like a cancer survivor, relieved to have finally had her disease—me—cut out.

When I accepted her call, all I could hear down the line was heavy, labored breathing. A sound I was all too familiar with, and one which I had come to associate with the last gasps of the dying. I said her name numerous times but never got an answer. The car was already turned around, speeding toward Crown Point. The sickening feeling in my gut only increased the closer I got to the house, for all I could think about now was Callie. What if something terrible had happened to her as well? What if she was dead? What if they both were?

Oh, Jesus God…you cannot fucking do this to me, you can't fucking—

I pulled up at the house to find the front door locked. Without thinking, I kicked the door twice until it flew back on its hinges, the sound of splintering wood punctuating the heavy, almost ominous, silence surrounding the house. Before stepping inside, I took out my service pistol—a standard-issue Glock 19—and held it up in front of me as I walked into the hallway. "Angela! Angela, where—?"

The coppery scent of blood was thick in the air, and my stomach turned over. Not because of the blood itself, but because of who it belonged to.

Angela lay on the hardwood living room floor, unmoving as a huge pool of blood expanded around her, most of it pumping from the ragged wound in her neck. The phone she had used to call me was still in her red-slicked hand. "*Oh Jesus…Angela…*"

I went to her, thinking she was dead. The wound in her neck was deep, as were the wounds in her chest. She looked like she had been attacked by a wild animal. I quickly checked the kitchen before taking my phone out and calling dispatch for immediate backup and emergency services, even though I knew they would never get there in time to help Angela. "*Callie…*" she whispered as I kneeled beside her, kneeled in her blood. "*Callie…*"

"Where is she?" I held her, but she didn't answer, and her head rolled over slightly in my hands as she died.

As I walked into the house now and entered the living room, my eyes immediately went to the huge bloodstain on the floor. It was like a reflexive action at this point, like walking into your house and tossing your keys on the table, only you walk in and stare at the spot where your wife was murdered instead. Maybe if I'd driven the car a bit faster, I might've got here in time to save her. Or if I'd known magic, I could've healed her injuries. Or maybe if I'd just never met her in the first place. If I'd never bought her that drink in that shitty dive bar, she would never have married me. She'd still be saving people at the hospital while I darkened the world with my presence far away from her. Callie would never have been born either. I could've saved my angel so much pain by never helping to conceive her in the first place. She'd still be nothing but a blissful thought of the universe, unburdened by the pain of existence. Instead, I helped drag her here kicking and screaming, only to help send her back out the same way six years later.

That night, covered in Angela's blood, I called Callie's name as I headed up the stairs, fighting the sickening dread with every step, fighting to keep my imagination from throwing up all sorts of horrifying scenarios as I moved toward Callie's bedroom, noticing the large, bloody footprints on the cream carpet, vaguely thinking that they didn't look human, that they looked like animal footprints. I didn't stop to examine them. My only concern was finding Callie, even though a part of me half-hoped I didn't find her in case—

So much blood…

The room was covered in it. The ceiling was stained with crimson. Blood ran down the posters on the walls. The books on the shelves were splashed with it. The carpet was sodden and sticky with it. And the bed. Oh my God, the bed—

An agonized moan escaped from my mouth as I saw my six-year-old daughter—my angel—lying atop the bed in a deep pool of her own blood. She had been shredded so much that it was hard to tell what was skin and what was her pajamas. Her little hands were over her stomach as she must've tried in vain to keep her intestines from spilling out. And her face…I can't even talk about her face. Let's just say that never in my life had I felt such gut-wrenching horror as I did right when I saw that beautiful, angelic little face butchered beyond recognition, and done with a savageness I struggled to comprehend. I've seen men injured so bad they looked like they'd been put through a meat grinder. But seeing my little girl so mangled and bloody bred a horror that has never left me, and probably never will. The only thing keeping it from destroying me is the job and finding out who caused the horror in the first place. That, and the Mud. Without those lifelines, I'd just eat my fucking gun, no question.

I was still holding her when the uniforms arrived, and then the EMTs, who tried to pry her off me, but I barked at them to stay away at first because I didn't want to hand her over. She was dead. Even if I handed her over, it was too late anyway. So I just growled at them all to get the fuck out, and they all did, leaving me to weep over my angel's lifeless body. I didn't give her up until Walker eventually showed. She talked me into handing Callie over to the EMTs, and when I did, it felt like my heart was being ripped from my chest.

"You torture yourself, Ethan," a deep, almost whispering voice said from the shadows in the living room. The curtains were drawn, and because it was dull outside, little light penetrated the room. "What do you hope to find this time that you didn't find before?"

"Something," I replied to the tall figure concealed in the shadows. "Anything."

Richard Solomon, looking as always like death incarnate, stared at me like he was trying his best to suck out my soul. Stick thin for his size, dressed in a black suit, he stepped forward as the shadows peeled back from his gaunt, chalk-white face. "As I keep telling you, I'm a necromancer, not a miracle worker."

I put a cigarette in my mouth but hesitated before lighting it. Angela banned me from smoking in the house, and even though she wasn't around anymore to enforce such a ban, I refrained from lighting the cigarette, holding it between my fingers instead. "They died violently. Their souls have to be near."

"You've stated that before, and in most cases, I would agree. But for some reason, your wife and child's souls are…nowhere."

"Check again. Run the ritual."

"But—"

"Do it."

"Very well." He looked like a ghost himself as he remained in the corner of the room. "But as always, you must give me something in return."

"What this time?" I'd dreaded him asking. Solomon liked to play mind games, to probe the psyche, which in my case was dark and murky according to him. I don't know what the hell he got out of it. Solomon was one of the most perverse motherfuckers I'd ever come across, even when I first met him at Blackstar, where he used to work intelligence. Back then, he was one of the best spies in the business, helped by the fact that he was a complete sociopath. He got results, however, and results were all that mattered to the company. Something I knew as well as he did.

Solomon walked into the middle of the room and kneeled on the floor, right on the spot where Angela took her last breath. From his pocket, he took something and hung it around his neck. A necklace made from a piece of thin wire threaded through several severed human fingers. Each of the fingers looked fresh, recently cut from the hands to which they once belonged. Blood dripped from at least two of them. "Tell me about your mother, Ethan," he said in a gentle voice. The sort of voice you would use if you were trying to get a child to open up to you. A tone that I hated, for it carried with it Solomon's perverse pleasure in hearing me speak about things I took no pleasure in talking about. Things that should rightly stay buried in some far-flung corner of my mind. "Tell me what happened to her."

"Fuck you, Solomon," I said.

A slight smile creased his thin lips. "Do you want me to do the ritual or not?"

Why am I even doing this? I know it will be a waste of time. So does he, and yet I'm allowing him to drag me into that dark place again. No, I'm dragging myself into it because...my angels might still be here somewhere.

Lies, Ethan, lies. What's the real reason you're descending into the dark past again? Is it because some part of you likes it there? Because you enjoy cavorting with the darkness as much as Solomon does?

"Ethan?"

"What?"

"I'm waiting."

I sighed, then lit the cigarette in my hand as I sat on the couch. "Start the ritual."

"Start talking then. I'm listening."

When I next looked at Solomon, his eyes were rolled up into their sockets, so only the whites were visible now. In his hand was a long, thin blade, which he drew slowly across his left palm, filling his hand with blood that dripped onto the floor. Then he switched the knife into his left hand and made the same cut in his right palm, before placing the knife on the floor in front of him. As he held both his hands out as if in praise, his blood dripped to the floor, each drip making a tiny sound in the silence of the house. "What do you want to know about my mother?" I asked through gritted teeth.

"Who was she?" he whispered, though his voice still sounded loud to my ears.

"She was a prostitute." I sat back in the couch, the same leather couch I had sat in for years while I pretended to be a family man. "She was in her early twenties when she got pregnant with me. Fuck knows why she didn't just get rid of me when she found out, but for whatever reason, she decided to keep me. I don't know, maybe she thought having a kid would straighten her out."

"Did it?" Solomon asked in a whisper, at the same time as gently chanting the syllables to the magic working he was doing.

I pulled on my cigarette for a moment before answering, flicking the ash into the palm of one hand. "Not really. Maybe she tried, I don't know. I just remember being left with strangers a lot while she went out every night, to work the same corner she'd always worked on Derry Street in the Warren. Most of the time, she would leave me with one of the neighbors in the apartment building where we lived. Sometimes with my father, but that was a rare occasion. I don't know, I was young. I barely remember."

"Did she…abuse you?"

That didn't take long.

"No, she didn't, not in the way you're implying anyway."

"You felt her love?"

"Yeah, she loved me, in her own fucked up way, I suppose. I don't think she had it in her to be a mother, though."

"Tell me…how she died…Ethan."

"You're a sick fuck."

"Glass houses," he said, smiling to himself.

"By the time I was five, she would often leave me on my own while she went out to work," I said, glad that enough of the Mud was still in my system to null the pain the memories were bringing. "Sometimes, I would go out and just wander the streets. Usually I would go to the comic store a few blocks away. The guy there would stay late so him and his buddies could play D&D. I think he felt sorry for me, so he would let me sit in the store and read comic books while they all played. When they finished, I'd walk back to the apartment, or sometimes one of the guys would give me a lift. This one night, I stayed out late, like three in the morning or something. It didn't matter, though, because no one cared what I did and my mother wouldn't be home yet anyway…or so I thought."

The intensity in Solomon's face increased as he continued to chant, the blood still dripping from his palms. He looked like he was doing some dark, twisted version of Buddhist meditation. "I'm listening. Carry on."

Why do I insist on associating with these fucking freaks? Is it because I am one myself?

"I knew something was wrong before I even got to the apartment," I continued. "It was just a feeling and one that proved right. When I got there, the front door was lying open. At first, I thought someone had broken in, which had happened before, but the locks and hinges were intact, so I figured my mother had come home early, probably drunk or high and hadn't closed the door properly. So I went inside—"

A sharp intake of breath from Solomon made me stop and look at him. "I see them this time," he said, his eyes still completely white, his mouth hanging open slightly.

"See who?" I asked.

"Your wife…and the creature that killed her."

My stomach turned over as I sat forward on the couch, the cigarette burning between my fingers, though I barely noticed. "What creature? Is it a wolf?"

Solomon nodded. "Yes…*lupinotuum pectinem*."

"I fucking knew it," I said, more to myself. "How transformed is it? Can you see a face?"

"Yes, but it's too misshapen to recognize."

"What about clothing?"

"No clothing, only a naked male."

"Fuck."

Solomon took another sharp intake of breath, this time as if he was experiencing pleasure. "So much blood…"

"Alright, enough, Solomon."

"Such powerful precision…"

"I said enough!" I shouted as I jumped to my feet to stand in front of him with my fists balled by my sides.

Solomon's eyes returned to normal a few seconds later as he lowered his bloody hands. "You really know how to spoil the fun, Ethan."

"The fun?" I pulled my weapon and pointed it at his head. "That's my fucking wife you were watching get torn to shreds."

Solomon showed no concern for the fact that a gun was mere inches from his head. "You asked me to look, Ethan, knowing what I am. Don't act so shocked when I feel pleasure at the sight of blood."

"What about their souls? Are they still here?"

"If they are, I can't feel them. As I said after the last time we did this, either they've moved on, or something is preventing me from finding them on this plane."

"What like? Another entity? A demon?"

"Maybe. I really don't know. You should just accept that they are gone, Ethan—"

I pressed the gun onto his forehead. "Don't fucking tell me what I should accept."

"As you wish. But don't threaten me either, or..."

Pain shot through my skull just as blood exploded from my nose and mouth, and I staggered back, gripping my head with both hands. The pain only lasted a few seconds before it ended as suddenly as it had begun, but it was enough for him to make his point. He stood up with the knife in his red-slicked hand, as though ready to cut me. I stood wiping blood from my nose and mouth, resisting the temptation to spit it out onto the floor, swallowing what was left in my mouth instead. Putting my gun away, I sat back down on the couch, taking out a small hip flask from my trench pocket. The whiskey inside I used to swill the coppery taste from my mouth before swallowing. Lighting a cigarette, I sat in silence and stared around the room, every piece of furniture, every picture on the wall reminding me of what I'd lost. Of what I'd lost long before my angels were killed.

"You've seen so much death, Ethan," Solomon said, still standing there with the knife in his hand, his blood still dripping to the floor. "But death is harder when it's so close to you, isn't it? Harder, yet more exquisite."

"Exquisite to you maybe," I said.

"Perhaps. Finish telling me about your mother."

Fuck it, there was no point arguing with him. He'd only insist. "I walked into the apartment to find her in the bedroom," I said in a low voice. "There was someone on top of her, some john I thought, even though she never brought any of her johns home. She had some seedy hotel room for that. But there was a man on top of her, and his head was buried into her neck. My mother wasn't moving at all, and when I called her name, the man on top of her raised his head and slowly turned to look at me with these eyes that were blazing red. His mouth was open, and I saw he had fangs. My mother's blood ran down over his mouth and dripped off his chin onto the bed."

"Did you know what was happening?" Solomon asked, a look of rapt fascination on his face.

I nodded. "I'd read enough horror comics at that point. Some voice in my head was telling me it was a vampire, but I didn't believe it because vampires didn't exist. They weren't real."

"And yet they were."

"This one was. The bastard smiled as he got off my mother, and if I hadn't run out to one of the neighbors' apartments, he probably would've killed me too."

"Did you go back?"

"Later, yeah, after the neighbor had called the cops."

"What was her body like?"

"Cold. Lifeless."

"And how did you feel, seeing her dead and drained of all her blood like that?"

"How the fuck do you think I felt? I was fucking devastated and angry and—"

"You wanted revenge."

"Yes, and I fucking got it, years later."

Solomon smiled and nodded, seeming satisfied by my reluctant admissions. "Thank you. I appreciate your candor," he said as he retreated back into the shadows. "I'm sorry the ritual came to nothing…again."

I went to say something, but Solomon had disappeared, swallowed up by the shadows.

5

After Solomon had gone, I sat on the couch smoking a cigarette, staring around the living room as I struggled to remember even living in this house. Being a Homicide cop, I was out more than I was in. Same with Angela, who worked long hours at the hospital. Her sister, Karen, would look after Callie most days. Toward the end, before Angela decided she didn't want me around anymore, I sometimes wouldn't arrive home at all for days. I would have one-night stands with strange women, and I worked as many hours as I could, all the while drinking heavily, often sleeping in the back of the car before landing straight into work again. I didn't blame Angela for not wanting to be with me anymore. If I'm being honest, that's the outcome I was looking for, only I was too chicken shit to come right out and say it. I pushed her to her limits and forced her to do what I couldn't. She hated me by the end.

Callie, bless her soul, never did, despite me not being around enough for her, missing her first school concert because I was out working a case, not turning up to three of her six birthdays. She deserved more than she got. A lot fucking more.

I didn't want to, but I went upstairs to Callie's room and

sat on the bloodstained single bed, every detail of the night I found her flashing through my mind as if it was happening all over again. Ever since the murders, I've done this, come and sat in Callie's room, because in some twisted way, it allows me to feel connected to her again. Sometimes, as with this time, I would hear her little voice in my head as I fingered the locket in my pocket, saying, "*Are you going to catch the person who killed Mommy and me and put them in jail, Daddy?*"

"Yes, angel," I said aloud. "I'll catch them. I will."

"It's *cold and dark here.*"

"I'm sorry, angel."

"*I want to go home. I miss you, Daddy.*"

"I miss you too." As I sat on the edge of the bed with my eyes squeezed shut, there was a sharp drop in temperature. Alarmed, I flung my eyes open to look around, just as a warm, tingling sensation in the back of my neck signified the arrival of the Infernal Itch. The Infernal Itch was a sixth sense I'd cultivated since the night I found the vampire with my mother, reinforced by the tattoos that snaked around my back, the ink moved through the layers of my skin, everything combining to warn me of the presence of a MURK close by.

I stood up quickly and drew my gun, unsure of what was in the darkened room with me. "Solomon?" I said, just in case it was him hiding somewhere, knowing he liked to play games sometimes. But even before I said his name, I knew it wasn't Solomon, who despite his necromantic ways, was still human, though just barely these days. No, this was a different presence, and one I could scarcely fathom it was so dark and strange. My first instinct was there was a demon in the room with me somewhere, but it wasn't like any demon I had ever felt before. The presence was so dark and otherworldly as to be beyond comprehension. Rarely did I feel much in the way of fear in the presence of a MURK, but I was feeling it now, deep in the pit of my stomach. Even the tattoos on my back swirled as if they too didn't know what to make of this suffocating presence.

"I know you're there." I turned on the spot to look around the room. "Show yourself."

My command was met by the sound of laughter, a sound that could not have been made by any human throat, so deep and unearthly was it.

"I said fucking show yourself!" Anger flooded my system now; anger at the fact that some filthy demon could penetrate the sanctity of my angel's bedroom. Not just her bedroom, but the very place where she was killed. "You're going to regret coming here. I'm going to—"

A powerful force cut me off by slamming into my chest and sending me flying back onto the bed. Upon landing, I rolled off onto the floor, taking my gun out as I crouched by the bed. Bullets can't stop a demon—not entirely anyway—but they can slow it down. Although that's only if the demon is possessing a human body. The presence in the room with me was incorporeal, though no less powerful as I soon discovered after it slammed into me again, sending me crashing into the dollhouse that I had built for Callie one Christmas, the force of the throw and my full weight combining to smash the wooden structure to pieces.

"Fuck you," I shouted after getting back to my feet. "What do you want?"

The presence took on the form of an indistinct figure in the middle of the room, a murky form that was almost human-like, but bigger. The gravelly voice that issued from the dark figure spoke in English. "I want you, Ethan," the demon said.

"Yeah?" I said. "Well, join the fucking queue, asshole."

The figure remained still for a second and then raised a smoky arm out in front of it, an action that somehow led to me raising my gun and jamming the barrel under my chin, my finger dangerously on the trigger. No matter what I did, I was unable to move the gun again, and the demon figure drifted almost languidly forward, coming to stop right in front of me, at which point two points of light appeared in its head, burning yellow orbs that bored into me. "I want your vessel, Ethan. Make it easy on yourself and give it to me now."

I laughed with the gun still jammed under my chin. "You might as well fucking pull this trigger now then because you will never get my body *or* my soul."

"You think that now. But I will have both soon enough."

I stared into those yellow orbs for a moment before smiling. "Why don't you take me now then? Because you can't, can you? You need me to submit, to give myself willingly to you. That's never going to happen."

The gun pressed harder into my chin as the demon moved closer, his incorporeal form swaying in front of me. "There will come a point when you will surrender to me of your own accord. I will break you, Ethan Drake. I will make you so weak and broken that you will beg me to take your body and soul, just so you no longer have to experience the pain and crushing defeat that I will inflict upon you."

"I'll put a bullet in my brain first before surrendering myself to some filthy fucking demon like you. I'd pull this fucking trigger now if I could."

"You would do that?" the demon asked.

"You're fucking right I would."

"Then you are more broken than I first thought. It will not take long to break you completely."

"What the fuck am I to you anyway?" I asked the demon. "There are plenty of sad sacks out there you could possess. Why me?"

"There are many vessels indeed, but few as strong as you. There aren't many bodies that could hold me for long."

"Oh yeah? And what makes you so fucking special, huh? Who are you?"

"You will find out in time."

"Yeah, I will, and when I do, I'm going to fucking destroy you."

"I've no doubt you could, but I will break you before that ever happens. Trust me on that, Ethan. In the meantime…watch."

The demon figure turned around to face the bed, his spectral hand pointing toward it. As I watched, I noticed the dried blood that was soaked into the mattress begin to rise, as though it had metal properties and was being drawn out by a giant magnet. The blood, appearing to be wet and alive again, rose in thin tendrils that began to swirl and interweave, sculpting itself into a form that I soon saw with horror was a small human-like figure. A figure made entirely from my dead daughter's long since desiccated blood. My eyes widened as the bloody figure formed human features: eye sockets and a gaping mouth, as well as long spidery fingers and numerous tendrils around the head that resembled hair.

"What is this?" I said. "What the fuck are you doing?"

"I'm bringing your daughter back," the demon said. "Or what's left of her."

I felt sick as I gazed at the eldritch horror coming to life before me, even more so because it was forming from my dead daughters very DNA. "Stop this! Fucking stop it!" The blood-figure on the bed turned toward me, its newly formed mouth wide open, and issued a bloodcurdling scream that made me wince in response.

"I must be going now," the demon said. "I'll leave you to spend some quality time with your daughter. I'm sure you have a lot of catching up to do."

"Did you kill her?" I shouted. "Did you kill my wife and daughter?"

The demon drifted back into the center of the room, answering my question with silence before vanishing, the previous cold in the room disappearing along with him. The second he left, I had control of my arm again. Taking the gun away from my chin, I instinctively pointed it at the abomination on the bed, even though I knew bullets wouldn't do much to stop it. The thing had now grown spindly arms and legs, and overall resembled a tangled mass of nerves, every one slick with blood—Callie's blood. It was difficult to look at the thing and not think of her, especially when it stared at me with its empty eye sockets and reached its arms out toward me, even managing to issue a twisted sound, which to my ears sounded like it was saying, "*Daddy...*"

"I'll kill that demon fuck for this," I said. I raised my gun and thought about shooting the thing in the head, but I didn't want to have to explain the gunshot when the neighbors inevitably reported it.

The creature screeched again as it started to crawl on all fours off the bed. "*Dad-deeeee...*" it mewled as it inched toward me, one arm outstretched as if it wanted me to go to it. My face twisted up in disgust at the sound. It was bad enough Callie was murdered, but to be brought back in this sickening fashion? And what was worse was that some part of me couldn't help but think this *was* Callie, that some semblance of her *had* been brought back to me. It was all I could do not to go to the pathetic creature and pick it up in my arms, just to see if I could feel my Callie's presence once more.

But it wasn't her, and I knew I had to destroy it. And if I couldn't do it myself, I would summon something that could.

The Hellbastards.

While the bloody abomination crawled down off the bed, still screeching my name as if all it wanted was for me to pick it up and hug it tight, I spoke a series of syllables that combined to summon the Hellbastards to me. Six of them appeared in the room, coming to stand by my side. Scroteface was closest to me, the others standing around him, all of them standing no more than three feet tall, the smallest of the two barely a foot in height. The blood creature froze on the floor next to the bed, as it must've sensed the presence of the Hellbastards. It even gave a high-pitched scream as if warning them not to come near it.

"You rang, boss?" Scroteface looked up at me with his large, cat-like eyes.

"Yeah," I said, my gaze on the creature by the bed. "Kill that fucking thing. Now."

The Hellbastards jumped around excitedly at the thought of descending on the creature. Nothing got their rocks of more than killing things.

"Let's get it, boys," Scroteface said as he began to advance slowly forward, the other five Hellbastards behind him, saliva dripping from their pointed teeth as they made little noises of anticipation. The smallest of the bunch dragged sharp claws along the carpet as he went, ears nearly as long as his body twitching from side to side. His name was Cracka, and he was the most vicious of the bunch, suffering as he did from small demon syndrome.

The monstrosity that was supposed to resemble my daughter began to back away now in fear, crawling back up onto the bed to stare down at the advancing demons, its mouth twisting from side to side as it hissed defensively, though it was clearly frightened as well. As it should be, for the Hellbastards didn't fuck around when it came to killing. When they attacked, Scroteface jumped up onto the bed first, his short but powerful legs carrying him up with ease to land in front of the creature who backed away immediately, climbing down off the bed on the other side and moving back until it hit the wall, soon realizing it had nowhere else to go. As did the Hellbastards, for they all smiled with glee knowing their prey was trapped. Scroteface launched himself at the creature from atop the bed, raking his claws over the creature's face as he came down, causing a large clot of blood to come away from the gruesome organism and splat against the wall. After that, the other five Hellbastards dived off the bed all at once, landing on the creature in a frenzy as they tore the thing apart piece by bloody piece, biting and clawing until blood began to fly everywhere, splatting against the walls where it ran down in thick rivulets. And even among all the frenzied violence, the creature continued to screech, "*Dad-deeee...Dad-deeee...*" over and over until it was no longer capable of making sounds at all.

Several seconds later, the violent frenzy was over, and there was nothing left of the creature except what ran down the walls and dripped from the ceiling. Scroteface and the rest of the Hellbastards came around the bed to stand in front of me like they expected me to throw them a treat for being good little puppies. "Job done, boss," Scroteface said, licking the blood from his lips.

Cracka was jumping up and down, his long tongue hanging out the side of his mouth as his pointed tail swished from side to side. "More blood! More blood!" he barked.

"More! More! More!" the others chanted in unison.

"Enough!" I shouted, silencing them all instantly.

"Steady on, boys," Scroteface said to his gang.

"You've had your fun," I told them. "Now fuck off." With the syllables I used to summon the demons, I used the same ones to banish them back to the apartment by saying the syllables backward. Soon enough, it was just me in the room and the silence that was left behind. Over on the blood-spattered nightstand was a photo in a pink frame, one of the last photos taken of Callie and me with her sweet smile and sparkling blue eyes. With my heart aching, I looked toward the picture and sighed. "I'm sorry, angel," I said, before turning and leaving the room.

6

I'd seen a lot of horror in my life—things that would drive most people insane—but no horror as personal as the creature formed from my dead daughter's own blood. The way it reached for me, pathetically calling my name, had left me shook up as I sat out in the car. The house now seemed like some infected entity as I stared through the side window at it. There was a gas can in the trunk, and for a moment I thought about grabbing it and dowsing the whole house so I could raze it to the ground, as if doing so would somehow erase the pain I felt. Instead, I took out the dropper bottle and took a double dose of the Mud. Which I probably shouldn't have done at this time of day because it affected my vision, causing everything to swirl in and out of focus. But I didn't care, as long as it put a heavy veil between me and my thoughts and emotions. By the time I pulled off, what happened in the house seemed like a dream I had trouble recollecting.

~

On the way back to the precinct, I stopped off at the

scrap metal yard on Mulberry Street, which wasn't far from The Warrens where I grew up. I drove through the main gates and along the dirt roads between the wrecked cars and other scrap that was piled high on both sides, continuing right to the back of the massive yard until I came to a battered old trailer and the man sitting outside it in a tattered leather armchair. The man made no move to get up as he continued sitting in his chair, a bottle of beer in one hand and a cigarette in the other.

His name was Caleb Grimes, and he owned the scrap business, though he did little to run the place these days. He had other guys on site to do that for him. Cal mostly spent his days sitting outside his trailer, drinking and occasionally seeing to his other business, which involved mainly making bladed weapons for hunters and others who required something that would do real damage to a MURK. In his late fifties, with long gunmetal gray hair and a thick mustache, he wore blue jeans and a leather half-cut that he'd had for as long as I'd known him, which was over twenty-five years now. Not only was he a mentor, but he was also the closest thing I ever had to a father, given that my real father had been garroted to death right in front of me when I was four years old.

"Ethan," Cal said as I got out of the car and joined him, coming to sit in a folding chair right next to him. "What brings you around? Things slow in cop land today?" His voice was gravelly from years of smoking, his demeanor languid, as if he didn't give a fuck about anything but drinking beer. I knew different, however. Despite his laid-back exterior, Cal was always deadly serious about everything, especially when it came to his real job of making things that were designed to cut MURKs into bloody pieces.

"It's never slow in cop land, Cal," I said, my speech slightly slowed from the Mud as I opened a cooler box next to him and helped myself to a beer. "The only thing that's slow today is me."

"Oh yeah?" He swigged on his beer. "And why's that?"

"I'm just back from Angela's house," I said as I cracked open my bottle and took a long swallow from it.

"Torturing yourself again, were you?"

"Trying to find evidence."

"Bullshit. There is no evidence. If there was, you'd have found it by now. What were you really doing, apart from getting high?"

I stared into his slate-gray eyes for a second before looking away. "Doing a ritual with Solomon."

"Jesus, you really are a glutton for punishment, aren't you? What did I teach you about grief?"

"Wallow in it for a while, then lock it up tight and throw away the key."

"Precisely. So why are you still wallowing? It does you no good."

"Because it's my wife and daughter, not some fallen comrade."

"Ex-wife."

"Screw you."

"Just saying. You want to help little Callie move on? Then get your head in the game."

"That's just it," I said. "I don't know where she is, or whether she *can* move on. She died violently, they both did, so their ghosts should still be on this plane. They aren't."

"Nothing to say they aren't upstairs somewhere. You don't know."

I took another swallow from my bottle and then lit up a cigarette as I stared at the mountains of scrap metal surrounding us. When I was younger, I practically lived in this yard, helping Cal sift through the scrap to find materials to forge weapons from. It was a simpler time, a time before Blackstar and the police department, and one I wished I could go back to sometimes. "Something's not right, Cal. I can feel it. Solomon said something might be holding Angela and Callie's souls."

"Solomon is a manipulative psychopath," he said, tossing his cigarette butt away before immediately taking another out of the crumpled packet resting on the arm of his chair, stabbing the cigarette into his mouth and lighting it up with a dulled zippo lighter. "Fuck that guy."

"It's not just that," I said. "While I was at the house, I had a run-in with a demon. Bastard made me jam my gun under my chin while he—"

"What?"

"Brought Callie back to life, or some terrible fucking version of her anyway."

"Shit."

"Yeah. I summoned the Hellbastards. They killed it."

"What about this demon? Did it say what it wanted?"

"Me, apparently. It wants this gorgeous body of mine and isn't going rest until it gets it."

"I don't know about gorgeous."

"You wish you had this bod, old man," I said smiling.

Cal smiled back. "Screw you. You ain't as tight as you used to be."

"You been checking me out or something?"

"I just saw your belly wobble as you came over."

"Ha-ha."

Cal laughed. "So aside from his poor taste, why does this demon want you and no one else?"

I shrugged as I pulled on my cigarette. "It needs a strong body, it says."

"So, it's powerful then."

"Yep, as powerful as I've come across, maybe even one of Hell's bigwigs, who knows."

A barking sound made me look to the left, and I saw two large black dogs come bounding toward me as if they were going to attack, though I knew they wouldn't. The dogs were a

German Shepherd/black Labrador mix, and their names were Ace and Apollo. When they reached me, they both shoved their heads in my lap, expecting me to pet them as always. Putting my beer on the ground and holding my cigarette between my lips, I said, "What's up boys?" as I roughly ruffled their fur and pushed their heads around, the dogs responding by jumping up and licking my face, Ace managing to lick the cigarette out of my mouth at the same time.

"Down," Cal commanded, and the two dogs immediately got down off me and sat on their haunches, their long tongues hanging from their mouths as they stared at me. I knew what they wanted, so I got up and found an old baseball that was full of teeth marks sitting by the trailer. As I picked up the ball, the two dogs ran over and sat in front of me, their ears pricked as they practically shook with excitement at the prospect of me throwing the ball for them. I waited a moment, drawing out the expectation, and then launched the ball across the yard. The two dogs barked as they bolted after it, fighting with each other to see who could reach the ball first. As it turned out, Ace got there a second before Apollo, but as Ace was running back with the ball in his mouth, Apollo poached it from him, keeping a hold of it as he brought it back to me.

"Good boy," I said, ruffling his ears as I took the slimy ball from his mouth. I launched the ball again, but in a different direction this time, so it landed somewhere in the piles of scrap, knowing it would take the dogs a while to find it. When the two of them ran off again, I sat back down next to Cal, picking up my beer to finish it.

"So how you gonna handle this demon?" Cal asked.

"Kill it or banish it back to Hell," I said. "I'm easy either way."

"If it doesn't kill you first."

"It needs my body."

"Yeah, and once it has it, your soul goes bye-bye."

"It won't come to that."

"Well, you'd better find a way to deal with this asshole then."

"I will. I always do."

"Try getting off that shit that you're on as well," Cal said. "It dulls the senses. You need to stay sharp."

"I am sharp," I said, looking away from him.

"Bullshit you are. You're looking at an ex-junkie here, remember?"

"I'm not a junkie, Cal."

"That's what I used to say, right up until that hellot cut my throat because I was too fucked up to sense him behind me." Almost unconsciously, he ran his fingers over the pinkish-white scar across his throat. "I wouldn't like to see the same thing happen to you."

"It won't."

"That's what they all say."

"It's just for a little while, to get me over the worst. I'll come off it soon."

Cal said nothing, thankfully letting it go, and we sat in silence for a few moments, watching the dogs as they hunted for the ball.

"Many customers coming around?" I asked him after a bit.

He nodded. "A few. Collectors, mostly."

"No hunters?"

"Not many, thankfully. I hate dealing with those guys, they're fucking crazy, man, most of 'em. Paranoid mother-fuckers. I prefer to deal with collectors these days. They pay more anyway."

Cal's weapons were works of art. Over the last few years, word has spread through the collectors' circles of his prowess when it comes to making blades, every design bespoke and finished to the highest standards. Collectors paid a lot of money for something they knew no one else had. "Not that you need fucking money. All you buy is beer."

A throaty chuckle left his mouth. "A man can live on beer alone. And pussy."

"Beer and pussy," I said. "You got it all figured out, Cal."

"Maybe *you* should get yourself some pussy," he said. "It might do you some good."

"I don't need the complication right now."

"I'm not saying you have to fucking marry them. Just fuck them. Christ, you were practically a fucking sex addict before you strapped a ball and chain around your ankle, which you're still fucking dragging around with you."

I shook my head at his lack of sensitivity, though I wasn't angry at it. No one could ever accuse Cal Grimes of being tactful, and I knew this better than anyone. "You hear about the body-snatching at Cave Hill?" I asked him to change the subject.

"Yeah, I saw the news. You on the case?"

"Yeah. Seems like a bunch of teenagers are fucking with stuff they shouldn't."

"Leave them to it then. They'll get what's coming."

"That's what I'm worried about. There'll be collateral damage unless I find the little shits before they do whatever it is they're planning on doing."

"If they haven't done it already."

"Let's hope not."

"You find them, send them here. I'll give them an education they'll never forget like I did to you all those years ago."

I thought back for a moment to the trials and tribulations Cal put me through in the name of toughening me up. "I wouldn't wish that on anyone."

Cal smiled. "Maybe you're right. Just throw the little fuckers in jail then."

"Jail would be easier."

"Pussy."

I couldn't help but chuckle. "After the shit you put me through, no one could ever accuse me of being a pussy." I drained what was left of my beer and stood up. "I gotta get back to it."

"To being a pussy?"

"To being a cop, smartass."

He reached down and got himself another beer from the cooler box, twisting off the cap and tossing it away. "I said it before, and I'll say it again. Why they ever gave a guy like you a fucking badge, I'll never know."

"A guy like me?" I said with a wry smile. "What are you trying to say, Cal?"

"You know what I'm saying."

"After I turn in my badge, I'll come straight here and spend the rest of my life sitting next to you drinking beer. How's that?"

"Son," he said. "Just don't lose that fucking badge, for the love of God."

"That's what I thought. Later, old man."

"Yeah, later…pussy."

7

After leaving Cal's place, I drove back to the precinct to see what was happening with the forensic evidence found at the graveyard. I also had a text from the commissioner saying he was looking to see about something. Didn't say what about, so I figured it was about the Keane case, or about my earlier conversation with the captain. I texted Lewellyn that I'd call in to his office shortly.

On the ride over, I noticed I was being followed by a dark gray sedan, which had stayed on my tail despite me taking a few obscure shortcuts to shake them off. I even drove into a derelict street, and the sedan kept right on behind me, barely trying to hide the fact that it was following me.

"What the fuck's this?" I strained into the rearview to see who was in the car. The sedan was ten yards behind me, the sun reflecting off the windshield making it difficult to see who was inside. I eventually saw there were at least two people in the car, neither of whom I recognized, at least from this distance. Near the end of the derelict street, I slammed on the brakes, and the car behind did the same, still staying ten yards back. "Motherfuckers," I said as I sat debating whether to drive on or get out and confront them.

A moment later, I opened the door and stepped out onto the street, just as my Infernal Itch flared up. Something was coming, I realized, something worse than the sedan parked behind me. A second later, a van with blacked-out windows screeched around the corner and came to a halt in front of my car.

"Fuck's this now?" I said as four robed, hooded figures jumped out of the van's side door into the road, each one carrying what looked to be a baton similar to the police issue ones.

The figures in the black robes stood in a line next to each other, their heads bowed so I couldn't see their faces. As I drew my gun, I afforded a glance behind me, realizing I knew who was following me now. I recognized the driver from the precinct. His name escaped me, but I knew he was IAB.

What the fuck did those motherfuckers want? I wondered.

Not that I would get the chance to ask them, for they were already reversing back down the street, wanting nothing to do with the robed figures blocking the road in front of me.

Bastards, I thought, unable to believe the IAB assholes had left me in the lurch. They were supposed to be fucking cops and yet here they were, leaving one of their own to face off against four, and possibly more, armed threats. I gritted my teeth as I watched the sedan get farther away, eventually turning the car so they could speed off around the corner, leaving me to it.

Wait till I see those assholes back at the precinct, I thought. *IAB or not, they won't fucking know what hit them.*

Turning around, I raised my gun to point it at the robed figures, who had now raised their heads to stare at me, though I still couldn't make out their faces, the sun now blocked out by preternatural darkness that had come from nowhere.

"Just so you know," I said. "Halloween's a whole two months away. This robed thing you've got going on…a bit theatrical, don't you think? You want to intimidate me, you want to scare me, you do it to my face, not behind some fucking costume."

Another robed figure got out of the van and came to stand in front of the others. But unlike the other four, this one peeled back their hood to reveal a bald, Caucasian male underneath, black tattoos across both sides of his head. His eyes were dark, and as far as I could tell, he seemed to be human. If he was a demon, I couldn't see any Visage hovering behind him. "Ethan Drake?" he said, a black baton in one hand.

"I think you know who I am, asshole," I said. "You'd better tell me what you want before you get shot."

I pointed my gun at the bald guy who never flinched. "We're here on behalf of our Dark Lord," he said. "Praise his infernal darkness."

"Praise his infernal darkness," the other four said in unison.

"Your Dark Lord?" I said.

"I think you met him earlier."

Hellots, I thought. Humans who had pledged their allegiance to a demon master for power. "What the fuck do you want? I already told your demon lord he had no fucking chance of getting his hands on me."

The bald guy smiled. "The Dark Lord always gets what he wants."

"Maybe so," I said. "But not in this case. I'm advising you now to back off. This is the only chance I'm giving you. Get back into your little cult van and get the fuck out of here. Now."

The hellot's smile widened for a second, before disappearing altogether. Then his four acolytes stepped forward, each of them slapping their baton into the palm of their other hand, a gesture which was supposed to scare me, I guess, but these motherfuckers didn't know who they were dealing with. If they thought I was going to back down, they had another thing coming. Holding my weapon tighter, I squeezed off a shot that was aimed at the nearest guy's chest. Fuck it, my life was under threat. I was within my right to defend myself as a police officer. Besides, I couldn't care less about killing some fucking cultist who'd sold his dirty soul to an even filthier demon. The city was coming down with these fucks, all of them serving the darkness for their own gain. Killing them would be like cutting out a cancer that was infecting the city and beyond, and I had no qualms about doing it.

Only, my bullet missed. Not because my aim was off but because the asshole I'd shot at had dodged the fucking bullet. His hood had come down as he moved with abnormal speed, and I saw he was human like his bald leader. The smug smile on his face told me he'd traded his soul in return for supernatural speed and God knows what else. Demons weren't stupid. They needed the belief of their followers to maintain and increase their power, and the best way to ensure that unerring allegiance was to grant the followers their own powers. It was a win-win. It also meant there were thousands of these hellot motherfuckers all over the city, and that number increased every day.

As Speedy went on smiling, I shot the person standing next to him, hitting him square in the chest. But the guy didn't go down. He just threw his hood back and slowly looked down at the bullet wound in his chest as if he wasn't worried about it at all. And just to prove he wasn't, he pulled open his robe to show his bare chest, and as I watched, I saw the bullet hole seal right up as if nothing had happened.

"That's cute," I said. "You all have superpowers."

"More than you can handle," the guy I shot said.

I put my gun back in its holster, a wave of calm coming over me as I got ready for what was to happen next. I'd like to say my adrenaline was flowing, but I didn't get adrenaline kicks anymore, having been through way too much shit in my life for that, not to mention the genetic tinkering I went through at Blackstar. "We'll see about that," I said. "You want me? Come and fucking get me."

Speedy came at me first, moving so fast I didn't see him until he was right beside me, swinging his baton into my ribs, a blow I took easily enough before I grabbed the baton and pulled him into a head butt that smashed his nose into his face. "Let's see how fast you move now," I said, my grip transferred to his wrist. As he went to pull away, I swung my forearm down and around, connecting with his elbow joint, hearing that satisfying crack as his whole forearm bent away from the joint, followed by his scream of pain. I finished him by driving my elbow down onto his skull, releasing his arm as he hit the ground and lay there groaning and unmoving. Just to be sure he didn't get up again, I stamped his head with my boot, pushing his face into the dirty asphalt.

Asshole, I thought as blood pooled around his head. *Everyone thinks they're a fucking killer…until they aren't.*

The guy I shot came at me next, running at me with his baton raised high, bringing it down toward my skull as he got close. Before the baton could connect, however, I blocked it with my forearm and the hardwood weapon broke clean in two, and my assailant froze for a second. "I got a few enhancements of my own," I said, taking advantage of his surprise by moving faster than he expected, considering my size. In no time, I had him turned so his back was against my chest and he was caught in a chokehold that he wasn't getting out of. "You might be able to take a bullet, asshole, but you'll go to sleep like all the rest…right about…now." By the time I released the chokehold, he was unconscious, and I tossed him to the ground, discarding his limp body like a piece of trash.

Considering I just took out two of those assholes with relative ease, I had expected the other three to back off.

But that's not what happened. Instead, they all came running at once, the bald leader coming straight at me, the other two flanking me either side.

I went for the leader first, driving a kick toward his midsection, surprised and annoyed when my leg and the rest of me went right through him as if he was no more than a ghost. By the time my foot hit the ground, his baton had whacked into my back, quickly followed by blows on both sides of me, inflicted by the other two assholes.

I was forced to cover up then, using my arms to protect my head as the baton blows rained down. Realizing I had to do something, I kicked out to create some space and then fell back into a roll, drawing my gun as I came up into a crouch before double tapping two more of my assailants.

The bald-headed leader froze as his two acolytes went down either side of him, both of them dead as far as I could tell, given that I'd just shot them in the chest.

I stared at the leader for a second as I stood up. Then I shot him in the head. The bullet went right through him, however, as he used his power to become incorporeal, floating at speed back to the van, which was already reversing around the corner. I got two more shots off before the van disappeared, both bullets impacting the windshield, though I don't think I hit the driver. Not that it mattered. I doubted the cultists would be back anytime soon, although you never know with these assholes. They'd do anything their demon masters told them to do.

Turning around, I surveyed the four bodies on the ground, two of whom were dead, the other two just unconscious, although the one I choked out was beginning to wake up, so I put him back to sleep again by kicking him in the head.

"Now, what am I going to do with you assholes?" I said, holstering my weapon just as the darkness began to lift and daylight—or what was left of it—began to return.

Arresting the two surviving cult members would mean a bunch of paperwork and a whole load of questions that I didn't feel like answering. Besides, their demon master would probably arrange for their release somehow, so arresting them would be a waste of time.

Instead, I dragged them both into one of the derelict houses, dumping their unconscious bodies into a filthy room littered with dirty needles and other unsavory detritus. Grabbing some zip ties from the car, I secured the cult member's wrists and ankles so they couldn't go anywhere when they woke up.

In the meantime, there were still two dead bodies lying out on the street, so I summoned the Hellbastards to take care of them.

Scroteface and the other five Hellbastards gathered around the two corpses, Cracka jumping up and down at the thought of getting his way with the dead meat. "Take them into one of the buildings across the street," I said to Scroteface. "Make sure they never get found. Dig out the slugs as well and dispose of them."

"Yes, boss," Scroteface said, just as I realized he had the pelt of a tabby cat on his head, wearing it like a hat, the cat's front legs swinging over the demon's shoulders, its long tail hanging down his back. The cat's dead eyes stared at me as Scroteface did.

"Is that the cat from the fire escape?" I asked.

"It is, boss, yes."

"I thought I told you to get rid of it, not wear its fucking pelt as a hat."

"You did, boss, but it has such pretty fur…so soft," he said as he ran his scaly fingers down the length of the dead cat's leg.

"Cracka want one too," Cracka shouted in his tiny but powerful voice. "Me want cat hat."

"Calm down, Cracka," I told him.

"He can't help it," Snot Skull—a four-armed, heavily muscled, mucus-dripping demon—said. "Dead meat turns him on."

"It turns us all on," said Reggie, a little dreadlocked demon with tiny yellow eyes who had taken up smoking since coming topside. He stood now, all two-and-a-half feet of him, puffing on a huge cigar, inhaling the pungent smoke deep before blowing it out again in a huge plume.

The other two Hellbastards were Khullu and Toast. Khullu had tentacles that hung from his face, which he was currently using to probe one of the corpses, and Toast looked like someone had run a blowtorch over every square inch of him.

Every one of the Hellbastards stood with massive hard-ons. Cracka was slapping his against the face of one of the corpses, laughing as he did so, as if he found it hilarious.

"Right you bunch of degenerates," I said. "Get to it and make sure these two get gone. I don't want their remains turning up on the nightly news, you got it?"

"Yes, boss," Scroteface said. "You can rely on us."

Leaving the Hellbastards to it, I went back inside the derelict house where I'd left the two unconscious hellots. The one I'd choked out and kicked in the head was beginning to come around. The other was still out of it and must've been in worse shape than I thought, given how hard I'd cracked his skull.

Standing over the one who was almost awake now, I said, "What's up asshole? Two of your friends are dead and your leader high-tailed it in the van, so it's just you and your other friend here, who to be honest, might be brain-damaged, given that he hasn't come around yet, so I guess it's just you and me for now."

The hellot, in his late twenties with sandy-colored hair and bad skin, groaned as he woke up, probably with a raging headache thanks to my kick to his head. "You'll not…get away with this," he said as his light blue eyes regained their focus.

"Get away with what?" I said. "I haven't done anything yet."

"You killed two of us."

"And?"

"The Dark Lord will make you pay. He'll have your soul."

"You're deluded if you think your Dark Lord gives a shit about you or the two assholes I shot. You're all expendable to him. There are always more chumps like you out there willing to sell their souls for a little power." I crouched down in front of him as he maintained his defiant stare. "No one's coming for you. However, if you answer my questions, I might consider turning you loose."

His response was to spit in my face. "Fuck you."

You're gonna regret that, asshole, I thought as I wiped his blood-flecked spit from my skin before drawing my slick hand across his chest. "I'm trying to give you a chance here—"

"Fuck you," he said again.

"Fine," I sighed. "Have it your way."

Scroteface, send Cracka to me.

Within moments of sending the telepathic command to Scroteface, Cracka came bounding into the room, the tiny demon coming to stand beside me, so wired he could barely keep still as usual. "Yes, boss? Watcha want?"

The sandy-haired hellot drew back against the wall at the sight of the Hellbastard. "What the fuck is that thing?" he said.

"This little fella is Cracka," I informed him. "Cracka is a little crazy, hence the name. Ain't that right, Cracka?"

The tiny demon nodded his oversized head with vigor, resembling one of those nodding dogs you see on the dash of cars. "Crazy boss, yeah, yeah…"

I smiled at Cracka like he was adorable and then looked at the hellot again, whose face said he found Cracka anything but adorable. "Here's the thing …what's your name again?"

"Screw you."

"Not much of a name. How about I just call you Asshole? Seems fitting to me."

Asshole shook his head as he glared at me. "You're the fucking asshole here, not me."

"Whatever, Asshole," I said. "Anyway, here's the thing. If you don't answer all my questions, I'm going to get Cracka here to rip open your stomach with his razor-sharp claws so he can crawl inside you and rip you apart from the inside. I've seen him do it, and it ain't pretty."

"Can I, boss, can I?" Cracka asked, jumping up and down. "Can I please, please?"

"Let's see what our friend here says first," I told Cracka, who made a loud noise of disappointment as I patted him on the head like he was just the cutest thing.

"Keep that fucking thing away from me," Asshole said.

"But you took one of my bullets without flinching earlier," I said. "Surely you aren't afraid of what a cute little demon will do to you?"

"I've sworn allegiance to the Dark Lord," he said. "I can't tell you anything. He'll—"

"Kill you? Motherfucker, Cracka will kill you in the most horrible of ways if you don't start talking."

"I—I—"

"Go to it, Cracka."

Asshole screamed as Cracka jumped on his belly, then screamed again as Cracka began to tear away his robes with his claws, exposing the soft flesh of Asshole's abdomen underneath. With one vicious swipe, Cracka raked his claws across Asshole's stomach, drawing blood and causing him to scream once more.

"Hold up, Cracka," I said, and Cracka stood balancing on the hellot's blood-soaked belly, ready to go again on my command.

"Please—" Asshole said.

"Why aren't you healing?" I asked him.

"I—I need time to build up my power again…"

"I see. So by the time you build your power up again,

Cracka will have ripped you to shreds, and it'll be too late for you. Great. Go to it, Cracka."

The little demon swiped his razor claws across Asshole's gut again, creating another row of deep slices that immediately filled with blood.

"Alright," Asshole screamed. "Alright. I'll tell you what you want to know, just get it off me, get it off me..."

"Down, Cracka."

Cracka made a noise in the back of his throat to signal his frustration at not being able to carry on eviscerating the hellot. "But, boss..."

"I said down, Cracka."

The demon snarled at Asshole before jumping down off him, coming to stand by my side once more, his claws dripping blood. "Alright," I said. "Your demon lord, what's his name?"

"Astaroth, his name is Astaroth."

"Astaroth?" I'd heard the name before. He was one of the Fallen, and as far as I knew, he was also one of Lucifer's Grand Dukes in Hell. "What does he want?"

"He wants a body to possess, one strong enough to hold his great spirit. He's been through so many—"

"How did he hear about me?"

Asshole shook his head. "I don't know. I'm just a follower, a believer, that's all."

He seemed to be telling the truth. I also knew from experience that the Fallen keep their plans to themselves, operating on a need to know basis only. This is how they maintained power over their followers and kept themselves safe from outsiders. "Okay," I said, moving in close to the hellot. "I'm only going to ask you this once, and I want the truth, or else Cracka will go to town on you." I paused for a second to make sure he was listening. "Did Astaroth have my wife and daughter killed? Did he have anything to do with it?"

Asshole shook his head. "I don't know anything about that, you have to believe me..."

I stared at the hellot for a long time, finally concluding that he was telling the truth. "Alright, Cracka. You can go."

"Ahhhhh," Cracka whined. "But boss—"

"Go. Help the others."

Cracka, huffing indignantly, scurried away to join the other Hellbastards.

"Are you going to let me go now?" Asshole asked.

"You fucking demon worshippers are a blight on society." I drew my gun. "You cozy up to these demon fucks for personal gain, helping them spread their filth and enact their vile plans. As far as I'm concerned, you're worse than they are. Demons are demons, but you? You had a choice, and you chose to help the darkness at the expense of the light."

"No, please," he said as I pointed my gun at his still unconscious friend on the floor next to him. He jumped and screamed when I put a bullet in his friend's head. "You're a fucking cop, you can't do this."

"This is the consequence of siding with evil," I said as I trained the gun on him. "Now you get to go to Hell where the real action is."

"You'll never get away with this!" he screamed. "Astaroth will have your fucking soul—"

I squeezed the trigger and his brains formed a red rose on the filthy wall behind him, his body slumping onto a bed of dirty needles on the floor. "No one's getting *my* soul, asshole. *No one.*"

8

After leaving the Hellbastards to their work, I drove to Bedford to meet up with the commissioner, whose office was in the swanky 1st Precinct.

Before going inside the post-modern steel and glass building, I changed my bloodstained shirt, putting on a fresh one that I kept in the car for just such occasions, and threw the old one in the trunk for disposal later.

Freshly changed and blood free, I headed up to the commissioner's office on the third floor, ignoring the looks I got from the cops inside, some of whom thought they were above those of us in Old Town just because they worked nicer looking streets.

Which was bullshit. There was as much filth and corruption in Bedford as there was across the river. But in Bedford, the filth and corruption were hidden behind layers of wealth and supposed respectability. The criminals in Bedford were as degenerate as the ones in Old Town—they just wore nicer clothes and drove more expensive cars here, that's all. Though that still didn't stop my fellow officers on the Bedford side looking down their over-tanned noses at my Old Town colleagues and me. They weren't all snobs—I knew some good cops this side of the river—but most of them were. Some were even hellots, enthralled to demons who helped them rise through the ranks quicker than they would have on their own.

The captain here was one such person, being the youngest captain ever to take up the position. I knew the asshole was a prominent cult member, and one of these days, I was going to take him down. The trouble was, there were so many of these demon-worshipping bastards—in all walks of life, not just in the police department—that taking them all down would be impossible, though I was willing to try if someone like Lewellyn gave me the go-ahead to do so.

When I reached Lewellyn's office, his secretary sent me straight in. Rarely did I have to wait long before Lewellyn saw me, even if I turned up late for a meeting. Lewellyn, it had to be said, was one of the better guys. He at least understood the importance of what we were doing in Unit X, which is more than I could say for any of the other brass who knew of the unit's existence.

"Ethan," he said as I entered his office. "I expected you here earlier."

"Sorry, sir," I said, taking a seat opposite him at his large oak desk. "I got held up."

"Oh?" Lewellyn, a tall, heavily built man in his early sixties, raised his bushy eyebrows.

"Yeah, just working on the Keane case, that's all." I could've told him the truth and he likely wouldn't have batted an eyelid, given he felt the same way about hellots that I did. But we had already agreed from the beginning that he should be afforded a certain amount of plausible deniability, given his precariously political position. He wanted to police the city's occult underground, but at the same time, he wanted to keep his job and all the nice benefits that came along with it. When it came right down to it, it was a rare individual who was willing to sacrifice everything in the name of justice.

"And how are things going with the case?" he asked. "I had Captain Edwards on the phone earlier complaining his department wasn't handling it. He also remarked on your attitude."

"My attitude, sir?"

Lewellyn settled back in his leather chair, looking the part in his expensive dark suit and impeccably groomed mustache. "Yes, specifically your lack of respect for his authority."

"I was nothing but respectful, sir."

He looked at me with a wry smile. "I'm sure you were."

"Captain Edwards just doesn't like being out of the loop. He's also in denial about what's really going on in this city, like the rest of the Precinct is, sir."

"I know." He opened a drawer on his desk and took out a bottle of Johnnie Walker Blue and two crystal tumblers, pouring a generous amount in both glasses before sliding one across to me. "And that's why we started this unit of yours, but we have to be careful not to piss people off. The department is full of hellots who'd like nothing better than to have you tossed out on your ass and me along with you. Even the ones who aren't enthralled to some demon are uncomfortable with what we're doing because we're looking into things that they've always preferred to ignore."

"I realize that sir," I said, sipping from my glass, nodding approvingly at the taste of the expensive whiskey. "I'm trying to keep things low-key, as we discussed."

"This has never been done before. As I told you in the beginning when we started all this, I'm going out on a limb here."

"I appreciate that, sir. You're doing the right thing."

"I suppose we'll see about that, won't we? What about Walker, how is she working out?"

I tried not to think of the earlier incident at the Hawthorn residence. Lewellyn had no idea Hannah Walker was now a demon, and I had no intention of telling him. Doubtless, he'd see it as a step too far, working with the enemy, so to speak. "Fine, sir. She'll do okay. She's a good investigator."

"She was also a drug addict on suspension. To be honest, Ethan, I'm surprised you chose to have her work with you."

"I didn't have much choice, sir. I can't think of a single cop who would work with me on this, especially given the sensitive nature of what it is we're doing. Walker will do fine… once she gets used to her new role."

"I'll take your word for it. What about the other thing?"

"What thing, sir?"

"The murder of your wife and daughter."

"Oh." As a memory of Astaroth in Callie's bedroom flashed through my mind for a second, I rubbed my forehead as if to try to banish the image. "No leads yet, sir"

"Sorry to hear that. Hopefully something will turn up."

"Hopefully, sir."

A silence elapsed as we both drained our whiskey glasses and I placed mine back on the table. Lewellyn then took the empty glasses and placed them along with the bottle back in the drawer. "Listen," he said. "The reason I called you here today is that I wanted to ask you about your former employer."

"Blackstar?" I frowned. Lewellyn was the only one who knew I used to work for Blackstar. There was no mention of it in my employment record, which stated I used work classified security for an unnamed company. "What about them, sir?"

"I got a phone call from one of their representatives yesterday, a man named Eric Pike. Do you know him?"

I nodded. "Yeah. He's the head of security at Blackstar. He's an asshole. What'd he want?"

"He was asking questions about the newly formed unit."

"Figures they would find out. What'd you tell him?"

"Nothing, of course," Lewellyn said. "I told him to fuck off and stop asking about confidential police business. Why would they be sticking their nose in?"

"Because that's what they do, sir. They believe they have authority over the occult underground and everything that goes on in it."

"And do they? Are they backed by the government?"

"Their position is murky, to say the least. They have dealings with the government, yes."

"But that certainly doesn't mean they have authority over the FPD, does it?"

"No, sir, not as far as I know, although when I worked with them, cops didn't get a look in. I'd say be careful, sir."

"Careful? Why?" His tanned, lined face reflected his worry. As much as he believed in what we were doing, I knew he would only go so far to keep Unit X in existence.

"Blackstar has money and power, sir. They could make things difficult for us, and I'm not going to lie, for you as well. They've been known to discredit anyone who gets in their way."

"But we're not *in* their way, are we?"

"Not yet, but we could be at some point. We'll just have to tread carefully." I paused. "Are you having second thoughts, sir?"

Lewellyn stared at me for a moment before shaking his head. "No," he said. "I'm still committed to what we're doing. These MURKs as you call them, have had their way for far too long. They need to know their actions come under the arm of the law like everyone else."

As usual, I admired his resolve and willingness to initiate change. It's what helped him rise through the ranks in the first place and the reason he was appointed commissioner by a mayor who got elected partly on the basis that he would root out corruption within the police force and local government.

But at the same time, his experience with MURKs and the occult underground in general was limited, especially compared to mine, which made him naive. I knew things he didn't, and I especially knew that fighting the darkness, along with the corruption it breeds, was a losing battle. If he thought he was going to change anything, he was sadly mistaken, and I hadn't the heart to tell him that yet. I doubted I ever would. He would find out for himself at some point anyway, and then he'd become mired in despair like all the rest of us, those who thought they could drive back the darkness, only to become consumed by it. "Yes, sir, I agree. The law should apply to everyone, human or not."

He nodded as if that's what he wanted to hear. "Just tread carefully and keep me apprised of all developments, good or bad. Do you understand?"

"Yes, sir." I stood up and walked to the door before turning around. "There's something else you should know."

"What is it?"

"I caught IAB tailing me earlier. Do you know anything about that?"

"IAB?" He sighed and shook his head. "I'm sorry, I don't. I'll look into it."

"Should I be worried, sir?"

"Just carry on doing your job, Ethan. IAB won't be a problem."

Whether or not he meant it, I can't say I believed him. As I left his office, I knew full well that IAB would be a problem.

The only question was how big of a problem.

Back in my car, I checked my phone to find a text from Walker, telling me she was in a blues club in Old Town waiting on me. I sat for a minute, wondering what she wanted to talk about and whether I was even interested in hearing it. Working with Walker— demon that she was—was one thing, but I didn't think I had any desire to be friends with her outside of work. I was never one for socializing with people from work anyway, preferring to drink alone most of the time, or with Cal at the scrap yard. Walker knew this about me, so whatever she wanted to discuss, it must have been important, at least to her. In any case, Lewellyn's whiskey had whetted my appetite for more, so if nothing else, I'd meet up with Walker just to get a few more drinks.

Once I hit the expressway going across the river, I initiated a telepathic conversation with Scroteface, just to make sure the Hellbastards had done their job properly.

You get it done?

Yes, boss. All done as you asked.

Good. And the slugs?

Cracka ate them.

Jesus, I suppose that's one way to get rid of them.

Yes, boss. Acid in the belly.

Alright, good job.

The boys think they earned themselves some fun.

Define fun.

The orphanage…

No, no way. That's out of bounds, as you well know, you little shit.

But, boss, the kiddies there are so sweet and juicy and—

I said no, Scroteface. Find somewhere else to get your kicks, somewhere that doesn't have kids.

The boys are sick of homeless bums…

I know of a kiddie fiddler who lives a couple blocks away. Apartment 224 on the corner of William's Avenue. He's a young guy, and should suit your needs well.

Sound's good, boss. Sounds real good.

Just clean up after you.

We will, boss. Not a trace left.

And Scroteface?

Yes, boss?

Make the cunt suffer.

We will…

The club I met Walker at was called The Brokedown Palace, a blues club in Milford not too far from where I lived. It was a surprising choice of venue for Walker, and I wondered if she knew I was a regular in the place. If she did, I didn't recall ever telling her.

After parking the car, I walked one flight down from street level to get to the main entrance of the club and was met by two burly bouncers known as Fred and Ted, brothers who'd been working the door since I started coming to the place over ten years ago. I greeted them both as I walked past them into a semi-circular room with a stage in the far center, tables covering most of the floor, and a bar to the right, where I soon spotted Walker sitting.

It was too early for one of the house bands to be playing, so deep blues music played through the PA system instead. Carlito Martinez, the club owner, ran the place properly, keeping illicit trade and undesirables out, which is partly why I liked going there. I knew him well and had even done him a few favors over the years, though I saw no sign of the aging Cuban now.

"You made it," Walker said as I approached the bar and sat on a stool beside her. "I wasn't sure if you would."

"Neither was I, but here I am," I said. "You wanna drink?"

"I'll get them." She signaled to the large-breasted blonde girl working the bar, who smiled at me when she came over.

"Hey, Ethan," she said. "Usual?"

"Please, Tamara," I said. "She's paying."

"I'll have another Jack and Coke," Walker said.

"Nice," I said. "Glad to see you're getting into the spirit of things."

"Hannah liked it. I suppose I do too."

"What about the other stuff?" I asked her. "You get any urges for that?"

"The drugs?" She shrugged slightly. "I've managed to purge this body of that stuff, physically at least."

"And mentally?"

"Not quite. It's a constant battle."

"Welcome to the human life," I said as Tamara brought the drinks. "Where the battle never ends as long as you're breathing. Probably a far cry from when you were Elohim serving under the Creator, no doubt."

Walker's Visage hovered behind her, barely visible in the club's gloom, a mere outline of the angel she once was. "My memories of that time are vague and unclear, as are thankfully my memories of Hell and the torment I suffered there."

"Do you remember your name at least?"

"My celestial name was Adrielis," she said. "My demon name was Xaglath. My true name I have no idea. I expect my memories will return in time. From what I gather, that's the process when a Fallen One takes a human vessel."

"What was your role as an Elohim? I know you all had your specific jobs to do for the Creator."

"I can't remember. I'm not sure I want to either."

"Why? Surely you can't enjoy being human?"

"One thing I remember from my time as an Elohim before the Fall was looking at the humans, these divine creations of the Maker, and wondering what it would be like to be one of them. Humans were endowed with all these feelings and emotions that we, as Elohim, didn't have. Humans always seemed somehow more complete to us, even though we were much more powerful than they were, but still—"

"And now you know what it's like, is it everything you hoped it would be?"

She smiled slightly; her pale face beautiful in its own way under the lights of the bar. "It's much different than I thought it would be. I suppose I'm enjoying it or trying to at least. It feels strangely superficial. It's hard to explain."

"And what about when you get all your memories back, and your powers along with them?" I said, lifting my drink. "What then?"

"What do you mean?"

"I've seen plenty of Fallen who turn nasty when they get their powers back. Am I going to have to put you down?"

"You've killed my kind?"

"More than you can count."

"Why?"

"Because most of them tried to kill me first, that's why, or they spent their time killing others, which meant I had to stop them."

"As a cop?"

"Before that, but a few times as a cop."

"What did you do before becoming a cop?"

I stared at her for a moment, wondering how much I should tell her, before deciding I wasn't ready to tell her anything yet. "Some other time. You asked *me* here to talk, not the other way around."

"Yes," she said after finishing her drink and signaling to Tamara for more. "I did."

When Tamara brought the next round, I told her to put it on my tab and get herself a drink as well, to which she smiled her appreciation, her eyes telling me that she would further demonstrate that appreciation later if I wanted her to, as she had done more than once before. "So spill," I said to Walker.

"Firstly, I want to apologize again for earlier," she said. "I don't know what happened."

"I do," I said. "Your inner demon took control, and it will happen again if you don't get a handle on it."

"I'm trying."

"Try harder. I need to be able to trust you if we're going to be partners, which means I can't have you doing random evil shit when the mood takes you."

"I don't want that to happen again," she said. "That's what I'm trying to tell you, Ethan. I feel I belong in this body, and that I was meant to be this person."

"Someone else, you mean."

"More like a different version of myself. It feels like fate. Hannah lost control by the end. This body would be rotting in the ground if I hadn't taken it over. This is a second chance for her as well."

"Except it isn't, is it? Hannah's soul is gone, and no matter how much you pretend to be her, you never will be her."

"You're wrong," she said, her face darkening, twisting for a second into the demon that she had become after the Fall. "I'm more her than you can possibly imagine. Everything she was, I am as well. *Everything.*" She stared hard at me for a moment until I looked away to finish my drink. Tamara had another set up even before I put the empty glass onto the bar.

"So, what are you saying?" I asked. "That I should look at you as human? Human's don't have demon Visages hanging over them like dark passengers."

"That's fair enough, but what I'm asking is, how well did you know Hannah? You don't figure in her memories very much, except in a work capacity a few times."

"I know she was a good cop, and she had her problems. She was a full-blown junkie by the end."

"Did you know she was from a Yakuza family?"

I stared at her with my glass halfway to my mouth. "Are you serious? You're saying Hannah was Yakuza?"

Before she got a chance to answer, Carlito Martinez came walking up from behind me and slapped his meaty hand on my shoulder. "Ethan," he said. "How ya doing?"

"Carlito. I'm good. How's business?"

Carlito came to stand in between me and Walker, a

permanent grin on his face as usual, dressed in a gray suit, gold chains hanging from his neck, his fingers adorned with rings. "Business is good," he said. "It would be better if more people listened to good music instead of the crap that's going around these days, but you know, I make up for it in other ways." He smiled like he expected me to know what he was talking about, which I did. As a businessman, Carlito had his fingers in many pies, from loan sharking to drugs to providing guns to certain select individuals. As a criminal, he remained discrete, dealing only with those he trusted. He ensured that trust by severely punishing those who broke it. As gangsters went, he wasn't the worst and was always willing to help with my investigations whenever he could. In return, I kept the heat on him to a minimum. When he turned his attention to Walker, she smiled somewhat awkwardly. "And who is this Asian beauty?" he asked.

"Half Asian," Walker said. "My name's Hannah Walker."

"You get yourself a new partner?" Carlito asked me. "I thought Ethan Drake didn't do partners."

"I don't usually," I said before finishing my drink.

Carlito smiled at Walker again. "You must be special then, huh?"

"Not really," Walker said. "Just unfortunate."

Carlito looked at me and then back at Walker before bursting out laughing. "I like you, Hannah," he said. "Tamara, get Hannah another drink. On the house."

"Thanks," Walker said, seeming somewhat amused now by Carlito, no doubt taken in by his jovial demeanor. I wondered what she would think of him if she saw him take off someone's fingers with a pair of bolt cutters, as he was inclined to do when someone crossed him.

"No problem," Carlito said. "A friend of Ethan's is a friend of mine. You're welcome here anytime, Hannah, and the first drink is always on the house."

"You're lucky," I said. "I always have to pay for mine."

Carlito laughed. "When you become as beautiful as Hannah here, that's when you stop paying, big guy."

"Beauty is in the eye of the beholder, Carlito, remember that."

"Then you be one ugly motherfucker then," he said, bursting out laughing, causing even Walker to laugh this time. "I'm going to go now before the big guy breaks my neck. I got business to attend to anyway." Before he left, he stretched up to murmur in my ear. "There's something I need to discuss with you. Come see me when you get a chance."

I nodded, knowing full well what he wanted to discuss. "Sure thing. I'll do my best."

"I know you will, big guy," he said before walking away.

When he was gone, having disappeared through a door that would take him into the back office, Walker smiled and raised her eyebrows at me. "He's an interesting guy. You two seem close."

"I've known him for a long time, that doesn't mean we're close," I said. "You don't get close to a guy like Carlito. Hannah would've known that."

"*I* do know that," she said. "I just meant—"

"I know what you meant." I turned to Tamara and asked for another whiskey, feeling like I needed a dose of the Mud as the alcohol wasn't doing much for me. I decided I would make this my last drink before going home and taking a double dose. That should be enough to get me to sleep, though it wouldn't be enough to stop the nightmares. Nothing ever stopped those.

"So, are we going to talk about Hannah's past?" Walker asked.

Before I could answer, a text came through on my phone from Gordon Mackey, which I read before looking at Walker. "It seems we got a hit on the fingerprints left on the cigarette packet found at the gravesite," I said. "A sixteen-year-old kid named Troy Turner. Has an address at Crown Point of all places. You wanna go talk to him?"

Walker finished her drink before nodding. "You okay to drive?"

"I'm fine. Let's go. We'll talk about that other thing some other time."

9

The address we had for Troy Turner was only a few blocks away from where I used to live at Crown Point, right around the corner from the small St. David's Catholic Church that Angela used to drag Callie to every Sunday.

Angela came from a staunchly religious family. Her views were deeply entrenched, despite being a surgeon of repute. She always said the intricacies of the human body were proof positive God existed, and I never argued with her on that front. Any arguments we had concerning her beliefs came from the fact I believed God had abandoned his grand experiment and had left his human creations to fend for themselves, like a father abandoning his children. To which Angela would reply, I must really be able to relate to such a god then, considering I had all but left my own child. This she said later in our marriage when I demonstrated to her just what kind of man I was—the type of man who would disappear for days at a time without so much as a phone call to say where he was or when he would be back.

Sometimes it felt like Angela openly embraced her religion just to spite me, knowing as she did how I felt about it all. Despite her trying to indoctrinate Callie with the same views,

Callie never really bought it, a fact from which I took secret pleasure. Callie may have been young, but she was wise enough to see through the bullshit spouted by the priest every Sunday. She told me herself she would rather stay at home and read her books, but she didn't want to upset her mother, so she allowed herself to be dragged to church every week, for her mother.

Callie was good that way. She always put others before herself. Fuck knows where she got that from. Not from me anyway.

"You alright, Ethan?" Walker stared at me because without realizing it, I had slowed to a near crawl as we passed my old house.

"I'm fine." I sped up again, cracking the window a little to let some cold night air into the car.

"I can't imagine how you must still be feeling."

"No, you can't," I said, staring straight ahead.

"If there's anything I can do to help…"

"There isn't."

"I've lost people too; I know what it's like."

"You mean Hannah has."

"Her memories are still here. The pain she felt. We discussed this earlier. I thought—"

"Let's just focus on the case," I said as I drove into the tree-lined street where Troy Turner lived. "Okay?"

"Okay." Walker turned her head to stare out the window.

Guilt gnawed at me for a moment. I knew she was only trying to help, to deepen her relationship with me—our partnership—but I wasn't ready to open up to her or anyone else about the pain I felt, and I doubted I ever would. That's why I never liked having partners because they always wanted to talk about everything, as if they considered themselves to be in some fucking marriage where all cards had to be on the table. If Lewellyn hadn't insisted I chose someone to work with, I'd still be working on my own. Walker would be anywhere but with me, working out her own shit instead of trying to drag me into it. Fucking Yakuza? What was that about? I had enough of my own shit to deal with without getting involved with fucking Yakuza, crazy bastards that they were.

"It's this one." Walker pointed to a large house on the right.

I pulled the car up to the curb and cut the engine. "Let's go see what Troy Turner has to say for himself," I said before fixing my gaze on her. "And don't forget, no funny business."

Walker sighed but said nothing as we both got out of the car and walked up the drive to the Turner residence. It was after ten-thirty at night, and by rights, we should've left this until the morning, but I guess neither of us felt like going home yet, not forgetting the pressure from above to get the case wrapped up quickly. The lights were on throughout most of the house, so at least someone was still up as I knocked on the red-painted door.

When the door opened, a black-clad teenager stood there, staring at us both like we were aliens who'd only just landed on the front lawn. The kid's long hair hung over his face, but I could still see his bloodshot eyes and slack jaw, indicating he was stoned even before I got a whiff of pot from him. "Yeah?" he said in that dismissive way that teenagers tend to have, trying very hard to show our authority didn't matter to him.

"Troy Turner?" I flashed my badge. "Detective Drake. This is Detective Walker."

If the kid was freaked out by the presence of two cops, he didn't show it, though I'm sure the weed he'd been smoking helped him stay stony-faced. He stared at us a minute longer before turning his head and shouting down the hallway, "Troy, man. The Terminator and some…Chinese chick is here to see you. They're saying they're cops."

Fucking little shit. I set my jaw, resisting the urge to reach out and grab him by his scrawny neck. "We *are* cops," I told him.

"Sure, whatever man," the kid said before disappearing down the hallway.

A moment later, another kid appeared from around the corner, slightly taller than the one who answered the door and dressed in black clothing. Even his shoulder-length hair was jet-black, though obviously dyed. The T-shirt he wore sported a pentagram with some unreadable band name written across it. His smug smile said he wasn't worried at the fact that there were two cops at the door, if indeed he was Troy Turner and not some other goth twerp. "Troy Turner?" I showed him my badge.

"That's me." He leaned against the doorframe with his arms folded as if he had nothing to worry about. "What can I do for you, officers?"

"Detectives. We'd like to ask you a few questions if that's alright?" I said.

"Questions?" he said, still with the same fixed smile that I wanted to slap off his face. "What about?"

He knew exactly what about. I could see in his dark eyes he thought he was playing some clever game in which he was too smart to get caught out. We'd see about that. "Can you tell us where you were three nights ago, between nine and ten p.m.?"

"Three nights ago?" He made a big show of thinking hard about it. Even Walker looked like she wanted to slap him. "I was here at home with my friends."

"So you don't know anything about a dog that went missing in Riverside Hills?"

"A dog? Why would I know anything about that?"

"Where were you two nights ago?" Walker asked.

"Home, all night," the kid replied.

"Can anyone corroborate that?"

"My friends."

"Anyone else?" I asked. "Like your parents maybe?"

"My mom works the night shift at Salem Hospital," he said. "I was here with my friends."

"What about your father?" Walker asked.

"Dead." Troy looked at each of us in turn as if this fact somehow exonerated him from any suspicion.

"So only your friends can corroborate your whereabouts on those two nights?" I said. "That's convenient."

"It's the truth," he said. "We were here watching videos on YouTube."

"Which videos?" I asked.

"Documentaries," he answered without hesitation.

"What on?"

He sighed. "Just some conspiracy docs."

"Which ones?"

"I can't remember the *exact* ones. I was a little hazy if you know what I mean."

"Yeah. You watch them on your computer?"

"I…think so. Yeah, we did."

"They'd still be in your history then."

He shook his head. "Uh-uh. I always clear my history. My mom, she doesn't like me watching some stuff."

"Convenient," I said. "Any chance we can come in and talk to your friends? Are they here as well? The ones you were with on those two nights?"

"They're here," he said, shifting uncomfortably now as he folded his arms tighter. "But don't you need a warrant or something to come in here? And as we're all minors, isn't there supposed to be an adult present if you wanna interrogate us?"

"This is isn't an interrogation," Walker said. "We just want to ask your friends the same questions, so we can rule them out of the investigation."

"What investigation?" he asked, his cockiness returning. "Is this about that dog they found at Cave Hill Cemetery?"

"You know about that?" I asked him.

"Sure, everyone does. It was on the news. Didn't a body go missing as well?"

"That's right. I suppose you know nothing about that either?"

"Why would I?"

"Well, can you explain why a cigarette packet with your fingerprints on was found at the scene?"

He smiled, not missing a beat. "Me and my friends hang out there sometimes. I must've thrown it away one of those times."

"When was the last time you were there?" I asked him.

He shrugged and made a show of thinking for a second. "Last week maybe? I can't remember."

"Don't you think it seems a little suspicious that the cigarette packet was found near the grave where the body was snatched?"

"No, not really," he said. "Maybe the wind blew it there. Or maybe someone kicked it there. Who knows?"

He was an arrogant little shit, I'd give him that. He had an answer for everything. "So can we come in and talk to your friends?" I asked him. "If we do it now, we won't have to come back and bother you. We can rule you all out of the investigation then."

The kid stared at us for a long moment as he probably tried to think which action would make him look less guilty, sending us away or letting us in. In the end, he decided on the latter. "Okay, you can come in," he said, and I smiled inwardly at his reliable arrogance.

"Thanks." I stepped inside, Walker coming in behind me. The house had the same layout as the one I used to share with Angela. Troy took us down into the basement where three other kids were sitting watching a huge wide-screen TV.

The kid who had initially answered the door was sitting on a couch along with another male, this one with short, spiked hair, dressed in black combats and a black T-shirt that had some gruesome death metal album art printed on the front.

On an armchair positioned to the side of the TV sat a young girl who seemed the same age as the others. Unsurprisingly, the girl wore all black in the form of tight-fitting PVC trousers and a sleeveless black top that had an inverted cross emblazoned on the front. Her hair was also black, but with a white streak down the side that matched the deathly paleness of her face, a paleness only broken by the heavy black makeup around her eyes.

Despite the smell of pot in the room, neither of them looked nervous. *Fucking kids these days*, I thought. *They think they can get away with anything.*

"Detectives," Troy announced as he stood by the side of the TV. "Meet the rest of my coven."

"Your coven?" I said as I looked around the large room, thinking the kid had some balls even mentioning something like that, considering the nature of the case we were investigating. *Does he think he's smart enough to play us?* I thought. *We'd see about that.*

"We're all witches," Troy said.

"Are you now?" I glanced at Walker, who was busy eyeing up the room. The walls were covered with posters, mostly of heavy metal bands and album covers, though I noticed a few others depicting occult symbols and Wicca spells. There was also a table in the corner, on top of which was two large black candles and a metal bowl next to a thick, leather-bound book I'd wager was a book of spells probably bought from Ebay or one of the occult bookshops in town.

"Yeah," Troy went on as his two male friends stared at the TV, at some heavy metal video that was playing, the band doing their best to look evil as they paraded around a dark wood wearing ghoulish makeup and pulling ridiculous poses while their nearly unlistenable raucous music played over the video. "We chose to walk the left-hand path, in the shadow of our Lord."

"Your Lord?" I said. "And who would that be?"

"Lord Satan, of course." Troy smiled as if he expected us to be shocked by this announcement.

"Can I get all your names?" Walker asked them, ready with her notebook and pen.

"Why?" the girl asked. "We haven't done anything wrong."

"We aren't saying you have," Walker said.

"They found a cigarette pack with my fingerprints on at the graveyard," Troy told his friends. "So now they think we have something to do with that body that went missing."

The girl sniggered as the other two males stared nervously at the TV. "Yeah, right. As if. Why would we want to steal a dead body?"

"Maybe to use in some sort of ritual?" I offered. "I mean, you're witches, after all."

"Yeah, but—" The girl looked at Troy, as if for backup.

"We had nothing to do with that as I already said," Troy said, going to sit between the other two on the couch as if he couldn't care less.

"We have a witness." I let the words sit in the room for a moment as I gauged each of their reactions. The two guys shifted on the couch, staunchly refusing to make eye contact with either me or Walker. The girl started fiddling with a pendant around her neck, while Troy just smiled.

"What witness?" he asked.

"A witness that saw four teenagers matching your descriptions hanging around Riverside Hills three nights ago," I said. "The same night that a dog was stolen. The same dog that was found dead, hanging from a tree in Cave Hill Cemetery with a pentagram carved into its head."

Troy sniggered. "Sounds gruesome."

I came around and stood in front of the TV, much to the

consternation of the two kids on either side of Troy, who hardly knew where to look now. "You think this is funny?" I asked Troy.

"Not at all, Officer," he said.

"Detective," I said.

"Not at all, *Detective*."

It was all I could do not to rush forward and grab him by the lapels, lifting him up off his feet so I could dangle him in front of me and give him a serious eye-fucking. Instead, I switched my attention to the one who had answered the door. "You, what's your name?"

The kid rolled his eyes and was about to answer when Troy cut in. "His name is Shadow," he said. "This guy next me is Midnight. She's Raven, and I'm Crow."

"That's cute," I said, taking a step forward. "Now what're your real names?"

Shadow shook his head, and grudgingly answered, "Doug Winslow."

I looked at Midnight. "And you?"

The kid sighed. "Derick Randolph."

Finally, I looked at the girl who rolled her eyes before answering. "Lisa Crowley," she said, before looking at Walker. "You're really pretty for a Chinese girl, like one of those girls from those Asian movies we always watch. You ever think about becoming an actor?"

"No," Walker said. "And I'm half Japanese, not Chinese."

"Oh shit, I can never tell the difference," the girl said. "Anyway, I'd really love to be an actress, like Kristen Stewart, you know her? From the *Twilight* movies? I love those movies, I don't understand why people hate on them so much, they're just so, like...deep. I also love other stuff like—"

"Shut up, Raven," Troy said. "No one cares."

"Fuck you, Troy," Raven said. "You're always telling me to shut up."

"Well, if you'd shut up, I wouldn't have to," Troy said, barely looking at her.

"Asshole."

"Bitch."

As Walker wrote down all their names, my gaze happened to drop down for a second, and I noticed the book under the sofa, the spine facing out. Crouching down, I read the title out loud. "*The Hattusa Codex*. Now what would you be doing with a book like that?"

"Nothing," Troy said, covering the book with his large, black boot. "It's just a book."

"Just a book, huh?"

"Yeah."

"A very old and rare book. Where'd you get it from?"

"Nowhere," he said, looking nervous for the first time. "I actually think you need to leave now. You have no right to be here." He took out his phone. "I'm calling my mom."

"No need," I said. "We're going."

"Good," Troy said, folding his arms as he sat back on the couch. "You're blocking the TV."

I stayed where I was as I looked at them all. "I should inform you we have good reason to believe you four were involved in the kidnapping of the Hawthorn's dog, and in the body-snatching of Barbara Keane. The witness statement combined with the fingerprint evidence is enough for us to get a warrant and come back here to search your place." I stopped and looked at Troy. "You can phone your mom and let her know if you want."

"Fucking bullshit," Troy said. "My coven had nothing to do with any of that."

"We'll see."

"Just go. You can let yourselves out."

"See you tomorrow...*Crow*. Until then, I'll be sending a patrol car to watch your house, just in case you decide to get rid of any evidence."

"Like a corpse," Walker said.

All four kids stayed silent as they stared hard at the TV. The two either side of Troy looked like they were about to shit themselves. The girl seemed to have lost her cocky demeanor as well as she stared hard at the floor. Only Troy remained defiant as he proceeded to pretend we weren't there. "Just to let you all know," I said. "There's a lot of attention on this case. Whoever we get for it will have the book thrown at them, as my bosses will want to make an example of them. We can't have corpses being snatched from graveyards, or people's pets being kidnapped and killed. You can all do yourselves a favor by coming clean when we come back here tomorrow," I added, looking more at the other three, as Troy seemed unaffected by my scare tactics.

"Jesus, just go!" Troy shouted.

"Enjoy your MTV," I said as I moved to leave the basement. "I don't think they have it in jail."

~

"So, WHAT DO YOU THINK?" WALKER ASKED ME WHEN WE were back in the car. "Did they do it?"

"No question." I lit up a cigarette. "Did you notice the muddy tennis shoes in the hallway?"

"I did, yeah."

"I'm willing to bet they match the shoe prints taken from the scene."

"They did look guilty as hell," Walker said. "What was that book you found?"

"An old occult book. Fuck knows where they got it from. It's full of dangerous summoning rituals."

"How do you know that?"

"Because when it comes to the occult, I'm very well-read. Last I heard that book was in the Special Collections Wing of the Fairview Public Library. I'm willing to bet Troy and his friends stole it from there."

"You think that's why they stole Barbara Keane's body? To use in some ritual?"

"You heard them," I said after taking a drag of my cigarette. "They think they're fucking witches, deluded little shits, and Troy seems arrogant enough to think he can summon a demon and get away with it."

"They'll all die," Walker said as if she knew this for sure.

"Probably."

"You think they have the body stashed somewhere?"

"I know they do."

"Are you really going to have the house watched?"

"I'll do it myself after I drop you off," I said, tossing my cigarette butt out the window and starting the engine. "You can arrange the paperwork for the search warrant so a judge can sign off on it in the morning."

10

Once I dropped Walker off at her car, I drove to my apartment so I could refill the dropper bottle with Mud. I figured if I was going to be staking out Troy Turner's place all night, I would need something to make the waiting a bit more tolerable. *Mud, whiskey, and blues should do just fine,* I thought. Jed the homeless guy was sitting in his usual spot outside the apartment building, a bottle with a brown paper bag around it in his hand. I paused when I got out of the car to talk to him, as he was staring around with wild eyes as if he was looking for something unseen. "You alright there, Jed?" I asked him.

Jed turned his head slowly to look at me, his eyes remaining unfocused for a second. "There's evil about tonight, Detective."

"There's evil about every night."

"The Devil is stalking these streets. I saw him."

"You saw him, huh?" Something told me Jed saw more than the Devil most nights.

"He's coming for us all. He's gonna make us all pay, mark my words…"

Leaving Jed to his DT's, I went inside the building. When I

reached the floor my apartment was on, I came across little Daisy sitting on the landing, and I knew straight away something was wrong. Instead of sitting there reading a book like she normally did, she sat in shorts and T-shirt with her knees drawn tight against her chest, her thin arms wrapped around her legs while she rocked back and forth, weeping at the same time. "Daisy?"

She barely looked up when she heard my voice. As it was dark outside, the only light that shone through the grimy window she was sitting under was the pale light of the moon which was barely enough for me to make out her features. It wasn't until I went and crouched in front of her that she finally raised her head and I saw just why she was crying. "Jesus Christ," I murmured.

"I'm okay," she said, trying to sniff back her tears. "It doesn't hurt that much."

Anger coursed through me as I took in her face. The whole left side was a deep reddish color under the pale moonlight, and there was a dark patch around her left eye. Blood still trickled from her busted lip. "Who did this to you, Daisy?" I already knew who did it, but I needed to hear her say it.

"It doesn't matter."

"It matters. Tell me who did it. Your mom's boyfriend?"

She stared at me for a moment before nodding once. "Yes."

"Is he still in there?"

"Yes."

"Alright, let's get you up. You're coming with me to my apartment."

"He'll be gone soon."

I glanced over at her apartment door. "He'll be gone, alright."

"What are you going to do, Detective?"

"Don't worry about it. Here, take my hand. Can you walk okay?"

She nodded again as she took my hand, and I helped her up to her feet. On the way down the hallway, we passed her apartment, and from inside, I could hear music playing. I scowled at the door on the way past, resisting the urge to kick it in. Before I opened the door to my apartment, I telepathically contacted Scroteface to make sure he and the other Hellbastards weren't inside. A second later, Scroteface replied by telling me they were still playing with the kiddie fiddler. *Stay there,* I told him. *Don't come back here until I tell you to.*

Once inside the apartment, I turned on the lights and sat Daisy down on the couch, squatting down in front of her so I could get a better look at her injuries. The bastard that hit her had slapped her hard around the face. I judged he was a big cunt, going by the extent of Daisy's injuries. His hand must've covered the whole side of her face, blackening her eye socket, probably with a ring on his finger. She was lucky she didn't lose her fucking eye. As I checked her out, she barely made eye contact with me. "You don't have to feel ashamed," I said to her. "This wasn't your fault, you hear me?"

Tears fell from her brown eyes as she looked at me. "I only told him I didn't want him in the apartment," she said, her voice barely above a whisper. "Mama's been sick lately, and he wanted her to drink and do drugs with him. That's all they ever do. And then he..." She trailed off as she looked away and my anger flared once more, though I kept it in check, for the time being at least. Before I did anything—and I *was* going to do something—I had to make sure Daisy was alright first.

"I've got some stuff that will help your face," I told her. "But I have to make it up first. You want some cocoa to warm you up?" I used to buy the stuff for Callie when she stayed over, which wasn't that often. I think I still had some in the kitchen somewhere.

"Okay." Daisy's body trembled, probably out of shock more than cold, but I found her a blanket and wrapped it around her anyway, which seemed to help as she sat back on the couch and pulled the blanket up under her chin.

After making the cocoa, I brought the mug into the room and gave it to her. "Thanks, Detective," she said, managing a small smile. "You didn't have to do this."

"Call me Ethan," I said. "I'll be back in a minute with something that'll help your face. You want the TV on?" I turned it on before she even answered and handed her the remote. "I'm sure there's not much on, but you can have a look anyway."

I went to the bedroom and unlocked it, going inside and closing the door behind me, pausing for a moment as I considered the situation. *What motherfucker would slap a child like that?* I thought. It was a purely rhetorical question, for I knew plenty of motherfuckers who wouldn't think twice about slapping a child. But knowing and seeing are two different things and seeing Daisy's face all messed up like that only made me want to punish the fucker who did it.

With my anger still simmering, I took out my phone to call Walker. It was unlikely I was going to make it back to Crown Point anytime soon, so Walker would have to stake out Troy Turner's place herself, at least until I was able to get there. I had a feeling Troy and his coven were going to attempt something tonight, a ritual maybe, using Barbara Keane's corpse. I doubted they would do it at the house which meant they would have to go elsewhere. I wanted Walker there to follow them. But when I called her phone, it went straight to voicemail, which pricked my anger even more.

"Fucking pick up your damn phone, Walker," I growled after the third attempt, finally sending her an angry text telling her to get her act together and get over to Troy Turner's place right away.

Agitated by Walker's lack of response, I focused instead on the jars of ingredients lined up on the shelves before me. When I first started hunting down MURK's, I used to get injured a lot. It's par for the course when you go up against powerful beings, some of whom have claws and sharp teeth, others who have the strength to throw you around like a fucking rag doll. You pick up a lot of injuries that you can't exactly go to a hospital with because of all the questions you get asked. So, you have to learn to treat your own wounds and injuries. Over the years, I've learned exactly what ingredients to put together to help treat specific injuries. For superficial ones like Daisy's, I just needed to mix together a few hard to get herbs and the blood of a vampire because it had excellent healing properties. Pretty soon, I had made up a poultice that I brought into the living room to give to Daisy. "This will help heal your face," I said, handing her the mixture, which was wrapped in white gauze.

"That looks like blood," she said, staring at the soaked gauze in mild disgust.

"It's not blood, it's just some special herbs. Trust me, it'll help."

She placed her mug down on the coffee table and took the poultice from me, gingerly applying it to the left side of her face. "It's warm."

"It's supposed to be. Just hold it there for a while. If you need to sleep or anything, just curl up on the couch there."

Daisy mustered a smile. "You're a nice man, Detective."

"I told you, call me Ethan."

"Ethan then. Why are you doing this?"

"Doing what?"

"Helping me."

I stared at her for a second, thinking about Callie, and about what I would do if it was Callie sitting there on the couch with her face all busted up. "Don't worry about it," I said. "Just stay here and rest. You'll be safe here."

"Where are you going?" she asked.

"To your apartment."

"Are you going to arrest Jarvis?"

"Jarvis? That's his name?"

"Yes."

"No, I'm not going to arrest him."

"Then what are you going to do?"

"Don't worry about it," I said after a pause. "I'll be back to check on you soon."

She said nothing more as I left her sitting on the couch holding the poultice against her face. As I left the apartment, I allowed my anger to finally come to the surface. Walking down the hallway, I took a few deep breaths and cracked my neck from side to side. Inside Daisy's apartment, the music was still playing, some techno shit with a relentless beat. I banged hard on the door with my fist and waited. The music continued at the same volume and no one came to the door, so I banged on it again, harder this time. A second later, the door was opened by a man who I assumed was Jarvis. He was topless, his bulging, tattooed muscles gleaming with sweat, his eyes wide, his pupils massive. A sure sign that he was drugged up on coke or some other kind of amphetamine. There were so many different drugs on the streets these days it was hard to keep track of them all. I didn't give a fuck what he was on anyway. Nothing was going to stop me from making him pay for what he did to Daisy.

"What the fuck do you want, asshole?" he all but shouted as the music blared in the background. "Can't you see we're trying to fucking party here?"

"Who is it?" Daisy's mother shouted from the living room in a raspy voice. I'd never spoken to her, but I'd seen her a few times. She was a scraggy woman in her early thirties, her looks ravaged by a lifetime of drug and alcohol abuse, making her appear much older than she was.

"It's no one," Jarvis said, his glassy blue eyes boring into me. "He's just leaving anyway."

When he went to slam the door in my face, I stuck my boot in the threshold to stop it from closing and the door bounced open again. Before Jarvis could even say what the fuck, I was through the doorway, the webbed part of my hand between thumb and forefinger slamming into his Adam's apple, causing him to gag and stagger back as he clutched at his throat. He recovered fast, though, thanks to the drugs in his system, and blocked my subsequent kick to his balls before bouncing back into a fighting stance, his hands up near his face as he started to dance around like he was fucking Conor McGregor.

Oh goody, another asshole who thinks he's a cage fighter.

"Come on motherfucker," he shouted. "Come on!"

"Jarvis, don't," Daisy's mother said from the couch. "The guy's a cop, for Christ's sake."

"Even fucking better." He came at me with a straight right to the face. He was fast, I'll give him that, but he was so fucked up he misjudged the distance, and his punch fell short of my face.

My punch didn't, however, and my reinforced knuckles slammed into the bridge of his nose. A loud crack issued as the cartilage got crushed and blood immediately gushed from his wrecked appendage.

After that, I hit him again, and again, and again. Three solid punches that cracked his eye socket and probably his jawbone, but which didn't put him down. His face covered in blood, he came at me like a wild animal and tried to bite my nose, so I grabbed his oily face and started pressing my thumbs into his eye sockets until about half my thumb was buried deep in there. He screamed and panicked and grabbed a bottle from somewhere and hit me over the head with it, causing me to lose my grip on him.

As glass and alcohol rained down over me, he screamed once more and came at me again, this time wrapping his hands around my throat and squeezing. Unfortunately for him, it was a dumb ass move and easy as fuck to defend against. All I did was swing my right arm over his head as I turned my body away from him, which broke his grip and allowed me to immediately turn back with a hammer fist to his temple, followed by a tight left hook to his jaw which finally sent him down to his knees. Drugged up or not, he looked like he'd had enough.

"Leave him," Daisy's mother said.

But I wasn't finished.

As Daisy's mother continued screaming in the background for me to leave him alone, I grabbed Jarvis by the hair and dragged him outside to the hallway and out onto the landing. Holding him up by the hair, I said, "You like to hit little girls, asshole?"

His response was to spit blood at me before saying, "The little cunt deserved it."

That did it for me. My anger boiled over into rage and I started punching the fuck out of his face until he fell back and I was holding nothing but a clump of his hair in my hand while he lay on the grimy floor barely conscious. I dropped my knee down onto him then, before delivering a barrage of hard, deliberate punches to his face, hearing bones break as my knuckles pulverized him over and over again. I only stopped when I heard a scream behind me, followed by a voice saying, "Stop. You're killing him."

I got off Jarvis and turned around to see Daisy's mother standing there in the dimly lit hallway, tears streaming down her freaked-out face, her eyes full of hatred and fear as she glared at me.

"YOU'RE A FUCKING ANIMAL!" she screamed and went to move past me, but I grabbed her by the throat with my blood-soaked hand and held her in front of me.

"You're the fucking animal," I snarled back to her, before pushing her away from me. She staggered back and fell on her ass, where she sat crying. "If anyone lays a finger on that little girl again, I'm holding you responsible, you hear me?"

The hatred and fear remained in her face, but she nodded

anyway. I went to walk away from her but stopped when I saw Daisy standing in the hallway near my apartment door. She just stood staring at me for a moment, her face difficult to read, though a sense of shame came over me as I looked at her. She then walked down the hallway, stopping only to hand me back the poultice I had given her earlier, before wordlessly continuing to her mother. "Let's go, Mamma," she said as she picked her mother up and walked her back into the apartment. Before she closed the door behind her, she looked at me one final time.

"Daisy—" I said, but she closed the door on me, leaving me alone in the hallway with a half-dead man that I wasn't sure what to do with.

I went to him and nudged him with my boot, but he didn't move. His chest rose and fell, indicating he was still breathing at least. I could've dragged him downstairs and dumped him in the street before calling an ambulance, but then there would be questions when he woke up and he would lead the subsequent inquiry to me. IAB were already on my case and a serious assault charge—possibly even attempted murder—wouldn't help matters. It would be easier just to summon the Hellbastards here to get rid of Jarvis altogether. There would probably be an investigation into his disappearance which may or may not lead back to me, depending on whether Daisy's mother said anything, or even Daisy herself. But if there was no evidence trail to follow, there would be no case against me. Besides, cunts like Jarvis didn't deserve to live as far as I was concerned. The world wouldn't be losing a fucking cancer cure, that's for sure.

I was just about to summon the Hellbastards when Jarvis sat up as though he'd just been given an adrenaline shot. His face was a mess, one eye swollen shut, the other partially so. His nose was grotesquely swollen, and his jaw appeared to be off-center. At least a few teeth were missing as well because they lay in a pool of blood beside him on the floor. Incredibly, he was able to stand up and stare at me, his naked upper body awash with his own blood. He opened his mouth to speak, but the words that came out were so garbled I couldn't make them out. As I walked toward him, he backed off into the corner in fear, probably unable to even see me properly through those swollen eyelids. When I came to stand in front of him, he started shaking.

"Okay, Jarvis," I said in a level voice. "Let me explain the situation here. You put your hands on a little girl, so as far as I'm concerned, you got what you deserved. You're fucking lucky I didn't kill you."

"*Pwullesse…*"

"Shut your mouth. Right now, you're going to take yourself to a hospital and get yourself seen to. You're going to say you got jumped on the way home from a night out. It was dark and it all happened so fast you didn't see any of your assailants." I stepped in closer. "When you leave here, I'm going to find out where you live and where your family lives. If I find out you've mentioned to anyone what happened here tonight, I'm going to kill you, and then I'm going to kill your whole family. You understand me, Jarvis?"

Tears rolled down his cheeks, mixing with the blood. All he could do was nod.

"Good. Now get the fuck out of here and never let me see you anywhere near this building again."

Jarvis clung to the railing as he stumbled down the stairs, and I watched him go until he disappeared. A large pool of blood was on the floor next to me, along with a clump of Jarvis' hair and a few of his teeth. It was a mess that would need cleaning up, and I knew just the candidates for the job. Scroteface and his gang of miscreants would have the floor spotless in no time.

On the way past Daisy's apartment, I stopped for a second and stared at the door. The music was off, and it was quiet inside. For a brief second, I considered knocking on the door to see if Daisy was alright, but then I thought about the look on her face before she closed the door on me earlier, and I carried on walking back to my own apartment. No matter what Daisy thought of me, at least that cunt Jarvis would never lay his hands on her again. I was satisfied enough with that.

11

Punching Jarvis' head into a bloody pulp had taken the skin off my knuckles, exposing the thin titanium plates underneath that capped the bone. Steel knuckles were one of a few different enhancements I'd gotten from Blackstar. The company needed its grunts in the combat department to be tough enough to go up against the damage absorbing, ultra-violent MURKs we were being sent after.

The tech they provided us with was bleeding edge, stuff I thought never existed, like plasma guns (one of which I had in the trunk of the Dodge for emergency situations), blasters, and energy weapons that would cut right through steel never mind the thick hide of a monster or the soft skin of demon in human form.

Blackstar also dealt with biotech, subjecting most of its field agents to genetic tampering to make them stronger, faster, and more aggressive when need be—and there was always a need. Besides the steel caps on my knuckles, I had bone material from a werewolf grafted onto my radius and ulna, making both my forearms as hard as steel and great for blocking incoming attacks or for smashing bones. I also had the tendons in my legs enhanced with genetic material taken from the tendons of an undisclosed monster, allowing me to run as fast as any hellhound and kick as hard as a mule. The tendons have degraded with age now like the rest of me, and not being with the company anymore, I'm not eligible for maintenance or upgrades. I still got some speed, though. Try to run away from me and you'll soon find out.

Blackstar also fitted its field agents with a Combat Offense Booster. It's an instant response delivery system which allows the user to attack and counterattack with reflexes that would put a vampire to shame. The chip intercepts aggressive action signals and boosts their neural impulse, accelerating the action. That's about as sciencey as I get. The firmware of the chip hasn't been updated in years, though it still does its job well enough when it doesn't short out, which it has a habit of doing, usually at the worst time.

Another thing I used to have fitted was something called a Spock Chip. The more emotional recruits among us were fitted with this chip, meaning we never reacted emotionally to any situation, always maintaining a calm, intellectual outlook. I had mine taken out when I realized I was slowly losing my sense of humanity, but by the time I argued my case and had the chip removed, a fair amount of damage had been done already, leaving me in psychiatric terms, borderline sociopathic, and that's an optimistic way of putting it. Sometimes I see my fellow humans as nothing more than pieces of talking, walking meat. That's usually just the ones I don't like very much. The rest I can drum up an adequate amount of feeling for, which I suppose in some cases isn't enough. I'd say just ask my ex-wife about that, but she's dead.

Plenty of field agents opted to leave the chip in permanently, turning them into soulless robots, which suited the company just fine. In any case, the company also manufactured Personality Chips, making them available to those who had trouble passing themselves off as human. Those who worked in intelligence made more use of these chips than other departments, practically programming themselves to suit the needs of each mission they were on.

There were many other enhancements and so-called improvements that I never partook in, although some guys never had a choice. Many were used as guinea pigs by the company to test out new enhancements, chips, and procedures, more than a few of which would end in disaster. These guys usually ended up dead when shit went wrong in the field. Some would also go crazy from too much interfering with their neural system or DNA. The guys would end up on the "scrap heap" meaning they were either put down or, if the company were feeling generous, the malfunctioning grunt would have their memories erased before being dumped on the street somewhere. There, most of them would remain; homeless, lost, and completely alone.

Me, I got out relatively intact, but only because I was smart enough to secure the company a long-sought-after relic it had been hunting for years, which curried some favor with the suits at the top. If it weren't for that, I'd've been consigned to the scrap heap like all the rest the second I announced I wanted to leave.

I was now in the locked room of my apartment, applying ointment to my skinned knuckles. The stuff was strong. A few hours and the skin on my knuckles would be like new again. While I was in there, I refilled the dropper bottle with Mud, taking a dose before I left the room, sighing with relief as my overactive nervous system calmed itself.

In Blackstar, we used to get shots after every mission, a concoction designed to reset our nervous systems back to zero, so to speak. If we didn't get the shots, we would've gone crazy from stress and PTSD. The Mud is the best I got these days, even though I managed fine without it for years. But you know, holding your six-year-old daughter in your arms while her guts spill out tends to push you over the edge.

I tried Walker's phone again, and like earlier, it went

straight to voicemail. "Fuck's sake," I said as I threw the phone on the couch and began to strip off my bloodstained shirt, yet another casualty of the job. I swear I spend more on fucking shirts than I do on anything else. There was a stack of new ones in the living room that I dumped there a while ago, and I put one on, followed by my worn black tie and trench coat that's seen better days.

This is the uniform. The clothes that feel so comfortable these days they're like a second skin. Once upon a time, it was denim and leather and homemade body armor. Then it was state of the art tactical gear when I joined Blackstar. I missed the old school getup the most. There was just something cool about going out to kill MURKs in tight jeans and a well broken-in leather jacket that smelled of years of wear, with a Judas Priest or Black Sabbath T-shirt on underneath. I felt like the shit back then, cool as fuck. Nowadays, I feel more like a shuffling city worker in a generic uniform, which when all is said and done is what I am, albeit one who gets his hands dirty more than most, not to mention bloody.

On the way out the door, I tried Walker again, stopping halfway down the hallway to send her another angry text after I got her voicemail for the fiftieth fucking time. Jarvis' blood was still coagulating on the floor of the landing. The cockroaches had been running through it, leaving little trails of blood going off in different directions.

Down the stairs, I gave Scroteface another shout. *Hurry up and get this fucking mess cleaned up here or I'm going to have to rethink our working relationship.*

What boss?

Just get your finger out of your scaly ass and do as I say.

Yes, boss. On our way.

How was the kiddie fiddler? Did he scream much?

Oh yes, boss, he screamed…until we cut out his tongue and shoved it up his anus.

Sounds like you had fun.

We sure did.

Outside, Jed the homeless guy was sleeping, wrapped up in dirty blankets and old newspapers. As I walked past him to get to the car, I noticed he was twitching and mumbling in his alcohol-induced sleep, as if he was having nightmares, probably about the Devil, whom he said earlier was out stalking the streets, and I realized he was right, that Devil was me. Jed just didn't know it.

Up the street, the dealers stood on the corner as cars drove slowly by, some of them stopping so the drivers could score, and for a second, a crazy thought went through my mind: I could market the Mud as a new drug. It would go down a treat with the opiate crowd and I'd make a fucking killing. Then I could retire from this life once and for all, leaving the MURKs behind as I withdrew from society and moved to the wilderness where no one could bother me ever again. It was a pleasant thought until I remembered that my angel's killer was still out there somewhere and that I wasn't going to rest until I found them and made them pay. Maybe then I would run for the hills and stay there. Maybe.

Inside the Dodge, I lit a cigarette, the first inhale combining with the Mud in my system to give me a light head, and for a moment, the night outside became a kaleidoscope of swirling colors as if some other world was overlapping with this one and all I had to do was sit there and let the colors swallow me up, taking me somewhere far, far away. But after blinking a couple times, the swirling colors disappeared, replaced with the drab colors of the night once more. I put Muddy Waters on the car stereo and turned it up loud as if to block out my thoughts, then I started the engine and screeched toward Crown Point, my Infernal Itch telling me I wasn't going to like what I found there.

~

DRIVING THROUGH THE CITY WAS AT TIMES LIKE DRIVING through a neon-lit dream, the Mud giving everything a surreal quality as I drove on autopilot through streets that contained, for the most part, little in the way of traffic. With Muddy Waters still filling the car with his quintessential blues stylings, my thoughts turned to Astaroth and his crazy hellots. The last thing I needed right now was to be targeted by a demon for possession. It was bad enough that I was devoting more time to my job than I was to finding out who killed Callie and Angela. Now I would have to try to face down a demon with probably incalculable power and a mind that wouldn't be changed unless I made him change it somehow. If I could get the fucker's true name, I could make him do whatever I wanted, but the chances of discovering that were as slim as Truck Driver Junior discovering who his real daddy is. Like trying to find a needle in a haystack, in other words. I'd probably have to find some other way to sort out old Astaroth.

In the meantime, I had other things to worry about as I arrived at Crown Point, pulling up across the road from Troy Turner's house. Stepping out of the car with a fresh cigarette between my nicotine-stained fingers, the stars in the clear sky appeared more as streaks through the filter of the Mud. There was also a ringing in my ears as though I had been listening to loud music for too long.

Taking out my phone to call Walker again, my Infernal Itch started to go a bit haywire as the back of my neck burned, and the tattoos on my back and arms began to swirl with agitation. Something had gone down inside Troy Turner's house in my absence, I realized. *God damn it*, I thought. I should never have left. I might've been able to stop Troy and his friends from doing whatever it was they did.

Though if I'd stayed, I'd never have come across Daisy, and Jarvis would still be partying in her mother's apartment while Daisy sat outside in the cold quivering from shock. But so what? I'm not a social worker, I'm a cop. Abuse of one form or another was a staple of my younger life, and it didn't do me any harm, did it? I'm being sarcastic. Of course it fucking did, though it also made me tough. But little girls shouldn't have to be tough. At least not in the sense that they had to learn to take physical abuse from cunts like Jarvis. They had a right to be little girls for as long as possible. Plenty of time to thicken the skin when they were older. Only my Callie never got that time, did she?

Fuck it, focus on what you're here for. Go inside that house and see what's what.

I put the phone to my ear just as Walker's phone went to voicemail. "Walker," I said, keeping calm despite the anger boiling beneath the surface. "Where the fuck are you? I'm at Troy Turner's house now. Something's happened. I'm not sure what yet, but I'm about to find out. It would be nice if my fucking partner were here with me. Get here when you get this."

The phone went back into my trench pocket as I approached the house. It was after four a.m. Troy's mother wouldn't be home from the night shift yet. All the lights were off inside the house, and as I got to the door, I noticed it was slightly ajar. Not a good sign, unless one or more of the kids had left and just hadn't closed the door properly behind them, though I doubted it.

In the stillness of the night, the house itself seemed agitated, as though its boards and foundations were reacting to some energy that had been unleashed within it. The tattoos on my back were swirling like angry snakes as the fabric of my reality continued to glitch in an annoying manner as I stood staring at the front door, half expecting someone or something to come running out at any second.

A pregnant anticipation hung in the air, caused by an unleashing of foreign energy that I immediately equated with MURK activity. When a new MURK arrives in this world, they bring with them a strange sort of energy that causes the air to crackle with tiny sounds, like the sound ice cubes make in a glass as they melt. Sometimes it's like an invisible frost is growing over everything, making its way under your skin at the same time.

"Hello?" I shouted as I took out my gun. "Police. Anyone home?"

My question was met with silence, which was no surprise. I already knew there was no one home. The silence was too deathly for there to be anyone there, though my instincts said there was some other presence lurking somewhere. A ghost maybe, I couldn't be sure at that point.

"I'm coming in now." I pushed open the door with one hand, knowing I had probable cause to enter the premises and therefore had no need for a warrant. "Troy? You here?"

The house was ice cold inside, the ambient temperature more suited to a freezer than the inside of a house on a mild September night. Another sure sign of MURK activity. When an eldritch being arrives here, they almost always bring with them an energy that lowers the temperature in the immediate vicinity to an Arctic degree. It's the temperature of the Void; the freezing cold of emptiness.

Then there was the smell drifting up from the basement as I made my way past the kitchen and down the hallway. A sulfurous smell with undertones of burned meat and ecto-plasm. Heading down the steps to the basement, I was also hit with the unmistakable stench of blood and offal, a stench I had come to know so well over the years, yet I still wrinkled my nose in disgust and smacked my lips as the coppery scent entered my nostrils and seemed to settle on the roof of my mouth, creating a metallic taste there. "Police," I said again as I kept heading down the steps. "Anyone here?"

As if in answer, my phone rang, and I stopped to fish it out of my pocket. It was Walker. I glared at the screen for a second before rejecting the call. "Fuck you, Walker," I said as I put the phone back in my pocket. "You're a bit fucking late."

The basement was in darkness when I reached the end of the stairs, the stench overwhelming now. In the darkness, lights flashed across my vision like tiny fireflies, which, in combination with the foul smells, made me feel nauseous. As bile stirred in my stomach, I swallowed hard to keep it down, glad I hadn't eaten today. It doesn't matter how many scenes of death you come across, they always elicit the same gag response. The only time I didn't gag was when I had the Spock Chip implanted. Back then, I felt nothing at all, no matter how horrific the scene. At times like these, I often wished I still had the chip implanted because it sure did make all the death easier to deal with.

I took a breath before flicking on the light switch to illuminate the room, my eyes having already picked out certain shapes in the darkness. Dead shapes. When the lights came on, it was like a flash grenade had exploded in front of me, and I found myself temporarily blinded for a few seconds. Given how the Mud was affecting me, I should've known to cover my eyes first. With my vision whited out, the loud ringing returned in my ears, and I shut my eyes for a few seconds until the ringing had died down. Only then could I take in the full extent of the bloody and brutal scene before me.

All the furniture had been pushed to one side of the large room to create a space in the middle of the floor, onto which a magic circle had been drawn with what seemed to be red chalk. The circle was about six feet in diameter and around its ill-drawn circumference were scrawled various occult symbols. A pentagram was also sketched out inside the circle, and black candles stood at each of its five points. It was a standard set up for an occult ritual, and one I had seen many times before. Most amateurs think the circle will afford them protection from whatever MURK they summon.

But said amateurs find out magic circles offer little in the way of protection from wily, determined entities who see amateur magicians as no more than children playing with things they don't understand. The summoned entities will often take great pleasure in teaching the amateur magician—or in this case, magicians—a lesson. A lesson that said magicians will never have the chance to learn from because they'll be dead before they do. Which is clearly what happened here in the blood-drenched basement.

I wasn't surprised to see the rotting corpse of Barbara Keane laid out in the center of the circle either, the skin covering her crumbling bones a sickly greenish-gray color. The clothes had been stripped from the corpse to give it further indignity, revealing the autopsy scars underneath. Her abdomen had also been ripped open, revealing a hollow cavity underneath, inside of which was placed a little Wiccan figure that seemed to be soaked in blood.

But there were more gruesome things in the room than the corpse of Barbara Keane. To my left, splayed across the couch, was the body of Lisa Crowley, aka Raven. Her body had been split open from crotch to gullet as if by some giant claw and pulled apart so that her innards spilled out onto the floor. Her once pretty face was split horizontally from cheek to cheek, making it seem like she was smiling ghoulishly in death.

On the wall across from Lisa the body of Doug Winslow, aka Shadow, had been pinned there by a kitchen knife driven through his throat and into the plaster. His feet were two feet above the floor, which meant he'd been held up by someone or something and pinned like a dead butterfly in a display case. His belly had also been slit open, and his steaming intestines dangled like ropes of thick sausages, a pool of blood on the floor beneath him that glistened under the tube lighting.

And on the floor itself lay the body of Derick Randolph, aka Midnight. He lay flat on his belly, but his head had been twisted right around so that his horrified face looked toward the blood-spattered ceiling. As if that wasn't enough, his left arm appeared to have been ripped from its socket, the arm itself lying a few feet from him, immediately discarded by the killer no doubt.

The blood from all this carnage had also been used to paint occult symbols on the walls, none of which I particularly recognized. The only body that was conspicuous by its absence was Troy Turner's. That meant one of two things. Either Troy had managed to escape from whatever MURK had killed his friends before it killed him as well, or Troy himself had killed his friends before making his escape. The former scenario seemed unlikely, given the ferocity of the attacks on the others. The latter scenario seemed unlikely as well. There was no way Troy could've caused this much damage by himself. Plus, why would he? Unless whatever entity the coven had summoned had possessed Troy. If that was true, then some MURK was running around right now in Troy's body, probably planning to cause a whole heap of trouble and further bloodshed.

I stood at the bottom of the steps for another few minutes taking in the scene, looking for details that would explain exactly what happened here, even though I had a pretty good idea already. The book that lay half-hidden underneath a bloodstained coat was the last piece of the puzzle I needed. The *Hattusa Codex* lay on the floor outside the magic circle, at the feet of Barbara Keane's corpse.

Stepping carefully across the floor, I kneeled in front of the book and used a pen from my pocket to move the blood-stained jacket aside. The book was open to a page that was written in Hittite, an ancient Indo-European language that I could only decipher a few words from. Those few words were enough, however, along with the illustrations and diagrams, for me to work out that I was looking at the instructions for a summoning ritual of some sort, though a summoning of what, I had no idea. Nor could I work out how Troy Turner was even able to read the instructions himself. He didn't translate it on the internet, which meant he must've used another book to do so or found someone else to translate it for him. Whatever the case, it didn't really matter how he deciphered the text. All that mattered now was that he did.

After photographing the open page of the book with my phone, I left the book and everything else where it was and turned to leave the basement. But as I crossed the floor, the hairs on the back of my neck stood on end and the tattoos on my back burned beneath my skin as the ink flowed like hot lava. After freezing for a second, I turned back around slowly to see the corpse of Barbara Keane sit bolt upright. Slowly, and with a horrible cracking sound, the dead woman twisted her head around so she could look right at me with milky eyes that still managed to communicate her fear and pain.

When she spoke, her mouth moved slowly as though her jaw was fighting the rigor mortis. The words that came forth from her were uttered with a drawn-out death rattle. "Don't… let him…use the…keeeeeyy!"

I blinked once, and Barbara Keane was back lying on the floor as though she had never moved a muscle, leaving me to stare for a moment as I wondered if what I'd seen had really happened. I might have been hallucinating from the Mud, but it was rare for that to happen. No, this was real. Barbara Keane had spoken. *Don't let him use the key*, she had said. What did she mean by that? Was that the purpose of this whole ritual carried out by Troy Turner, to obtain some sort of key? Or more likely an entity that *was* the key to something else. And if so, what?

Fuck knows, I thought as I left the basement and went outside, glad of the fresh air to dispel the fumes of human offal from my lungs. Taking out my phone, I called in the incident. Pretty soon, the place would be crawling with cops and forensics. Before that happened, however, I made another two calls. One to Salem Hospital as I briefly explained the situation to a shocked Jacklyn Turner who said she was on her way over, and another to Walker, who picked up this time. "Where the fuck are you, Walker?" I asked.

"Sorry," she said. "I'm on my way to you now."

"I'll talk to you when you get here."

I hung up on her and lit a cigarette as I stood outside the house waiting on a phone call from Troy's mother so that I could try to explain the situation to her, letting her know that her son was missing, and his three friends were dead. If Routman and Stokes were here, they'd pin the murders on Troy without a second thought, and in one sense they'd be right. But I knew better. Troy was out there, possessed by some evil power.

And he was going to kill again if I didn't find a way to stop him.

12

Walker arrived on the scene before everyone else. She came down the driveway in her tight black jeans and leather jacket while I stood outside the house smoking a cigarette. Her expression as she approached was as serious as it always was. I didn't remember Hannah Walker's face being quite so fixed the handful of times I'd spoken to her before her soul parted ways with her body.

"What the fuck, Walker?" I said, blowing a stream of smoke into the damp night air. "You know how many times I called you?"

"I'm sorry," she said. "Can I get one of those?"

"I didn't know you smoked."

"I don't. Hannah quit a few years ago. She thought smoking would kill her."

I almost laughed at that as I took a cigarette out of the packet and handed it to her. "I'd say the drugs would've got her first, which they did."

"It doesn't matter now." She took the cigarette and put it between her pink lips. "This body is resistant to all forms of disease now. I can't get cancer."

"Knock yourself out then." I handed her my zippo,

watching as she lit the cigarette and coughed on the first drag before handing me back the lighter. "Why haven't you been answering my calls? Do you know what happened in there?"

"I just had some personal business to take care of," she said, looking away as she drew on her cigarette, the taste seeming to disagree with her.

"Personal business?" I stared at her for a second. "Yakuza business, you mean?"

She took another drag, managing not to cough this time. "Maybe. I didn't think I'd be needed after I sorted the paperwork for the warrant."

"You were needed."

"Like I said, I'm sorry. What happened in there anyway?"

"It seems like Troy killed his three friends," I said after a second, giving her the out she was looking for. "After they all performed some summoning ritual with Barbara Keane's corpse."

"Any sign of Troy?"

"Do you think I'd be standing here if there was? He's gone."

"What state is he in do you think?"

"I'd say a bloody one, after what he did to his friends. I think he's also possessed by whatever power or entity he summoned."

"Any ideas on how to find him?"

I stamped out my cigarette on the ground. "As he's on foot, I might be able to track him. We'll see. First, I have to talk to his mother. She's on her way here now."

"Does she know anything?"

"Just that her son is missing, and his three friends are dead. I don't think she knows very much about what Troy and the others were up to. We'll see what she says when I interview her."

Walker tossed her cigarette away and fished a pair of black

evidence gloves out of her pocket before putting them on. "I'm heading in for a look."

As she went to move past me, I stopped her by grabbing her arm. "You okay, Walker?" I said, aware I was asking a demon if everything was rosy in the garden. Still, demon or not, she was my partner, and I was concerned, which to be honest, surprised even me.

Just to be clear, you're looking at a guy who sat by while his last partner gambled away everything he owned, resulting in him losing his badge and then his family and later his own god damn life. I could've helped him, steered him onto a better path, but I didn't even try, content as I was to watch the train wreck happen. I often blame the Spock Chip for these lapses in empathy and absences' of compassion, but deep down, I know there's more to it. I just haven't cared to look yet, or maybe I'm just afraid to. Either way, if you want saving, look elsewhere, for I'm not your guy.

Walker smiled just the tiniest bit, enough for me to know she was oddly touched by whatever modicum of concern I had for her. I had to admit, though, it was a tad tough to wrap my head around the concept of a demon being touched at all by human compassion. "I have days where I have trouble coping. Hannah had a lot going on inside her, and I'm still trying to adjust to it all."

"You mean with this whole Yakuza thing?"

"I suppose so, yes."

I let go of her arm. "Once we get this case wrapped up, we'll talk about the Yakuza thing, and you can let me know what's going on."

Her dark eyes seemed to well up with emotion for a second, then she nodded once before going inside the house to inspect the scene. I remained outside. The last thing I wanted was for Troy's mother to come home and see the mess left in her basement. Doctor or not, I doubted she would react too well to the carnage.

While I waited outside, a car pulled up by the front of the house, and I frowned when I saw it was Routman and Stokes. "What the fuck are they doing here?" I asked no one as I walked up the drive to meet them, just as two squad cars arrived, followed by the forensics van.

"Ethan," Routman said by way of greeting as he and Stokes started walking up the drive toward me.

"Jim?" I said. "What the fuck's going on?"

Routman looked apologetic, but Stokes smiled when he said, "Sorry, Drake, but you're off the case. We're taking over."

"What?" I looked at Routman, whose face confirmed what Stokes was saying. "This is my fucking case."

"It was," Routman said. "But as of half an hour ago, the captain put *us* on it instead."

"Why?"

Routman shrugged as Stokes smiled once more. "Rumor has it you were a bad boy, Drake," he said. "IAB wants you over something."

Fucking IAB. I might've known.

"Don't get too comfortable," I said to Stokes. "This is still my fucking crime scene."

"I'm sorry, Ethan." Routman rolled his broad shoulders against the cold. "We have our orders. You need to sort things out in the precinct. Until then, this is our crime scene now."

"Good luck with IAB," Stokes said, still smiling as he walked away, the fucking weasel.

I put a hand on Routman's shoulder as he went to move past me. "What is this all about, Jim?"

Routman sighed. "I'm not supposed to say anything."

"Jim, it's me," I said, squeezing his shoulder as I stared at him.

"IAB's saying you're a suspect in a murder."

"What fucking murder?" I thought of the cult members I'd put down earlier today, but there was no way those bodies were found, not after the Hellbastards were done with them.

Routman shrugged. "That's all I know. Captain wants you back at the precinct. I'm sure he'll explain everything. Sorry, Ethan."

"Yeah, as I said, Jim, don't get too comfortable. This shit will be sorted soon enough, and I'll be back on the case."

Routman nodded as if he didn't hold out much hope before walking away. When he left, I stood for a moment while I wondered what the hell was going on, and why Lewellyn hadn't pre-empted this shit, whatever it was. There was no point phoning him now as he'd probably still be in bed at this time, so I decided to head to the precinct to find out what was going on first. IAB had been building a case against me, though whatever evidence of misconduct they thought they had they could shove up their asses as far as I was concerned.

As I was heading to my car, a blue Mercedes pulled up behind one of the squad cars just as the uniforms were cordoning off the area. A woman with light brown hair tied in a ponytail got out of the car, a distressed look on her cherubic face as she walked up to one of the uniforms wearing surgical blues. Guessing it was Troy Turner's mother, Jacklyn, I told the uniform to let her through, and I met her at the end of the driveway. "Mrs. Turner?" I asked her.

"It's Ms. Where is my son? I want to see my son." She went to barge past me so she could enter the house, but I stood in front of her, my hands held out as I explained she couldn't go in. "But it's my house. I have a right to go inside. Move aside, please."

"Your house is now an active crime scene, ma'am," I said. "I'm afraid you'll have to wait until it's been processed. Is there somewhere you can go in the meantime?"

Her blue eyes welled up with tears. "Where is my son?" she asked in a voice that said she was about to break.

"We aren't sure, but we're trying to find out." I looked

behind me for a second to make sure Routman and Stokes were still inside before turning back to her. "Ma'am, I'd like to ask you some questions about your son if that's alright."

Her hand was over her mouth as she struggled to keep herself together. "You said his friends were...were dead, is that right?"

"Yes, I'm afraid so. Did you know your son was involved in the occult?"

"What? I—" She paused to compose herself for a second. "He's a teenager, it's just something he uses to rebel, like the heavy metal music he listens to. Ever since his father died…" She trailed off, clamping her mouth again as tears streamed down her face, finally saying, "I just want to see my son."

"Rest assured, ma'am, we're doing our best to find him. In the meantime, it would be beneficial if you could tell me if there's any place your son might go. Any other friends, for instance? Or places he liked to hang out?"

Jacklyn Turner stared at me a moment as she swallowed back her emotions, her training as a surgeon kicking in now it seemed like. "Are you going to tell me what happened here, Detective?"

"Well, we think your son may have killed his three friends," I said, not seeing any way of breaking it to her gently. "Forensics will have to confirm that, but it seems likely that's the case, I'm afraid."

Her modicum of professional distance dropped away as tears sprang from her eyes, and she clamped her hand over her mouth again as if to keep from screaming. She took a minute to compose herself, then said, "My son would never… would never…"

"I know, ma'am," I said. "I think there's more to the story. Your son may not be completely to blame here."

"What?" She shook her head in confusion. "What are you saying?"

"I'm saying there are other forces at play here, and that—"

"Drake." I turned around to see Stokes standing by the front door, an angry look on his weasel face. "I thought I told you to leave this crime scene."

"What's he talking about?" Jacklyn Turner said. "Aren't you a detective?"

"I am, ma'am, but—"

"Wait, don't I know you?" A look of recognition came over her face. "You're Angela's ex-husband, aren't you?"

"Drake," Stokes said again, louder this time.

"Excuse me, ma'am."

Setting my jaw as my anger threatened to boil to the surface, I stomped away from Jacklyn Turner and over to Stokes, whose face dropped when he realized he'd pushed me too far. "Drake—" he began.

"Say my fucking name again, Stokes," I growled as I towered over him. "I dare you." My eyes bored into him as he did his best to maintain eye contact.

"Ethan?" Routman was outside now. "I think you should go now. Let us handle this."

I stared at Stokes for another second. "Yeah, I'm sure things will be in good fucking hands." Then I turned to look at Routman. "Be sure to whitewash everything like you usually do, Jim."

"What the hell does that mean?" he asked.

"You know what it means," I said as I walked away, stopping by Jacklyn Turner, who was still standing on the edge of the drive, her arms folded across her chest as if to hold herself together. I handed her my card. "Call me if you can think of anything that might help with finding your son," I said.

"But aren't the other detectives handling this?"

"Not for long."

~

I wasn't surprised to find Captain Edwards absent from the precinct when I got there. Son of a bitch had probably phoned Routman from home to tell him to get me off the case. Not that it mattered anyway. I had nothing to say to Edwards. Whatever I had to say, I would say to Lewellyn, no one else. Anyway, that's not why I was in the precinct. I was here to see Internal Affairs, assuming anyone from that department was even here at almost five a.m.

As it turned out, rats never slept, and I found a Detective John Striker at his desk in the IAB. He was a tall man with broad shoulders and a smooth, shaved head. Wearing a dark suit, he looked more like an FBI agent than a cop. I also realized that he had been the one driving the car that had followed me yesterday. He didn't seem surprised to see me as I walked up to the desk in his small office. "You want to tell me what the hell you're playing at?" I asked him. "Pulling me off a case that doesn't even concern you?"

Striker remained composed as he put down his pen and closed the folder in front of him. He was in his early thirties and had an air of arrogance about him. He was the type of guy who thought he held all the cards in every situation he was in, including this one. He struck me as the high and mighty type, and the way he glanced down his sharp nose at me said plenty for the contempt he held for his fellow officers, maybe even for his fellow human beings. I'd seen him around but had never spoken to him before. His reputation preceded him, and he was known for doggedly pursuing any cop that got onto his radar, never giving up until he got his man. He knew people hated him, but that didn't seem to bother him much. In fact, he seemed the type to be spared on by such hatred and animosity, as most of these IAB fucks seem to be. It was them against everyone else, and that's how most of them liked it.

They had a lot in common with hellots in fact, and as soon as I thought it, prickly heat started in the back of my neck, and my tattoos twitched just enough to get me thinking further. It wasn't beyond the realm of possibility that this IAB fuck was a hellot, and that if he was, then maybe he might be affiliated to that other fuck, Astaroth.

It was tempting to goad this guy into unmasking himself, maybe by confronting him directly with accusations, or maybe by subtler means via insinuations, peeling away at the mask until it fell off. But I decided to let things play out. *Let's see what this asshole has to say*, I thought, as my Infernal Itch started up once more. "Detective Drake," he said. "Please take a seat. You may also wish to have a rep sit with you, but good luck finding one at this hour."

"I'm fine," I said, grudgingly taking a seat opposite him. "Commissioner Lewellyn will sort all this out anyway."

Striker smiled as if he knew better. "Don't be so sure, Detective." The way the son of a bitch smiled, it made me think he knew more than he was letting on. He was involved at a higher level, and he enjoyed hiding that fact from me.

"What do you mean by that?"

"The commissioner does not have the authority to quash IAB investigations, despite what you may think."

"That's what this is, an investigation?"

"Very much so."

"Feels a bit witch-hunty to me."

"Witch-hunty? A bit dramatic, Detective, not to say grammatically incorrect."

"Conspiratorial then."

"Again..." He trailed off as if continuing with the sentence was beneath him.

"Alright, hotshot. Why you investigating me? I haven't done anything, apart from my job."

"Was it your job to beat a man to death?" His clear blue eyes bored into me, a look of smug satisfaction in them. He was enjoying himself because he thought he had me by the balls.

And then it clicked. Jarvis. The motherfucker had only gone and died on me. "I have no idea what you're talking about," I said.

Striker placed his hand on top of the folder in front of him, as if it contained his next surprise that he couldn't wait to pull out. "Maybe we should postpone this interview until you can get a rep in here," he said. "Maybe even a lawyer."

"I don't need either," I said, confident he had nothing on me.

"Okay, have it your way." He opened the file and took out a photograph of a man whose face looked like ground beef. "Do you recognize this man?"

Recognize him? I doubted Jarvis' own mother—if the fucking cretin even had a mother and weren't just shat out by some MURK—would've recognized him. I made a show of peering at the photo, then I shook my head. "Should I?"

"His name is Jarvis Heath. He died in hospital from injuries caused by massive blunt force trauma to the head. He was beaten to death."

"I know what blunt force trauma means. What's this have to do with me?"

Striker interlocked his fingers as he placed his hands on the desk, his gaze steady and probing as he fixed it on me. "The last words he said to the doctor who was treating him were, *A cop did this*."

I stared at Striker for a moment as if waiting for the punchline. "And?"

"And then he gave an address." He paused for a moment, as if for dramatic effect. If he expected to see me squirm at this stage, he was sadly mistaken. "The address is the building where you currently live, and as it happens, you're the only cop who lives in the whole building."

Fuck you, Jarvis. You couldn't just make up for your no doubt countless sins and die like a fucking man and keep your mouth shut. No, you had to die as you lived, like a fucking rat…

"Tell me about this guy's rap sheet."

"What does that have to do with anything?"

"I doubt he has much credibility if he used his dying breath to tell lies about a serving police officer."

"Lies, Detective?" Striker said, seeming to refrain from rolling his eyes too much.

"Well, clearly he made this shit up. I mean—" I held up my hands, knuckles facing out, the skin completely healed now. "Do these look like hands that recently beat someone to death?"

"You could've been wearing gloves."

"Gloves? I like to feel something when I hit it, Detective Striker," I said, my eyes boring into *him* until he eventually dropped his gaze to the folder on the desk. "When was this beating supposed to have taken place?"

"Between midnight and two a.m."

"I wasn't even home then. I was in a club called The Brokedown Palace."

"Of course you were. Can anyone vouch for you there?"

"The owner, Carlito Martinez. Call him. He'll tell you I was there until after three."

Striker wrote the name down before looking at me again. "The victim gave a name before he died as well."

Well, it wasn't fucking mine, for as far as I know, Jarvis didn't even know my name. "Oh yeah? Who?"

"Just a surname. *Donovan*. And as it turns out, an Ashlene Donovan is living on the same floor as you."

"Really? I don't know anyone by that name. I'm not very neighborly, keep myself to myself."

"I'll be paying Ashlene Donovan a visit later, so we'll see," he said. "And just in case you have any thoughts of trying to talk to this woman beforehand, I've posted a man outside her door."

"That's very thorough of you," I said, trying to remain stony-faced as I cursed my damn luck. No good deed, eh?

"I'm going to go now, as you have no evidence I was involved in this man's assault."

"Death, Detective, not assault."

Scroteface?

Yes, boss?

Did you do as I asked? Is all the blood gone from the landing?

Yes, boss. Cracka sucked up most of it, then we all licked it clean.

Good boy.

I went to get up, but Striker told me to sit down again, which I didn't do immediately, pausing as I hovered over the chair for a second. "The truth is, the death of Jarvis Heath was not the original reason we opened an investigation against you."

Here we go.

I sat back down. "So why did you then?"

"Who were the men in hoods who stopped you on the street yesterday?"

I frowned. "Men in hoods? I have no idea what you're talking about."

"We were following you, Detective. You looked right at me when you exited your car."

"No." I shook my head. "You must be mistaking me for someone else."

"Really, Detective? You are going to bald-face lie to me?"

"I'm not lying. I was out working the Keane case all day yesterday."

Striker gave a small sigh as he tried to contain his annoyance. "You aren't doing yourself any favors by lying, you know. This will go against you at the official hearing."

"What official hearing?"

"The one that will examine the so-called Unit X and your role in it."

It was my turn to sigh. "Like I said, witch-hunty."

Striker leaned his forearms on the desk. "It's a unit that officially doesn't exist, that doesn't file any reports, and which picks and chooses its own cases. What makes you think such a unit isn't worthy of our scrutiny when every other cop in this precinct is held accountable? As far as I can see, Detective, Unit X has no accountability at all."

"You're wrong. My accountability is to Commissioner Lewellyn."

"Yes, Commissioner Lewellyn," he said with some disdain. "A man who seems to be abusing his position of power to start up some crackpot unit that no one else is allowed to know about. Tell me, Detective, what is your unit's brief? This unit that only contains two people, you and Detective Hannah Walker, who by the way, was previously suspended due to allegations of drug abuse, but who was reinstated, at Commissioner Lewellyn's behest, I might add." He paused before asking, "What's the true purpose of Unit X, Detective Drake? Tell me."

"As keen as you seem for answers, I'm not at liberty to disclose any of that information," I said. "You'd have to ask the commissioner about it."

"We will don't worry."

"I'm going now." I stood up. "You want to talk to me again, you arrange an official interview."

"Not so fast, Detective," Striker said, standing up at the same time as me. "Pending further investigation into the death of Jarvis Heath, you are now officially suspended from duty."

"What?"

"Please turn in your badge and gun, Detective."

"You can't fucking do this."

"I *am* doing this. Your badge and gun. Now please."

I glared at Striker as the heat on the back of my neck intensified, and my tattoos began to swirl continuously beneath my skin. My hands clenched into fists, and I had to stop myself from swinging hard at this fuck's jaw, smashing it to bits so he couldn't ever again speak his sickening brand of smug superiority. But like it or not, he had the power here because he was IAB and we both knew he had me by the balls. Maintaining eye contact with him, I calmly took my gun from its holster and placed it on the desk between us, on top of the photo of Jarvis Heath's mangled face. "You'll regret this," I told him.

"That's what they all say, Detective," he said. "But funnily enough, I never do."

"Asshole," I said as I turned and walked away.

"Detective?" I stopped without turning around, said nothing. "Your badge?"

Reaching down, I unclipped my badge from my belt and held it in my hand for a second, gripping it just right. Then I spun around and flung the badge right at Striker's face. It was a good throw, well-aimed. It would've hurt like hell if it had hit his face. It didn't though, because as I half-expected, Striker reflexively used his supernatural power to stop the badge mid-air six inches in front of his face. The badge stayed there for a full three seconds before he calmly reached up and took it, a smug smile on his face now as if this was the real him and all pretenses could now be dropped.

"How did you know?" He put my badge on the desk next to my gun.

"Lucky guess," I said. "Or maybe I could just smell the demon stench coming off you. I'm very attuned to that sort of thing. Maybe your boss didn't tell you that."

He feigned confusion. "My boss?"

"Astaroth. It makes sense. He says he wants to break me."

"He does. He *will*. He's coming for you, Detective."

I walked right up to Striker until I was only inches away from his face. "And what about you, Striker? Are you going to come for me too?"

"I already am coming for you," he said, his voice lowered now as though he no longer felt the need to try to browbeat me. "Unlike the other feeble schmucks in this building, I'm not afraid of you, Drake. I possess more power than you can possibly imagine, graciously given to me by Astaroth himself, the most powerful of the Fallen next to Lucifer."

"I get tired of hearing you hellot fucks drone on about how powerful you are," I told him. "You think knowing a few magic tricks gives you power? It doesn't." I stepped forward an inch, my eyes boring into his. "You know what true power is, Striker? It's the power that comes from having owned countless motherfuckers like you over the years, ever since I was a kid. There's hardly a monster in this world that I haven't faced and fucking owned, even if it damn near killed me doing it. You know what that makes me, Striker? A survivor. Now tell me—" I stepped forward another inch. "How many motherfuckers like me have *you* owned in the past?" When he stared back, saying nothing, I said, "That's what I thought. Watch your fucking step with me, and that goes for your asshole demon lord as well. You decide to come for me, you better be ready for a whole world of pain, because right now, I got a lotta fucking pain to give." I turned and walked away, but the asshole had the audacity to stop me again. Fucking hellots, always having to get the last word in.

"You're not a god, Drake," he said as I turned around. "You're barely even a man. You're just an animal who likes to kill anything that doesn't adhere to your ridiculous moral code. Don't even pretend you don't have one. I know you do. Men like you always have a moral code, even if it directly contradicts everyone else's. You're nothing but a bully who's been allowed to get away with far too much for far too long."

"And what the fuck would you know about it?" I said through clenched teeth.

"I know more than you think…Detective. Knowledge is power. I know exactly who you are."

Instinctively, my right hand went for my gun, only to find it wasn't there, as it was still sitting on Striker's desk.

"Really?" he said tutting as he took my gun from the desk and held it. "You were going to draw on me in here?"

"This isn't over," I said. "You might be coming for me, but I'll be coming for you as well, asshole, you hear me? And that includes your fucking demon boss."

I turned and walked to the door. As I was walking out, Striker said, "May the best man win, Detective."

13

Back outside in the Dodge, I slammed my palms against the steering wheel. "Fucking IAB bastards," I snarled. Taking my fucking badge and gun. *What fucking right did they have anyway?*

It was a rhetorical question of course, since they had every right. There was also the fact I *did* kill Jarvis Heath, although to be fair, he wasn't dead when he walked away from me in the apartment building. It must've been the drugs keeping him going. Asshole. He probably died happy thinking he was getting some sort of revenge on me. Fuck him. He still deserved what he got. And there was no way I was going to allow a scumbag like that to lose me my badge or land me in fucking jail.

No way.

And speaking of scumbags, the same went for Striker and his cult buddies. They could go fuck themselves as well if they thought they were going to railroad me into giving up my body to some fucking demon. I'd cut my own throat first before that happened.

Hopefully Lewellyn would sort things out with IAB. Astaroth and his cult, I would sort out myself.

But Jesus, these motherfuckers were everywhere these days. Ever since the last big wave of Fallen arrived here over a decade ago—and despite the bloody war that took place after—the demons have used their hellots to infiltrate every level of society, making me wonder just how many of them were at the top. Who was above Striker, for instance? Was his boss a hellot too? Was the fucking chief of police a hellot? Or the mayor? How high did this demonic grasp for power go? How far was I willing to go to stop it, if it even could be stopped at this stage?

I called Carlito Martinez's number. Even though it was after five a.m. I still expected him to answer. Carlito didn't sleep much, mainly because he spent his nights snorting lines of coke from the silicon tits of strippers and escorts. After half a dozen rings, he picked up. "Yeah?" he said, sounding like he was in the middle of something.

"Carlito, it's Ethan Drake. Can you talk?"

"Can I talk? I'm in the middle of getting my dick sucked, but sure, fire away, Ethan."

I rolled my eyes and shook my head in mild disgust. "I need you to vouch for me being in the club until three this morning. Can you do that?"

"Sure," he grunted. "Oh yeah baby, that's it…what for, Ethan?"

"I'm being investigated by IA over something. They might come calling."

"Oh fuck…oh yeah…sure, I'll…I'll…" He trailed off, lost in his drug-fueled ecstasy.

"Carlito?"

"Yeah, hold on. Fucking suck it, baby, yeah, oh yeah. Oh, fuck I'm gonna come, baby, yeah…"

I held the phone away from my ear just as Carlito's loud as hell orgasm came ripping through the speaker. "Jesus Christ."

"Oh shit, oh fuck…"

"I'll call you later."

"Wait, Ethan. Just wait." He paused for several seconds

while he panted down the phone, sounding like someone who'd just finished a thousand-yard dash. "Alright, fuck... listen, you already owe me. Eighty large, don't forget."

"I haven't forgotten. I'll get it back to you, don't worry."

"How? On your shitty cop salary?"

"I'll figure something out. Just do this one thing for me..."

"I will, I will. I'm not going to see you in fucking jail, am I? What did you take me for?"

"Thanks, Carlito."

"At the same time, though, you're gonna have to do something to clear your debt. You feel me?"

I stared out the window for a second at the murky gray and the rain which was beginning to hit the windshield. "Sure. What do you want me to do, Carlito?"

"Not over the phone," he said. "Come by the club. We'll get a drink and talk it over."

He hung up, and I put the phone on the dash before reaching into my pocket and taking out the Mud dropper, depositing a dose onto my tongue, wincing at the taste before swallowing. Eighty grand was a lot of money. More than I could get anytime soon, at least not through any legal means. I had about eight grand or so in a bank account, that was all. Carlito wasn't a man you wanted to be in debt to for too long. He'd know better than to send his men after me, so he'd fuck me with subtler means. He'd already hinted when he first loaned me the money that he would ruin me with the police department and land me in jail somehow. He'd find a way to set me up and there wasn't a thing I could do about it, bar killing Carlito himself. Which was an option, but one I'd rather not take, especially since I needed his alibi. I had enough blood on my hands as it was, and with IAB chasing me over Jarvis Heath, killing Carlito probably wouldn't help my situation any. Besides, he helped me when no one else would or could. I owed him fair and square. Best just to turn up at the club and see what he wanted, then go from there.

Before starting the engine, I called Walker to see how things were going at the Turner place. "Mackey is here going through everything," she said. "I'm standing outside. Routman fazed me out. Says I'm not needed. As far as he's concerned, it's a cut and dried case. Troy is a psycho who killed his friends. Now we just have to find him. Stokes is organizing a search of the area."

"Assholes," I said. "I'll talk to Lewellyn later and see if I can't get this whole thing straightened out."

"Stokes says IAB is all over you," she said. "What for?"

"Don't worry about it. It's bullshit. Our priority now has to be finding Troy. He's dangerous, and he's going to kill again." I took out a cigarette and lit it. "I want you to try to track his movements from when he left the house. I'm sure you have *some* power in you that might help with that."

"Not much. I'm still struggling to access my powers. I imagine it will take time."

"You should get yourself a cult like most of your brethren have done," I told her. "They get their power from the belief of their followers."

"I know they do. I'm not starting a cult, Ethan."

"Up to you. I'm just saying it's fine if you do. In the meantime, *I* believe in you, if that helps any."

A small laugh echoed down the phone. "It does, actually."

"Alright. Keep me informed."

"Ethan?"

"Yeah?" When she didn't answer, I said, "What is it, Walker?"

"Nothing. I'll talk to you later."

When she hung up, I shook my head at her weird behavior and tossed the phone onto the passenger seat. *Jesus*, I thought. *Women were hard enough to deal with, but a woman with a demon inside her as well?*

Shit…

I ENTERED THE BROKEDOWN PALACE VIA THE SIDE ENTRANCE, which not too many people knew about. Most often it was used by the bouncers to throw unruly customers out, or by Carlito to take some poor schmuck outside to have the shit beaten out of them after they'd crossed him. Carlito even kept a bloodstained baseball bat behind the dumpster next to the door for just such occasions. One time he beat some guy so hard he killed him. He called me to help him get rid of the body, which I wasn't happy about, but I owed him for putting me onto a murder suspect who I'd never have found without his help. I covered up one murder to solve another. That's how things worked with Carlito, and with the city in general. Nothing was black and white, there was no good or bad, just shades of gray that I did my best to sort through.

Carlito was alone at the bar when I walked in, any customers long gone. Soft blues music played in the background as Carlito sat in a gray suit with no tie, nursing a drink and occasionally snorting, a side effect of all the coke he'd probably done that night. "Ethan," he said smiling, looking the worse for wear after a hard night's partying. "Come join me, big guy." I sat next to him at the bar while he leaned over and grabbed an extra glass, filling it with whiskey from the half-empty bottle on the bar. "There you go, my friend. Drink up."

"Rough night?" I asked, sipping the whiskey, the Mud already having landed me in surreal country as a sense of unreality washed over me in the dimly lit club.

Carlito nodded slowly in that way drunk people do. "Oh yeah, but in a good way." He smiled. "You know what I mean?"

"Sure," I said as he slapped my leg and grinned like a naughty schoolboy, which is what Carlito reminded me of sometimes.

"When's the last time you got laid? I got a busty blonde hooker in the back right now. You can have her if you want, on me. I'm telling you; she sucks cock like nobody's business."

"I'm sure she does. I'm fine, though. Thanks anyway."

"You've never struck me as a man who enjoys himself very much. Why is that?"

I turned my head slowly to look at him. "It's kinda hard to enjoy yourself when the two most precious people in the world to you get murdered."

"Oh, shit…I'm sorry. You know what I mean, though, right? Even when you were still married, you would come here and you would drink and cavort with other women, but you never seemed to enjoy it. You always looked like you were just…" He thought for a second and then threw his hands up. "Fuck, I don't know. I'm too fucked up to think about it. Who am I to judge anyway? I mean all the shit I do; you think I'm happy?"

I shrugged as I took a drink. "How would I know? Is anyone happy? Happy is bullshit. There's no such thing."

"You're a dark motherfucker. Let's change the subject before you kill my buzz."

"Knock yourself out." I turned in my stool to face him. "What do you need me to do to clear my debt?"

"You know, you never told me why you needed the money." Carlito leaned one elbow on the bar. "You're not a gambler as far as I know, so why did you?"

"It's personal." I took out my cigarettes, offering him one, which he took.

"Personal, huh?" I lit his cigarette for him before lighting my own. "That's all your gonna say?"

"Yep."

"Well, at least you've got discretion, Ethan. I like discretion, as you know."

"Are we gonna get to it or not? I still have a case to work on."

"You're wasted as a cop. You should come work for me. I guarantee the pay would be better."

"No thanks. I'm happy as a cop."

"How the fuck could anyone be happy as a cop? I mean, Jesus…" He snorted loudly and wiped his nose with the back of his hand. "I can't think of a worse job. Everybody hates you, and guys like me would sooner put a bullet in your brain rather than fucking talk to you."

"I've helped you out more than once, haven't I?"

"Yes, yes you have, and you're about to help me out again."

"In exchange for clearing my debt."

"Yeah, of course, should you get this thing I want done…*done*."

"So, who do I have to kill?"

"Who mentioned killing anybody?"

"Come on," I said. "What else would be worth eighty grand?"

"True." He nodded. "Though even for killing somebody, eighty grand would still be a big stretch. I'd be letting you off lightly."

"We'll see about that. Who's the target?"

He took a swallow of his whiskey before answering. "Scarlet Hood."

I paused with my cigarette halfway to my lips. "Scarlet Hood? Are you fucking kidding me?"

"Nope," he said, his dark, heavy-lidded eyes serious. "She crossed me bad."

"So, what did she do that was so bad that you want her dead?"

"She killed my cousin, Eduardo."

"Eduardo? Why?" I knew who he was talking about, having

met Eduardo on a few occasions over the years. He did most of his business in the next city over, which was Blackham. It was a few years since I last saw him here in Fairview, but I remember him being a sleazeball. His business was pornography, and he made no secret of the fact that he was into young girls. Rumor had it that he was also a trafficker, although Carlito would never confirm or deny that. I always had my suspicions that Carlito was involved in the trafficking business as well, but again, his business interests were a closely guarded secret for the most part. As far as Carlito was concerned, the less people knew about what he was up to, the better. "That's how I stay alive and out of jail," he told me once. "Discretion."

"I have no fucking idea why Scarlet fucking Hood would kill my cousin," he said now. "You know me, Ethan. I ain't got much in the way of family. All I had left was Eduardo and my brother in Cuba, and my brother don't even talk to me because of what I do, so…now I'm all alone, Ethan. I got fucking nobody." In a burst of anger, he pitched his glass at the bar, smashing other empty glasses in the process. "I GOT NOBODY!" He stood off his stool, his face fuming, his eyes wide and glaring. "NOBODY FUCKING DOES THIS TO ME AND GETS AWAY WITH IT!"

"Calm down, Carlito." I poured myself and him another drink.

"Don't fucking tell me to calm down," he said, taking a step toward me. "You better kill that fucking bitch for me, or I swear to God—"

"What?" I said, staring hard at him.

Snorting, he ran his thick fingers through his gray-streaked greasy hair, his hands coming away slick. "I just want her dead," he said, calmer now, or as calm as he could be with God knows how many grams of coke in him and fuck knows what else. He sat back on his stool and took the drink I poured him, downing it in one. "I just want her fucking dead."

"I can see that," I said after a minute. "Only, this is Scarlet

Hood we're talking about here, not some two-bit punk or half-assed assassin. Hood does contract hits; she doesn't just kill at random. Which means somebody hired her to kill your cousin. You want the real killer, you gotta find out who hired Hood first."

Carlito nodded to himself. "You're right," he said. "You gotta find out who hired her."

"Me?"

"Why do you think you're here, Ethan, huh? Kill Hood once you find out who hired her and then leave whoever hired her to me. You do that and we're clear, you and me. No more debt."

"And if I don't do this thing for you?"

"There are worse things than death, Ethan," he said, looking up at me. "Like if a man loses his job, and he loses his purpose along with it. What would you do if you weren't a cop, huh?"

A scowl came over my face. I didn't enjoy being threatened by anyone, though I understood why he did it. This was how the game was played, and as I was deep in the game, I couldn't very well complain about the rules, now could I?

Carlito raised his glass and held it out toward me. "So, what do you say, Ethan? Do we understand each other or not?"

Lifting my glass, I pressed it against his. "We do."

"Good, because I want that bitch's head on a fucking silver platter."

JESUS FUCK, I THOUGHT TO MYSELF AS I STOOD IN THE ALLEY outside the club in the cold dawn light, surrounded by dumpsters and scurrying rats. When I'd turned up to talk to Carlito, I'd expected him to ask me to do something crazy—like take down a drug gang or kill some fucking crime lord—but nothing as crazy as what he actually asked me to do. Kill fucking Scarlet Hood? You didn't just kill Scarlet Hood. When it came to killing, *she* was the one who did it. I'd heard of a couple of incidents where people had gone after her before, and none of them lived to tell about it. Their bodies ended up swinging from a lamppost downtown, or their heads were sent back to their bosses with a note telling them to back off or they'd be next. Even the cops and the FBI had given up hunting Scarlet Hood. Everyone was afraid of her and for a good reason. Now I was going to be the next fool to go after her.

As I lit a cigarette and started walking to my car, I wondered if it might not be easier just to kill Carlito instead. It was something I would have to think about before I jumped into anything. Besides, I had more pressing concerns, like the fucking IAB investigation against me, and the fact that Daisy and her mother were both witnesses to the beating I gave Jarvis Heath. If they told Striker it was me who beat up Jarvis, I was done for. My badge would be gone for good and I'd be looking at the rest of my life in jail for murder.

As I got into the car after tossing my cigarette butt to the ground, I decided to head to my apartment building. Maybe I could find some way to talk to Daisy before Striker and his cronies did. Rest assured, they'd be banging on Daisy's door soon if they hadn't done so already. On the way there, I called Walker and asked her if there was any progress in finding Troy yet.

"No, not yet," she said. "The dogs picked up a trail, but it went cold after about a mile. Stokes is widening the search area, I think."

"Didn't you use your powers?"

She paused before answering. "I tried. It's too soon, Ethan. My celestial powers are still too weak."

I shook my head as I turned a corner into Bricktown. "What about the mother? Has she said anything?"

"Not much. She's at the precinct now with Routman. He's taking her statement. What are you doing, now that you're off the case?"

"I'm going home," I said. "I'll call Lewellyn later."

"You think he'll put you back on the case?"

"I don't know. Things have gotten more complicated. Striker, the IAB detective leading the investigation against me? It turns out he's a fucking hellot enthralled to Astaroth. This is all part of Astaroth's plan to break me."

"You can't let him."

I snorted. "No one fucking breaks me."

"Is there anything I can do?"

"Just keep looking for Troy. I'll call you later."

As I pulled the Dodge up outside my apartment building, I got out and had a look around for any unmarked police cars, but I didn't see any. A pang of anxiety hit me as I realized that Striker had already been and gone, otherwise his car would still be here. But I also realized that if he wasn't here waiting on me and he hadn't called either, then maybe he hadn't gotten anything from Daisy and her mother. Which was great, if that was the case, but there was still the other matter of forensic evidence that would undoubtedly be lifted from Jarvis Heath's body. They'd find my fucking DNA all over the asshole, which is something I didn't consider earlier. Jarvis' body would already have been moved to the morgue as it awaited processing. Once the samples were lifted, I'd be done for.

"Fuck," I said as I entered the building and started up the stairs, stopping when I got to the landing. Daisy was sitting in her usual spot, still reading the same Clive Barker novel. She continued to read it as if I wasn't there. In the cold morning light coming through the grimy window above her, it seemed as if her face had healed pretty well. I was also glad to see the blood gone from the floor. "Daisy," I greeted her.

"Detective," she said, her eyes still on her book.

I walked toward her and leaned one hand on the railing. "Your face looks better."

"It still hurts."

An awkward silence grew, and I glanced down the hallway, glad to see there were no cops around. "Listen—" I began before she cut me off.

"Yes, your cop friends were here, if that's what you were going to ask."

"They aren't my friends. Far from it. What did you tell them?"

She put the book on her lap and looked at me, one eye still slightly blackened, her bottom lip still swollen a little. "Nothing."

"Nothing?"

"They asked if you beat up Jarvis. I said no, and that I didn't even know you."

Crouching beside her, I leaned my back against the railings. "Thank you, Daisy."

"Don't thank me yet," she said. "My mother wants paying for her silence."

"How much?"

"Five grand or she talks, she says."

Five grand. Jesus Christ.

"That's extortion."

"I'd say murder is worse."

"Fair point. Though I didn't intend to kill that asshole, just so you know."

"I know. I don't care that he's dead." She seemed to mean this, which saddened me.

"I'll get your mother her money."

"When?"

"As soon as I can."

"She wants it today."

"Of course she does. I'll get it to her later."

Daisy nodded before going back to reading her book.

"And for the record," she said without looking at me. "I don't agree with her blackmailing you. Jarvis got what he deserved."

"I'm just sorry you had to see it."

She took her eyes off her book and fixed them on me. "You shouldn't be. No one has ever defended me like that before. I should be thanking you, Detective."

"I told you, call me Ethan. We're friends, right?"

"Sure." Daisy smiled.

"You ever need anything, just come and see me." I reached into my pocket and took out my card, handing it to her. "My personal number is on the back. Call me anytime."

Taking the card, she looked at it for a minute before sliding it in between the pages of her book. "I will."

Leaving her to her reading, I started down the hallway to my apartment, but stopped when Daisy called out, "Ethan?"

"Yeah?" I said turning around.

"That cop that was here, Striker? He said he'd send my mother to jail if I didn't get her to talk. Can he do that?"

Motherfucker, I thought. *Threatening a fucking kid.*

"No," I said, reassuring her. "I'd never let that happen."

Daisy smiled and nodded before going back to reading her book. "I know you wouldn't. Oh, and by the way, there are strange noises coming from your apartment. I guess you must've left the TV on or something."

Almost as soon as she mentioned it, I heard the noise myself, like multiple voices shouting and arguing. By the time I reached the door to the apartment, I knew what the source of the noise was.

And it wasn't the damned TV.

14

I walked into the apartment to find Scroteface and the gang all crowded onto the couch, squabbling and fighting among each other as *The Muppet Show* played on the TV. Cracka clawed Toast's face, removing large flakes of blackened skin in the process as Scroteface tried to keep him back. Snot Skull, Khullu, and Reggie seemed to be having their own argument as Khullu slapped Reggie around the face with one of his tentacles. "Hey!" I shouted, and they all stopped dead to stare at me like kindergarten kids caught misbehaving by their teacher. "What the hell's going on here?"

"Khullu say Miss Piggy don't have pussy," Reggie said to me, his little yellow eyes full of indignation.

"They don't," Khullu said. "They puppets."

"Miss Piggy have pussy."

"No. Missy Piggy puppet. And ugly."

"Miss Piggy not ugly," Cracka screamed. "Miss Piggy bootiful!"

"Miss Piggy not even fuck you anyway," Khullu screamed back. "You ugly as shit."

"Fuck you, tentacle face!"

They went at each other again like angry ferrets, and

Scroteface dived into the middle of them this time to try and keep them apart, the tabby cat pelt still on his head.

"You suck Kermit's dick!" Reggie screamed, seemingly at no one in particular.

"Kermit don't have dick!"

"Beaker have biggest dick!"

"You have *no* dick!"

"Enough!" I all but screamed and they froze once more. "Cut it fucking out or I swear to God, I'll cut *you* all out right now, and you know what that means, don't you? *Don't you?*"

"I try to tell them, boss," Scroteface said. "They don't listen."

"How about this then?" I said and began to say aloud the evocation that would send every one of the Hellbastards back to where they came from in less than a minute.

"Boss, wait," Scroteface said, holding his clawed hand out. "Don't."

"We sorry," Reggie said. "We sorry, boss."

"Please stop, boss," Khullu said.

I cut the evocation off before I got to the end and glared at them all as they sat like frightened puppies on the couch, their heads bowed as *The Muppet Show* continued to play out on the TV, with Statler and Waldorf laughing in the background. "Sit quiet and watch the fucking Muppets. I need time to think. Do you think you can do that?"

"Yeeessss, boossssss," they all said in unison.

"Good." I went to the kitchen and made myself some coffee before taking it into the bedroom and closing the door behind me. I sat down at the old oak writing desk I'd picked up at a thrift store a few years ago. The desk was positioned next to the window, and I sat and stared through the grimy glass as the rain pelted down outside.

My mind and body were tired through lack of sleep, but there was no way I was getting anything approximating sleep anytime soon. There was too much to do, too much to think about, like Jarvis Heath's body for a start. His body should still be in the morgue at this point, at least until it was moved to the Medical Examiner's Office for a full autopsy. Once there, it would be impossible for me to get to it without arousing suspicion. At the hospital morgue, however, I had more of a chance. I just needed to get in and destroy the body somehow, or at least make it impossible for any forensic evidence to be lifted from it.

As a plan slowly formed in my mind, I got up and walked to the shelves of medicinal ingredients, selecting a small bottle filled with a dark red powder. After taking the rubber bung from the glass bottle, I poured a small amount of the powder onto the back of my hand and snorted it all in one go, throwing my head back and gasping as the powder entered my system, giving me a huge euphoric high, before settling down into something that approximated an amphetamine high. The stuff was made from a nocturnal plant found in the jungles of South America, which was mixed with a few other key ingredients, namely dried vampire blood and the ground-up bones of a Hell Toad. One snort would keep me wide awake and alert for the next six to eight hours at least. I refilled the Mud bottle and dropped a dose into my mouth, just to take the edge of the other stuff.

When I was done, I went to the gun rack and selected a Sig Sauer P226 pistol and a magazine filled with 9mm Parabellum rounds. I slid the magazine into the pistol and then put the gun into the holster on my belt. *Fuck Striker if he thinks I'm going to walk around unarmed*, I thought. I'd carried a weapon of some sort with me ever since I was a kid and I wasn't about to change that habit now.

Back in the living room, the Hellbastards still sat on the couch, having calmed down now as they sat giggling at the Muppets on TV. "Alright," I told them. "I have a mission to do. Cracka, Toast, and Snot Skull, I'm going to need your help." The three chosen demons started to jump up and down with excitement, while the other three moaned that they didn't get to go. "Wait until I summon you, which won't be long. And boys?"

"Yeah boss?" Snot Skull said.

"This is an important mission. I can't have any fucking about, you hear me?"

"Yes, boss," Toast said.

"We hear, boss, we hear," Cracka said as he gave Khullu, Scroteface, and Reggie a smug look, earning himself a slap around the face from Scroteface, which nearly started them all off again until I drew my gun and pointed it at them.

"Go ahead," I said. "Fuck around some more and see what a bullet to the head feels like."

The Hellbastards cowered into the couch as they stared at the gun in my hand, then Scroteface said, "Sorry, boss."

"Yeah, sorry, boss," the rest said.

Holstering my gun before walking away from them, I muttered, "Like a bunch of bloody kids."

Wilshire General Hospital is the smaller of the two hospitals in the city, the main one being Salem General in Bedford. Compared to Salem with its gleaming white front and designer glass and steel construction, Wilshire General was drab and rundown, even decayed in some parts, with guttering hanging off the roof that allowed rainwater to stream down the walls, leaving a green slime over time, and old sash windows rotting in their frames.

The place didn't receive a great deal of money from the city for repairs and upkeep, which was the same story across the whole of Old Town. Bedford was the jewel of the city because that's where all the money was and where all the investment went. Old Town had money, but it was in the hands of crime lords, slum lords, street gangs, drug dealers, and low-level gangsters. Such money was never spent on the repair of buildings or even investing in new ones unless it was money that needed laundering.

Wilshire General was a shit hole and likely a petri dish of viruses and disease. It was the last place you wanted to be sent if you were sick. The hospital dealt with the detritus of Old Town that inevitably blew through its doors: the gunshot victims, the stabbing victims, the victims of rape, assault and domestic violence, the druggies who overdosed at least once a week and those who landed in under false pretenses either for a warm bed and a hot meal or to try to get their hands on the hospital drugs.

I'd made use of the place myself on a number of occasions, and for the most part the doctors and nurses who worked there were good, caring people, though many of them eventually developed a more callous attitude toward their patients after years of putting up with abuse of all kinds, and all for very little in the way of pay. Angela worked in the place as a junior doctor and couldn't wait to get across the river to Salem for better money and better working conditions.

Because of my frequent visits to the place over the years—both personally and as a cop—I knew the layout well, and it wasn't long before I was able to make my way to the morgue via a series of dimly lit corridors and stairwells. The hospital was so understaffed, I knew there'd only be one person working the morgue. The morgue itself wasn't very big either, which I knew from visiting it a few times over the years as a cop. If memory served, there were only half a dozen drawers inside, so it shouldn't be too hard to find Jarvis Heath's body. I could've taken a chance and just walked inside, but if someone was there, they'd see me and later give my description to IAB when they inevitably came to investigate. Using my tattoo magic to do the memory wipe trick on the morgue attendant was another option, but one I knew I couldn't entirely rely on.

Best not to take chances, I thought.

Sticking to the original plan, I first summoned Toast, who materialized in the corridor beside me. The little blackened demon looked up at me with his fiery orange eyes, awaiting my command. "Go around the corner and start a small fire in the corridor," I told him.

Toast gave me a blackened grin. "Yes, boss."

"A small fire, you hear me? Don't try to burn the whole fucking hospital down."

"Small fire. Yes, boss."

As Toast ran off down the corridor, sticking to the shadows near the walls, I moved to the end of the adjacent hallway and waited where I could see the door to the morgue. A few minutes later, the smoke alarms were activated as the smell of smoke drifted from around the corner. "Come on…" I said, staring at the door to the morgue.

A moment later, the door opened, and a chubby morgue attendant ambled out just as I hid around the corner. The white-coated attendant had a magazine in his hand, which he rolled up before sighing and walking off in the direction of the nearest exit. As soon as he did, I moved quickly down the corridor to the morgue entrance, stopping when Toast came running up to me. "All done, boss," he said. "I do good?"

"You did good," I said. "You kept it small, right?"

"Small, boss, yeah," he said, holding out his thumb and forefinger an inch apart.

Summoning Cracka next, I sent his excitable self inside the morgue to knock out the one camera in there as I waited just in the doorway until he was done. When Cracka had ripped the camera off the wall, I hurried inside, taking Toast in with me, who fell in beside Cracka as the two of them followed behind me to the refrigerated drawers. As I opened the drawers in search of Jarvis' body, I heard childish laughter and turned around to see Cracka standing on top of a man's body that lay on a steel gurney. Cracka had his oversized penis in his hand as he used it to slap the dead man around the face, much to Toast's amusement, who was spitting fire he was laughing so hard. "Cut it out!" I hissed. "Cracka, get the fuck off that dead man."

Cracka made a groaning sound and shook his small head before jumping down off the gurney to stand by Toast. "I can't take you anywhere," I said, giving them both a look before opening the next drawer, which as luck would have it, happened to contain the battered body of Jarvis Heath. *Jesus*, I thought as I pulled the drawer all the way out. *I really did a number on him.* His body had ugly black bruises all over it, and his face…I won't even go there. It looked worse now than it did in the photo Striker had shown me.

Once I summoned Snot Skull, he jumped up onto Jarvis' chest to await my instructions. "What you need, boss?"

"Do your thing," I told him. "Vomit over this face."

Sounding like he was trying to regurgitate something more substantial than himself, Snot Skull soon released a stream of stinking vomit all over Jarvis' face, covering it in a dark green viscous liquid that immediately began to melt the flesh from Jarvis' skull. The fumes rising from the corrosive mess made my eyes water as I stood back away from it. "Toast," I said. "Finish it off. Burn the body."

As Snot Skull jumped down to the ground, Toast jumped up onto the steel drawer and unleashed a breath of fire that he directed right down the length of Jarvis's body, searing the dead flesh as the fat beneath caught fire. Standing in the flames, the demon looked proud of a job well done.

"Down you get." I stood back from the flames, covering my mouth and nose against the stench of burning flesh.

Let's see them get any evidence from that fucking charred mess.

I was just about to banish the three Hellbastards back to the apartment when through the gathering smoke, I spotted something sitting on the gurney a few feet away. It was a cell phone, belonging to the morgue attendant. As I stared at the phone, the fire alarm stopped sounding out, and then two seconds later, the door to the morgue opened and in walked the attendant. The fire Toast had started had been brought under control, and now the attendant was back. He stopped dead to stare first at the burning body on the open drawer, then at me, and then finally at the three Hellbastards, who started snarling at the shocked attendant as they advanced toward him. "What the fuck?" he said, his voice shaky with fear.

The three Hellbastards went for him before I could call them back, slamming against the door as the attendant made it out just in time.

"Shit," I said and ran for the door, telling the Hellbastards to stay in the morgue as I went outside to see the attendant running down the corridor, though as he was so overweight, his speed was abysmal, fear or not, and I was soon able to catch up with him before he made it up to the first floor to call for help.

"Please," he exclaimed as I grabbed him from behind and pushed him face-first into the wall. "Don't hurt me."

Gripping him by the shoulders, I turned him around and pinned him against the wall. "You couldn't have waited a few more minutes?" I said. "You couldn't have gone for a fucking coffee or something before coming back?"

"I—I—"

"Never mind. Look at my hand." Holding him with my left hand, I held my right hand up in front of his face. The tattoo ink had already moved down my forearm and was now swirling in the palm of my hand. As soon as the attendant glanced at the swirling ink, he couldn't take his eyes off it. "You don't know what you saw inside that morgue. It's all just a blur, isn't it?"

"Yes." He nodded slowly. "Just a blur."

"You can't remember any faces. You have no idea what I look like, do you?"

"No," he said, shaking his head.

"Alright," I said, letting him go. "Now fuck off upstairs and get yourself a coffee or something while you forget all about this."

"A coffee. Yeah. Good idea." Still in a daze, the attendant ambled off down the corridor toward the stairs, and I watched him go until he disappeared around the corner. The brain-jarring trick seemed to have worked on him, though its effects varied from person to person. Depending on how weak-willed the victim was, they could either completely forget the events they witnessed, or everything would be so fuzzy and indistinct in their head their credibility as a witness would be rendered worthless. Either way, the attendant should be of no use to Striker when he was later questioned. And without witnesses or forensic evidence, IAB no longer had anything on me, and Striker could go fuck himself.

Once I sent the three Hellbastards back home, I took the back way out of the hospital to avoid any cameras, then walked across the parking lot in the rain and climbed into the Dodge, lighting a cigarette before taking my phone out and calling Lewellyn. He picked up after three rings. "Ethan," he said. "I assume you're calling about this IAB thing?"

"Damn right." I flicked ash out the window. "What the fuck is going on? Why are IAB investigating the unit?"

"Come on, we always knew this would happen. We were taking a chance starting the unit up in the first place, and we always knew there'd be pressure from outside forces."

"Outside forces is right. Did you know this Striker guy is a hellot?"

"No, I didn't."

"Well, he is, and the bastard took my badge and gun."

"I'm sorry. I didn't think things had gone that far. I thought this was just some informal investigation."

"He's also trying to pin a murder on me."

"A murder? Whose?"

"It doesn't matter. I didn't do it anyway."

Lewellyn went quiet for a moment. "Are you sure?"

"What? Course I'm fucking sure. Sir."

"Okay, if you say you didn't do it."

"It's a witch-hunt, sir. You need to get it quashed."

"I'll do my best."

It wasn't what I wanted to hear, but it would have to do. "And while IAB is trying to cut my balls off, Troy Turner is running around with an otherworldly power inside him. More bodies are going to drop if he isn't stopped, and I don't think Routman and Stokes are the men for the job."

"Routman and Stokes?"

"Captain Edwards put them on the case."

"I see. Look, I'm heading to the precinct now. Leave this with me. I'll have you back on the case soon."

"I hope so, sir." I tossed my cigarette butt out the window. "For everyone's sake."

15

As soon as I left Wilshire General, I intended to drive to the bank to get Daisy's mother her blackmail money. I hated having to give her anything. She was nothing but a fucking waste of space, not to mention a terrible mother to Daisy, who deserved better than a junkie, alcoholic mouth-breather for a parent. Daisy would end up getting seriously hurt, or worse, fucking raped by one of the animals her mother liked to party with. If that ever happened, nothing would save her from my wrath. The bitch had me over a barrel though. If she spilled her guts to IAB about what happened to Jarvis, things would get even more difficult for me. As much as I didn't appreciate being blackmailed by anyone, this time I would pay. *This time.* If she demanded more after that, I'd have to put my foot down, preferably on her fucking neck.

For whatever reason, though, I didn't make it to the bank. Instead, I headed to Cave Hill Cemetery, not to see Barbara Keane's grave this time, but Angela and Callie's graves. The rain still hammered down hard as I got out of the Dodge with a lit cigarette in my mouth. I pulled the collar of my trench around my neck and shoved my hands into my pockets before trekking across the cemetery to where the graves were.

Both gravestones were identical—arched marble structures—differing only in the names etched into them. I hated even coming here. Every time I did, it reminded me I caused their deaths, and I was still no closer to finding who killed them.

Wherever their souls now were, Angela was probably raging, hating me as the cause of having her life—and the life of our daughter—cut short. Callie, as forgiving as she was, probably didn't hold it against me. Even if she did, she had every right to. It was a grim feeling—the grimmest actually—standing there in the pouring rain as you looked upon what remained of the only two people you'd ever loved in your life. I thought about saying sorry, as I always did when I came here, but the word was meaningless, so I ended up saying nothing as I walked away from the two graves with a feeling of emptiness that I knew would never leave me. And nor should it.

Almost without thinking, I found myself heading toward Barbara Keane's grave as I crossed the cemetery again, my boots sinking into the sodden grass as I weaved my way through the maze of tombs and gravestones. The tent that had covered the grave had been taken down, leaving the open gravesite exposed to the elements once more.

As I peered down into the rectangular hole, I noticed the broken coffin had been removed. Father Brown would no doubt arrange a fresh coffin, ready for when Barbara Keane's desecrated corpse was returned to the ground. I wanted a little time with Barbara Keane before she was covered in dirt again. She clearly had something to say when her ghost had appeared to me in Troy's basement. If I could get Solomon to work his necromancy on her, I might be able to glean some information from her that would help catch Troy or at least give me some clue as to what the power inside of him wanted.

But to access Keane's body, I needed to get my suspension lifted first. Hopefully, Lewellyn would see to that. If he didn't, I would go to fucking war with Striker myself. No one takes my fucking badge, least of all a hellot scumbag like Striker.

Walking away from the grave, I soon stopped when I felt my Infernal Itch flare up. Even before I turned around, I knew what I was going to see. The ghost of Barbara Keane hovered like a specter over her own grave, a look of anguish on her twisted features. Just like before, her mouth opened slowly to speak. "Don't let him…use the key," she said, her voice clearer than it was when she spoke to me before, as though she was getting a better handle on her new ghost form.

"What key?" I asked, but she didn't answer, instead floating back down into her own grave before disappearing. With the rain beating down on me, I stared at the grave for another moment in case she decided to make another appearance, but she never did. "As informative as ever, Barbara. Thanks."

After the cemetery, I made the trip to the bank and withdrew five thousand dollars in cash. I didn't care about the money, I never have, but I cared about giving it to a cunt like Daisy's mother, Ashlene.

After this, she better stay well fucking clear of me.

Back in the car, I noticed I had two missed calls from Walker, so I phoned her back straight away. "What's up?" I asked her.

"There's been a development in the Troy Turner case," she said.

"Oh?"

"The search team caught up with him about twenty minutes ago, at the home of a man who is like me."

"A demon?"

"I don't like to use that word, but yes, he was one of the Fallen."

"Was?"

"Troy killed him before we caught up with him."

"What happened? Is Troy in custody?"

She paused before answering. "No."

"Fuck's sake, Walker. Out with it. What the fuck happened?"

"Troy killed Stokes and two other cops."

I puffed my cheeks out as I processed what she just said. "How did it happen?"

"Stokes and the two uniforms went into the apartment first, after a witness had reported seeing a kid covered in blood walking into the building. They did a search and finally found a door that had been kicked open. They went in and—"

"Got themselves killed."

"Yes."

"Where were you at this point?"

"Checking the bottom floor of the building. Me and another uniform got to the apartment just in time to see Troy throw the vic to the floor, having beaten him to death first, and after he had broken Stokes' neck and killed the other two with a kitchen knife."

"Jesus fuck."

"There's something else," she said. "As I breached the apartment, I saw energy pass out of the vic and into Troy. It was like he had sucked it out somehow."

"You think he's targeting demons for their power?

"I don't know. That's just what I saw."

"How'd he get away?"

"He jumped out the window, three floors up."

"And survived?"

"I saw him land on his feet before running off."

"Christ, he's more powerful than I thought."

"Routman has every cop in the city out looking for Troy

now."

"Fuck, I'm not sure that's a good idea," I said. "Fucking Routman has no clue what he's dealing with. He's gonna get more cops killed with his ignorance."

"Maybe I should tell him."

"Tell him what? That Troy's possessed by a supernatural power? He'd never swallow that. I know for a fact he's seen stuff, but he's like all the rest, he just denies it ever happened."

"He's telling everyone Troy is drugged up, that's why he's so strong and could survive the jump from the window."

"My point exactly. I need to get back on this case."

"Any idea on how to stop Troy, or whatever's inside him?"

"Not yet, but I will."

"Routman said you got suspended. Is that true?"

"It's a temporary thing, believe me. I hope to be back running the case by this afternoon."

"I hope so," she said. "Routman treats me like a leper."

"Ignore him. Just do your best to prevent any more deaths until I'm back running things again."

After hanging up the phone, I lit a cigarette and stared out the window for a moment at the passing traffic as I thought about these latest developments. One thing was clear to me. Even if I didn't get my badge back, I was still going to go after Troy, but first I had to find out what I was dealing with. That meant getting the page from *The Hattusa Codex* translated first, and the only person I knew who could likely do that was Cal. Once I was done paying off Ashlene Donovan, I'd head over and see the cantankerous old bastard.

No sooner had I pulled out into traffic, however, when my phone rang. Thinking it was probably Walker again, I picked it up off the passenger seat and answered it without looking at the caller ID. "Yeah?"

"You think you can fuck with me, Detective?"

"Striker." I pulled up at a light, unsurprised to hear from him. "Whatever do you mean?"

"I know it was you who destroyed Jarvis Heath's body," he said, a level of spite in his voice that wasn't there last time I spoke to him.

"I've no idea what you're talking about," I said.

"You think you're smart, but you aren't as smart as you think you are. I figured you'd try something like this, so I had samples lifted from that body before it was ever sent to the morgue. I've even had them tested. And guess what?" He paused, probably loving this. "We found the DNA of a serving police officer all over Mr. Heath's body. Care to guess who that officer is?"

My left hand gripped the steering wheel hard as I held the phone to my ear with the other. "Fuck you, Striker."

"Yes, that's right. The DNA belongs to you."

"Whatever evidence you think you have, it's not enough. I'm still getting my badge back."

"I wouldn't be so sure," he said as if he was about to deliver the coup de grâce. "I paid Ashlene Donovan another visit earlier. I told her what would happen if she withheld vital information from the police and obstructed justice. Once she realized I could take her daughter and have her put into the system, she soon changed her tune. She gave us a full statement, naming you as Jarvis Heath's attacker. She told us everything, Detective. So—" He paused again. "Now we have DNA evidence and a witness statement. I'd say that's enough to get a conviction, wouldn't you?"

"Your witness isn't credible," I said, just as the car behind sounded its horn for me to move. "She's a fucking junkie."

"She seems credible enough to me. In any case, don't expect your badge back anytime soon." He laughed to himself. "Don't expect it back at all."

When he hung up, I roared, "Fuck" and threw the phone to the floor, just as the car behind blared its horn again. In a fit of rage, I got out and stomped around to the car behind, drawing my gun on the driver before I realized it was a woman with her kids in the back seat. The mother looked terrified, thinking I was going to shoot her. The kids in the back, two boys and a girl, just stared at me in horror, as did the people on the sidewalk.

What the fuck am I doing? Get back in the car, get back in the fucking car…

Lowering my gun, I rushed back to the car. Tossing the weapon on the front seat, I quickly put the car into gear and drove off, the tires screeching in my wake. Holding the wheel with one hand, I fished out the Mud dropper from my pocket and stuck a dose into my mouth, feeling its effects immediately as I pulled off the main street and parked up in a side street where there was less traffic and people. I left the engine running as I sat staring at the waves of rainwater running down the windshield, my hands gripping the steering wheel so tight it felt like my knuckles would burst through the skin.

Motherfucker, I kept thinking. *Motherfucker.*

"He's not going to get away this. I'll fucking kill the cunt if he thinks he can take my fucking badge."

I took a deep breath as the Mud made everything go fuzzy for a minute and a loud buzzing sounded in my ears that I tried to block out by turning the radio on, just in time to hear a newscaster say, "…*that news again. An unidentified male and three police officers—one a senior detective—have been killed in an altercation with a suspect in the Livingstone Heights area. We're still waiting on an official statement, but it is believed the three police officers and the man were beaten to death by a suspect who is said to be a sixteen-year-old boy. Quite how a sixteen-year-old boy was able to kill three police officers and another man with his bare hands, we still don't know, nor do we know why he did it. No official statement has been—*"

I switched the radio off before the newscaster could say any more. Stokes and the other two cops would still be alive if I was left to handle things, of that I was certain. There was no way I would've sent anyone after Troy, knowing what he is. *This is all Striker's fault.* In coming after me, he had gotten three cops killed, and all over the head of some child-abusing fuck who deserved to die anyway. If Striker thought taking my badge was going to stop me from going after Troy, he had another thing coming. The kid—and whatever power was inside him—had to be stopped before anyone else died.

I went to pull off again, but as soon as I did, the engine died for no reason. "What the fuck?" I tried the ignition a few times but to no avail. I was about to try again when the passenger door opened. Grabbing my gun from the front seat, I pointed it at whoever had opened the door, which happened to be a young girl of all people, maybe ten years old, soaked to the skin in ratty clothes. The girl stared at me a second before getting into the car and closing the door after her.

"What…do I know you?" I asked her, slightly stunned that this little street urchin would just hop into my car.

The girl smiled, tangled, dark brown hair stuck to her face as water ran off her in rivulets. "Know me?" she said. "I suppose you could say that."

I didn't need my Infernal Itch to tell me that there was something off about the girl. The way she talked, the way she held herself, even the look on her grubby face seemed incongruous, as though—

Someone else was wearing her body.

"It's you." I pointed my gun at her.

The girl smiled like she was happy I finally recognized her; or rather recognized the being who had possessed her body. "How's your little girl?" she asked. "Did you enjoy your reunion with her back at the house?"

"Fuck you." I put the gun to her head, pressing it into her temple.

"You wouldn't kill an innocent little girl, now would you?" she said, still smiling.

"You're no girl. You're…"

"Say my name, Ethan."

"Astaroth," I said.

"The one and only," he said. The girl's eyes turned pitch black. "Now lower that gun. I don't have much time before this puny meat sack disintegrates."

"And if I don't?"

"Feel free to shoot this child through the head. She was dying of malnourishment anyway. We both know you've done it before. But then, you won't hear my proposition."

"I'm not interested in any proposition."

"Even if it means seeing your daughter again?"

"My daughter's dead, as you well know, asshole."

"But you can still be with her, Ethan, if you want to, that is. Now—" Astaroth gave a small wave of the girl's hand and the gun I was holding to her head went flying into the back seat as though someone had slapped it out of my grip. "I already told you once to lose the gun. Maybe now you'll listen, or do I need to start breaking bones?"

Resigned to the fact that I wasn't going to get rid of him, I sat back in my seat and lit up a cigarette, purposely blowing smoke in the demon's face. "Say what you gotta say and then get the fuck out."

"Have you always held this level of animosity toward others?" he asked, his demon Visage hovering behind in the backseat like a dark specter.

"Just with assholes like you," I said, exhaling more smoke into the car.

"You're in pain. I can see that. That's why I want to take your pain away."

"By killing me?"

"By freeing you. Look me in these baby blue eyes and tell me you don't want to be free of all that pain."

I looked into the girl's eyes, eyes that were no longer innocent, but full of calculating evil. "The only pain I want be free of is you, asshole."

Astaroth sighed as he reached out and took the cigarette from between my fingers, bringing it to the little girl's lips so he could take a drag. "You could be with your family again, Ethan, with your beloved wife and daughter. I know where they are. Their souls are in Heaven. I've seen them."

As much as I wanted to believe him, I wasn't sure I could. "You're lying."

"They're waiting for you there, Ethan, waiting for you to come to them so you can all be together again."

Somehow, I couldn't see Angela yearning to be with me again, even in Heaven, if that's where they even were. The truth is, no one knew if Heaven existed anymore. The last reported sighting of an angel—one who wasn't Fallen anyway—was decades ago. There were also rumors going around Blackstar at the time that Heaven had been destroyed by the Creator a long time ago in a fit of rage. Blackstar had even done some experiments to try to find out exactly where a soul goes when a person dies. Some walk the earth as ghosts, but beyond that, no one knew, and the experiments were inconclusive at best. Some speculated that most souls ended up in the void left in Heaven's wake, which was nothing but deep, dark emptiness. Even Hell's gates were apparently closed these days. The Creator had abandoned His own creation and had left nothing but chaos in His wake.

"Fuck you, Astaroth. I don't care what you do or say, you will never occupy this body. I'll fucking burn myself to a crisp before I let that happen. Find some other mug to prey on."

Astaroth took the cigarette he was holding and stabbed it out in the palm of his hand, the ten-year-old flesh searing from the embers, filling the car with the smell of burned skin. "You are the one I've chosen to house my spirit, Ethan, and nothing will deter me from that. Once you realize that, you will give in to me, of that I am certain."

He didn't know me very well if he thought that. Speaking of which… "How did I become your target?" I asked him. "You didn't just randomly choose me. Did someone point you in my direction?"

Astaroth smiled. "That would be telling."

"Who else are you in league with? Do you know who killed my wife and daughter?"

"What if I did? Would you give up your body for that information?"

Staring at him for a long moment, I wondered if he really did know the identity of the killer, or was he just playing me again? And if he knew, would I really kill myself just to find out? No, I wouldn't, because then I wouldn't get vengeance for Angela and Callie. What good is knowing if I can't do anything about it, can't punish those responsible? I was about to say as much when Astaroth stiffened and arched his back like he was in severe pain. At the same time, the skin on his face started to bubble like it was being seared by an invisible blowtorch. "What the fuck is wrong with you?"

"It's time for me to go," he said, the little girl's voice strained. "This body is breaking down. Why don't you shoot me in the head?"

"What?"

"I said shoot this child in the head, or I'm going to step outside and start killing people." Using telekinesis, he moved my gun from the back seat into my lap. "Do it."

I picked the gun up but held it in my lap. "No."

With the skin still bubbling on the little girl's face, Astaroth said, "Fine, have it your way." Then he got out of the car, stepping out into the rain. Just down the street a bit, three guys were loading boxes from a van into a clothing store. Astaroth stared at me through the open passenger door as though he wanted me to know whatever happened next was my fault, and he made a big show of clicking his fingers and then smiling. Down the street, one of the workmen dropped to the ground, the box he was carrying falling along with him as the other two men rushed to his aid, but I knew there'd be no reviving him. He was dead. "There's one," Astaroth said.

"Stop!" I shouted.

Astaroth lifted his hand again, holding his thumb and middle finger together. "Shall we make it two?"

Before he could click his fingers again, I got out of the car and pointed my gun at him. "I said stop."

"Stop me then. Shoot me. Do it!"

"Oh my god," someone nearby screamed, and I turned to see two women backing away up the street, a look of horror on their faces as they realized I was pointing a gun at a little girl. One of them already had their phone out, probably about to call the cops. Until that is, Astaroth clicked his fingers again, and the woman holding the phone fell dead, causing the other woman to scream in panic. Others were coming out of the stores to see what was happening. Within seconds, at least a dozen people were lining the street, most of them staring at me in disbelief as I kept my gun trained on Astaroth and the girl's body he had stolen.

"Shall we make it three?" he said, his face looking like it was melting now, bits of flesh falling off the bone and slapping onto the wet sidewalk. The girl's body would fall apart soon enough, but Astaroth could kill everyone in the street by then, and I couldn't let him take any more innocent lives.

I pulled the trigger and shot him in the head, the crack of the shot followed up by the screams of the onlookers. "He just shot that little girl," someone shouted in horror.

The girl's body lay in a heap on the ground as the spirit of Astaroth rose out of it, a dark shadow with massive wings at its back. It hovered for a second while it stared at me with burning yellow eyes. Then it shot off into the air, disappearing into the dark gray sky, leaving me to stand there with a smoking gun in my hand and the body of a dead child lying on the wet sidewalk in front of me. And as I stared at the girl, all I could see was Callie's face, her eyes open as they gazed lifelessly back at me.

16

I didn't have much choice but to flee the scene after shooting Astaroth's stolen vessel, leaving the body of the little girl to lie there with her brains spilled out onto the sidewalk. Even if I had my badge on me, how was I going to justify shooting a little girl in the head?

I got in my car and sped off, going to the only place where I knew I could hide for a while. Cal's scrapyard.

I found him inside one of the big tin sheds near his trailer, which he had converted into a workshop to house every blacksmith tool you could think of: hand hammers, sledgehammers, a great number and variety of chisels, punches and drifts, and a selection of tongs with bits or jaws of various shapes and sizes.

The smithy also contained a large forge which over the years, had been used for more than just heating metal. Several bodies had been fed into it to be disposed of, and in more than one interrogation session, the forge had been used as a threat against the suspect, with more than one head or hand being placed dangerously close to the forge's intense heat. You'd be surprised what people tell you once they realize they might get their hand charred to a crisp.

Cal was in the middle of hammering out a length of metal with a large hammer when I walked in, sparks flying up with every swing as the hammer connected with the glowing hot steel laid across a huge anvil.

When he saw me standing there, he must've sensed I wanted to talk, for he downed tools and announced it was time for a beer break. As he took his heavy gloves off and wiped sweat from his brow, I walked outside with him.

The rain had stopped, but the chairs were still wet. Not that Cal seemed to mind as he sat down and grabbed a beer from the cooler, handing me one as I continued to stand.

"What's going on?" he asked. "You look haunted. More than usual anyway." Beer dribbled down his beard, which he wiped off.

"I'm fucked," I told him. "A crowd of witnesses just saw me shoot a ten-year-old girl in the head. That bastard Striker's gonna have a fucking field day when he finds out."

"Why the fuck would you shoot a kid in the head?"

"Gimme some credit, will ya?" I snapped. "It was a fucking demon. The kid's soul had long gone."

Cal looked around for a moment as he seemed to think. "It's as I said to you before," he said, bringing his gray eyes to rest on me again. "You can't do what you do and be a cop at the same time. The two jobs are incompatible."

He had a point, but it was one I wasn't ready to concede. "So, I just go back to being a straight-up killer again, is that what you're saying? I like being a cop. It gives me structure."

"You just like carrying that fucking badge around."

"Yeah, well, without it, I'm just a—" I stopped and shook my head. "I don't have a fucking badge to carry around anymore anyway."

Cal gestured to the chair next to him. "Sit down, will ya? You're making me nervous."

Sighing, I wiped off the rainwater from the seat next to him before sitting down. "That fucking demon knew what he was doing when he forced me to shoot him," I said. "It was probably Striker's idea, to put another nail in my coffin. He's enthralled to Astaroth."

"Can't you just kill the son of a bitch?"

"Striker? He's a cop, an IAB cop."

"He's also a cocksucking hellot. Seems like he deserves it to me."

"I'm not disputing that. I can't just kill a fucking cop, though."

"Why not? As long as you're careful."

I laughed and shook my head. "As always, you're such a positive influence on me."

Cal smiled and stroked his beard, his rough hands blackened from the work he was doing. "You can't be a cop and a savior at the same time. You want to stay a cop, you gotta forget about all this MURK business, which I know you could never do. You tried it already, and yet here you are, drawn back into the thick of it."

"I didn't forget about it," I said. "I turned a blind eye for a while, for my family's sake more than anything."

Cal focused his steely gray eyes on me. "And where did that get you?"

"Fuck you."

"I'm just sayin'. You were never meant to be a cop, Ethan."

"So you think I should just be a killer instead, like those crazy hunters that run around shooting and hacking anything with teeth and claws? Or like I was at Blackstar, nothing but a fucking walking killing machine? You know what that did to me, Cal? You know what that did to my mind? To my soul?"

He snorted slightly. "What fucking soul?"

I stared at him until he chuckled to himself. "Fuck you, Cal. You're one to talk anyway, the shit you've done."

"You need to lighten up."

"You need to stop being a fucking asshole."

"You wouldn't be here if it wasn't for this fucking asshole."

"Yeah, don't I know it. You never let me forget it."

It was his turn to stare at me now. "You kill a kid, so you come here to give me shit, is that it?"

"Give you shit? You're giving *me* shit."

He stared ahead of him at the machinery sorting out the piles of scrap in the center of the yard, the jaws of the machine crushing the metal as it picked it up. "All I'm saying is, justice in our world means killing most of the time, not apprehending."

He had a point. I'd lost count of how many MURKs I'd arrested, only to have them get off on some unforeseen technicality, or for the evidence against them to go missing, or for some judge to throw the case out of court. The vampires, the werewolves, the Fallen and all the other MURKs had been at this game for a long time now. Long enough for each group to have gained significant influence in every part of society, including the justice system. That's how they stayed out of the system and out of the public eye in general.

If you wanted real justice for some vampire that had killed an innocent victim after draining them dry, the only way to get that justice was to kill the vampire. End of story. And to those like myself who tried to go after MURKs within the system, well, we just got fucked eventually. Rather like I'm being fucked now. Why Lewellyn and I thought Unit X would ever work in the first place, I'll never know.

As I lit a cigarette, my phone rang in my pocket, and I took it out to see that it was Walker ringing. "Walker," I said. "What's up?"

"Just thought I'd let you know," she said. "Captain Edwards issued a warrant for your arrest. Did you shoot a little girl dead in the street?"

"It wasn't a little girl, it was fucking Astaroth."

"A bystander recorded the whole thing on their phone and posted it online."

"Jesus, already?"

"You're an internet sensation. Striker is gunning for you. So is Captain Edwards." She paused. "What are you going to do?"

Standing up, I pulled on my cigarette as I walked toward a huge mound of scrap metal, tons of the stuff piled up like discarded carcasses, sad remnants of a society that threw more away than it kept. "I don't know. I need time to sort things out. I'll think of something."

"People are hating you online," she said. "You're the psycho cop who shot an innocent kid in cold blood."

"And what about her face?"

"Her face?"

"Half her fucking face was melting at the time. Didn't anyone notice that on the video? Or the demon spirit that flew out of the body?"

"It was taken from a distance, in the heavy rain."

"Course it was."

"People see what they want to see anyway," she said. "That much I've noticed since arriving here in this world."

"What about Troy Turner? Any new developments there?" I asked, as much to get off the subject of my impending doom as anything else.

"Nothing yet, I'm afraid. The search is still on, but Troy has either gone underground, or he's very good at hiding in plain sight, because every cop in the city is looking for him at this point, at least the ones who aren't looking for you, which is most of them."

"So apprehending me is more important than apprehending a fucking multiple murderer? They must really fucking hate me."

"Technically, you're also a multiple murderer."

"Yeah, thanks for pointing that out, Walker. Let's see how long it takes *you* to start racking up bodies in this world."

"Not long, I imagine."

"What? What's that mean?"

She went silent for a long second. "Nothing."

"Who are you planning on taking out?"

"No one. Forget I said anything."

"Not likely. We'll discuss it later. In the meantime, what are you doing now?"

"Filing reports."

"No, you're not," I said as I began to walk back toward Cal again. "You're meeting me at Grimes Scrap Yard on Mulberry Street. Do you know where that is?"

"Yeah."

"Make sure you aren't followed. I'd be surprised if Striker doesn't have a tail on you."

"What are we going to do?"

"Find Troy, of course, before he kills anyone else."

Having finished talking to Walker, I went and sat back down next to Cal. "That your partner?" he asked.

"Yeah. Why?"

He shook his head slightly. "I just can't believe you're working with a demon."

"It just happened. Whatta ya want me to say? Who else was I gonna get?"

"Just sayin'. Watch your back."

"I always do." Placing my beer on the stony ground, I took my phone out again and brought up the picture I'd taken of the page in *The Hattusa Codex,* then I handed the phone to Cal. "Can you translate that?" Cal squinted at the phone for a second before taking a pair of spectacles from his shirt pocket and putting them on. "It's in Hittite, describing a summoning ritual. I need to know what it summons exactly."

Cal threw me a look before going back to peering at the phone. "Bet you wish you'd listened when I tried to teach this language years ago."

"Languages weren't really my thing back then," I said. "They still aren't."

"More like you were too busy killing and fucking back then to think of much else."

"That too. Can you read it, or do you need thicker glasses?"

He threw me a more disparaging look this time. "We can't all be like the fucking Bionic Man. Bodies do break down, you know, along with eyesight."

"Mine breaks down too, just not as quick…or as much. And I have a few modifications, which is hardly enough to constitute the Bionic Man reference. Steve Austin had bionic implants."

"And what do *you* have?"

"Implants, but more organic, apart from the Combat Offense Booster chip and the Infrared Vision Implant in my cornea."

"A regular fucking Terminator," he said, going back to staring at the phone. "This is a summoning ritual, by the way."

"I think I said that already. Your memory going now as well, old man?"

"I know you did, asshole. You didn't let me finish. It's a ritual to summon something called a Litchghin. You ever hear of one?"

"No, but I'm guessing it's not good, whatever it is."

"It's not. Litchghins were human once, but they were like super-humans. The story goes," he said as he fished another beer from the cooler, "that the Litchghins were direct descendants of the Adam and Eve race, and that they were nurtured by Lucifer before he was cast out of Heaven. Lucifer took the humans created by God and made them smarter, stronger, better in every way. The Litchghins built a great civilization before God turned around one day and destroyed them all, or most of them anyway. The ones who survived, thanks to Lucifer helping them, were sent to an outer dimension in the universe. Lucifer told them to wait until he could permanently relocate them somewhere better, but he never got the chance before he was cast down to Hell—"

"Leaving the Litchghins stuck in some awful dimension," I finished.

"That's right. They've been floating around in cold, empty space since, well, the beginning of time." Cal took a swallow from his beer before belching loudly. "Obviously the Litchghins weren't completely forgotten, though, since people designed rituals like this one to contact them. Your boy must've thought he was going to get something in return for bringing the Litchghin here."

"Don't they all?"

"Damn straight. Idiots."

"So this kid, Troy, he's been possessed by one these Litchghins?"

"Either that or he has a bad case of hormones."

"How do I stop this thing?" I asked, shaking my head at him.

"By stop, you mean kill."

"I'm also happy to send it back to where it came from. Whichever works."

"I take it you want to at least *try to* save this kid? Or do you plan on killing him as well?"

"Not if I can help it, obviously. *Can* he be saved?"

Cal shrugged. "I'm not sure. I'd have to do some checking. I think there might be a way of pulling the Litchghin out of him."

"How would that work?"

"If memory serves, you would need a spirit bottle. I'm sure you have one somewhere."

"I do. Been a while since I used one. Last time I did, it was on the spirit of that witch who possessed the fashion model. You remember that?"

"Yeah, I remember," he said. "I remember her going crazy

on the catwalk and everybody thinking it was part of the show."

"They didn't clap when the girl collapsed after I used the spirit bottle. She'd fucking aged by fifty years. You think the same'll happen to the kid?"

Cal shrugged. "What if it does? Serves him right for summoning a fucking Litchghin in the first place."

"Yeah," I said. "And even if he does age, he'll still have a few years left to contemplate his mistake, right?"

Cal looked at me, and we both laughed. "We're going to Hell, you and I," he said.

"Heaven, Hell…I think it's all the same now. We'll just be floating in the deep dark like everyone else."

"Like Angela and Callie?"

"I don't like to think about it." I leaned down to pick up my beer.

"I don't blame you."

Draining what was left of my beer, I put the empty bottle on the ground again. "Before I go, does it say anything on that page about a key?"

"A key?" Cal shook his head. "Not that I can see. Why?"

"Barbara Keane's ghost, in the two times she's appeared to me, mentioned something about a key. *Don't let him use the key*, she said."

Cal thought for a moment. "Maybe the Litchghin wants to open something, a doorway maybe."

"Like a portal?"

"Who knows? You'd have to ask your ghost more about it."

"Don't worry," I said standing up. "I intend to."

"Good luck." Cal got up himself, but before he could walk back into the smithy, I stopped him.

"You know where I can find Scarlet Hood, by any chance?"

Cal turned around to stare at me. "Why in the hell would you want to find a stone-cold bitch like that?"

"I just need to find her."

"More fool you if you do. She'll fucking kill you."

"She can't be that good, surely."

"Let me tell you about Scarlet Hood," he said, coming to stand closer. "One time she did a hit on a Mafia Don, Rudy 'Fingers' Agnello."

I nodded. "I remember, about five years ago, right? She garroted Fingers in his own home, in front of his two kids."

"That's right, and afterward, Fingers' brother Joey got a dozen guys and tracked Scarlet down to where she was living at the time, in the forest outside Charlesburg. She killed every last one of them and strung their bodies up in the trees. Left them there for the crows to peck at. Ever since then, no one goes after Scarlet Hood. If she hits one of yours, you take it and move on. If you don't…"

"She'll move you on anyway."

"Yeah. So *why* do you want to find her again?"

"I just need to find her, that's all. You know where she's at these days?"

"Maybe. By telling you, will I be sending you to your death?"

"I hope not."

"That's what I thought. Leave it with me. I'll find out for you."

"Thanks, Cal."

"Don't thank me. It'll be your funeral I'll be arranging."

~

I LEFT THE DODGE INSIDE THE SCRAP YARD AND WAITED BY THE front gates for Walker to arrive. As I stood smoking a cigarette, staying just out of sight behind a rusted fridge-freezer, I took out my phone and called Lewellyn, who answered straight away. "Sir," I said, hardly knowing what to say.

"Ethan," Lewellyn said, a noticeable distance to his voice. "I'm surprised to hear from you."

"Why? You think I'd be on the run by now?"

"Your situation is not looking good. You shot a child."

"Not a child, a demon, and if I didn't do it, people were going to die. People had already died."

"Yes, I know."

"Who's investigating it?"

"Richmond from Homicide."

"And how are they explaining the deaths of the man and woman who were in the street?"

"Natural causes, I believe. The shock of seeing a man kill a child."

"Jesus Christ," I spat.

"What do you expect?" Lewellyn said. "No one's going to say a demon killed those people."

"Are you going to sort this out, sir?"

"Sort it out? Ethan, you're all over the damn internet. How can I?"

"So that's it?" I said, tossing my cigarette butt away in anger. "You're bailing at the first sign of trouble?"

"I don't know what you want me to do. It's not just the shooting of the child—"

"The demon. The fucking demon, sir."

"It's not just that, it's also this evidence against you in this other man's death, Jarvis Heath. Detective Striker is alleging you destroyed the body. Is that true?"

"Striker is a fucking hellot," I said. "And I'm going to take him down before he takes me down."

Lewellyn went silent for a moment, then said, "I've been thinking. Perhaps this Unit X thing was a bad idea. I think maybe we need to stand down. All this heat, it's not—"

"Good for your fucking career, *sir*?"

"I'm sorry," Lewellyn said. "You're on your own."

When he hung up, I turned and slammed my fist into the fridge-freezer next to me, leaving a massive dent in the metal casing. "Fuck."

A few seconds later, a dark blue sedan driven by Walker pulled up by the gates. I took a deep breath to calm myself before walking to the car and getting inside. "You alright?" she asked.

"Not really," I said, reaching into my pocket and taking out the Mud bottle, dropping a double dose into my mouth. "But I soon will be."

"What's going on?"

"Well," I said, wincing at the taste from the Mud. "It looks like our unit has been disbanded by the man who started it."

"Lewellyn?"

"Asshole can't stand the heat. I'm on my own."

"No, you're not," Walker said, her deep-down eyes refreshingly free from judgment.

I nodded at her. "It won't do your career much good if you stick with me."

"My career?" She started laughing, which was the first time I'd ever heard her do so. It made her seem more human. "You know better than that, Ethan."

"I guess I do," I said, glad she was here. Glad that I wasn't alone for once.

"So, where are we going?" She put her hands back on the steering wheel.

"To talk to Barbara Keane," I said.

Walker frowned. "Okay. How exactly?"

I allowed a smile to begin on my face as the Mud did its work on me. "We're going to snatch her body."

17

The body of Barbara Keane was moved to the undertakers earlier this afternoon thanks to pressure from Father Mike Brown, who wanted the body cleaned up and back in the ground as soon as possible. Getting to the body in the coroner's would've been hard and may have drawn more attention than I'd liked. At least at the undertakers things would be easier.

The undertaker was a man named Patrick Wills. Patrick had no love for me since I arrested his father for murdering a prostitute three years ago. I also arrested Patrick, thinking it was he who had killed the woman.

But as it turned out, Patrick had fallen in love with this prostitute named Mary. Mary herself had once been a nun before she fell into drugs and prostitution. Patrick, being one of these darkly religious types who'd had a strict Catholic upbringing, was apparently trying to rescue Mary from her life on the streets, seeing her as an angel from the Lord put in his path to save his soul. Why his soul needed saving in the first place, I didn't know.

Once Patrick's father, John, found out—himself an ex-

Christian Brother—he took it upon himself to save his son from this harlot named Mary before she corrupted his son's soul for good. John went out one night and strangled Mary to death behind a dumpster.

When he tried to dispose of the body in the cremation oven back at the funeral home, his son caught him. Patrick wasn't happy that his father had killed the love of his life, so he beat the shit out of his father and probably would've killed him had I not burst into the funeral home and caught him in the act.

Unknown to John Wills, his act of murder had been caught on camera and immediately reported, which is when a warrant was issued and I went to the funeral home to arrest him, robbing his son of the chance for revenge.

Ever since, Patrick has hated me, as if I was to blame for everything. Our paths had crossed a few times since, his hate for me never seeming to lessen. So when we turned up at the funeral home, I wasn't expecting a warm reception from Patrick Wills. Not that I particularly cared, for I would strong-arm him into cooperating with us if need be.

The funeral home is on the corner of Malcom Road on the edge of Bricktown. It's a large brownstone building with an awning that stretches from the steps of the building to the edge of the sidewalk. It had just started to get dark as Walker pulled the sedan up outside the funeral home, and up the street I noticed a patrol car heading our way. "Shit," I said as I slid myself down low in my seat, turning my head away as the patrol car cruised by.

"You're clear," Walker said.

Sitting back up, I shook my head. "Fuck this, I hate hiding."

"Hopefully it won't be for long."

"I don't know." I lit a cigarette and stared out the window. "This might be it for me. Maybe I had it coming. All the shit

I've done…" I trailed off as I took a deep drag on my cigarette, cracking the window an inch and exhaling the smoke outside.

"Believe me," Walker said. "You only think you've done bad things. I was a demon in Hell, remember?"

"I thought you couldn't remember your time in Hell?"

"I remember pieces…fragments. It's enough."

"So what's your point?"

"That if I can look for redemption, so can you."

"Is that what you're doing here, looking for redemption?"

"Yes."

I took another drag of my cigarette, blowing the smoke toward the window again. Outside, the streetlights seemed especially bright, even psychedelic at times thanks to the Mud. "I have no interest in redemption. I can't change the things I've done or make up for them." I turned to face her. "How would I make up for getting my wife and daughter killed?"

"By finding who killed them. By getting them justice."

"That won't change anything. Justice won't bring my family back to me." I'd already lost them long before they were killed anyway.

"No, but it might bring you peace."

"Peace?" I couldn't help but laugh. "There's no such thing as peace in this world. To humans, peace is a foreign concept. There's no inner peace, and there's certainly no outer peace. There is only conflict of one kind or another. You'll find that out soon enough if you haven't already. You think you'll be able to redeem yourself somehow? You won't. You'll stay tormented for as long as you live, fallen fucking angel or not."

Walker stared at me before looking away, falling into silence as she gazed out the window. "Why are we still sitting here?" she asked, a note of sadness in her voice now, almost making me feel bad for her. As old as she was, she had a childish naivety to her I couldn't help ridiculing. If she wanted inner peace, she should've possessed the body of a Buddhist monk and not a fucking cop.

"We're waiting on someone."

"Who?"

"A necromancer named Richard Solomon."

"A necromancer?"

"How else did you think we were going to communicate with Barbara Keane? A fucking séance or something?"

Walker stared hard at me, anger flashing across her dark eyes. "Have you always been this much of an asshole?" she asked.

"More or less."

"I'm starting to see why the other cops don't like you very much."

"I just don't suffer fools."

"You ever stop to think that you're the fool, Ethan?"

I stared at her, then smiled. "All the time."

Walker smiled back and shook her head. "I never thought being a human would be so…"

"Torturous?"

"I was going to say interesting. As Elohim residing in the Heavens, I thought I knew what life was about, but I realize the only thing I really knew about was the building blocks of life, the energies that made it all work. It was like looking at a clock and all its intricate moving parts, but knowing nothing about time, or even what any of it really meant. I was nothing more than an observer, and now that I'm actually participating for once, it feels so much different. I feel so much more…*alive* than I ever did as an Elohim."

"You ever wonder what you are now? Do you still think of yourself as an Elohim?"

"Yes, partly, but that's not all I am. I feel like I'm much more than that now, and strangely, that I'm closer to the Maker than I've ever been."

"Are you telling me you still feel the Maker's presence? God's presence?"

"Some days I do, some I don't."

"That's more than I do."

"Do you hate God, Ethan?"

I smoked the last of my cigarette before throwing the butt out the window, just as a tall, dark figure appeared next to the tree a few feet up the street. "Let's just say I've never loved Him and leave it at that." I opened the door. "Let's go talk to Barbara Keane now."

When we got out of the car, the figure that was standing in the shadows around the tree emerged to meet us under the dark green awning. Richard Solomon was dressed as usual in a black suit that was topped by a black fedora hat that cast his gaunt face in shadow. "These favors are mounting up," Solomon said, his voice quiet but clear. "I hope you have something juicy for me, Ethan." When his eyes fell upon Walker, a smile spread across his face. "Or perhaps you have brought me something instead."

"Not her," I said. "Probe the recesses of my mind all you want later once we get this done."

"Don't worry, I intend to," he said, walking toward Walker as he outstretched his hand, his boney fingers seeming impossibly long. "Richard Solomon. Nice to meet you."

"Hannah Walker," Walker said as she took Solomon's hand, whose fingers immediately closed around hers, holding her in his grip.

"Ah, but you aren't, are you?" he said, his near-black eyes taking her in. "What is your real name, Fallen One?"

Walker threw a glance at me before looking back at Solomon. "Adrielis," she said.

"And your demon name?"

Walker pulled out of his grip. "You don't need to know that."

"So you're one of those," Solomon said.

"One of what?" Walker asked.

"One of those who are ashamed of who they were in Hell, of the torment they caused."

"What would you know about it?"

"More than you think."

Walker moved close to Solomon as her Visage hovered behind her, dark wings outstretched as if they were made of smoke. Her face subtly changed as she adopted a dark look, a wicked glint appearing in her eyes. Even her Visage twisted into a more demonic form as it appeared to grow horns. "You think you know torment?" she said, reaching up and grabbing Solomon's head, pulling him down lower.

"Walker," I said, but she either didn't hear me or just didn't listen as she continued to grip Solomon's head. Solomon himself looked halfway between frightened and ecstatic.

"Why don't you teach me?" he said, his tone suggesting he was enjoying this

"With pleasure," Walker said, just as an amber glow started in her dark eyes.

"We're in the middle of the fucking street here," I said to her, noticing some pedestrians had opted to cross the road rather than walk anywhere near us. Which was probably just as well, for Solomon sank to his knees as a wailing sound left his mouth, which soon turned to screams of agony or ecstasy, I couldn't tell which. Across the street, people were staring over with disturbed looks on their faces. The last thing I needed right now was people staring, given my wanted status, so I walked over and pushed Walker away from Solomon, pinning her against the iron railings at the front of the funeral home. "Enough."

Despite my warning, the demonic glow remained in Walker's eyes as her Visage loomed large over her, and in the blink of an eye she turned me and slammed me into the railings.

"Don't tell me enough," she said, a harsh edge to her voice now. "Don't ever fucking tell me enough."

It was tempting to punch her square in the face for talking to me like that, but I knew she was having another demonic episode like she'd had in Riverside Hills, and Solomon was to blame. He had goaded her into it. "Just calm down," I told her. "Remember why you're here."

At that, the fire faded from her eyes and her Visage began to shrink down into a more angelic form. "I'm sorry," she said after a moment, blinking as if awakening from a dream.

"It's okay," I said as I stared over at Solomon, who was still on his knees, his head tilted back, his jaw slack as he took in gulps of air like he'd just emerged from underwater.

"That was…magnificent," he gushed, turning his head to look at Walker. "I want more. I want to feel it again."

"Get up, Solomon, you fucking weirdo," I said. "People are staring. You're going to attract heat."

Solomon picked his hat up from the ground and placed it on his bald head before standing up. When he did, the crowd that had gathered across the street finally began to move on. I kept my back to them, in case someone recognized me from the internet. I hadn't seen the video yet, nor did I plan on watching it, but I was sure I wouldn't be hard to recognize from it.

Walker stared at Solomon. "You push me like that again," she said to him. "I'll leave you in so much pain and torment you'll be begging to die."

Solomon smiled as he straightened his hat. "Don't tease me."

Impressed by Walker's badassery, I told her to come on as I headed up the steps to the front door of the funeral home. Solomon came up behind us just as I banged on the door with my fist. A few moments later, the door opened to reveal Patrick Wills standing there. Wills was a small, uptight man in his late thirties, with dark eyes and jet-black hair that glistened with gel. He was dressed impeccably in a black suit and skinny black tie, looking every inch the undertaker, his creepy demeanor adding to the overall look. I always thought Wills was the type to flagellate himself as he kneeled on the floor with tears streaming from his eyes as he begged God for forgiveness, perhaps because he had just had sex with one of the bodies in his care. He stood staring at me for a moment before taking in Walker, a frown coming over his face when his eyes fell upon Solomon as he no doubt wondered what the hell was going on.

"Whatever this is," he said. "I'm not doing it. Piss off, Detective. I told you before not to come near me ever again."

When he went to slam the door, I jammed my boot against it to stop it from closing. "We can do this the easy way or the hard way, Patrick," I told him. "I'm easy."

Wills' nostrils flared as he glared at me. "Do what, Detective Drake. What is it you want?"

"We need some time with a body you have here," I said. "Barbara Keane."

"Do you have a warrant?" he asked.

"No, but this is important. Lives are at stake."

"I don't care," he said. "I'm not letting you in here. Now please remove your foot from the door before I call your superiors. If I'm not mistaken, Detective, you're a wanted man. That video of you is all over the news. Do you even have a badge anymore?"

"Mr. Wills," Solomon said, coming to stand next to me. "I can tell you're a man of, shall we say, particular tastes."

Wills looked uncomfortable as he shook his head slightly. "I don't know what you're talking about."

"Oh, I'm sure you do," Solomon said. "You and I, we have much in common, being lovers of the dead. I can show you things, things that will make your...relationships with your clients even more...sublime."

Wills couldn't take his eyes off Solomon. It sickened me a

bit to see how much Wills was being drawn in by Solomon. The look of deep desire in his eyes said it all. "I—I—think you've got me all wrong, whoever you are. Now please go—"

He didn't get to finish as I put my weight into the door and sent him flying back into the hallway where he stumbled and landed on his ass. "I gave you the option to do this the easy way," I said as I stepped into the hallway, with Walker and Solomon entering behind me, Solomon closing the door after him. Reaching down, I pulled Wills up onto his feet and held him as I glared at him. "Listen to me you creepy little fuck. Fact is, I saved you from going to prison when I stopped you from killing your father. The way I see it, you owe me. So why don't you put your petty grievances aside and just get out of the way so we can do what we came here to do, otherwise you're going to see a side to me that you haven't seen yet, a side you don't want to fucking see. Do we understand each other?"

Despite the fear in his eyes, Wills gave a tight smile as he said, "Perfectly."

"Good." I let him go. "I assume you have Barbara Keane down in the mortuary?"

He nodded. "I planned to finish working on her later."

"I'm sure you did," Solomon said with a sly smile.

Wills glanced uncomfortably at Solomon before looking back to me. "Exactly what do you want with Mrs. Keane's corpse?"

"She's going to assist us in finding someone."

"And how would she do that exactly, given she's dead?"

"Never mind." I looked at Walker. "Stay here with him, make sure he doesn't call anybody."

Walker's face tightened. "I'd like to be there as well. Can't we just tie him up or something?"

"No need for that," Solomon said, stepping toward Wills. "Mr. Wills, if I may—" He leaned down and started to whisper in Wills' ear, and as he did, Wills' eyes began to widen and that same look of desire from earlier returned in them. When Solomon stopped whispering and straightened up, he said to Wills, "Of course, all of that is contingent on you being a good little boy and doing as you are told."

There was a slight smile on Wills' face now, a smile of anticipation it seemed like. "I'll give you half an hour," he said.

"You'll give us as long as we need," I said.

"Fine," he said. "Just don't violate the body. I haven't finished with her yet."

"I'm sure you haven't."

"That's not what—"

"I don't care. Just stay up here until we're done. You fuck us, it's going to be your corpse on a slab next."

"Just don't touch any of my equipment," Wills said. "And whatever you plan on doing, don't damage the corpse any more than it already is, please. I'm an artist, not a miracle worker."

"Don't worry," Solomon said. "The process inflicts no damage to the corpse."

"What process?" Wills asked.

"Never mind," I said. "Just stay out of our way until we're done."

THE MORTUARY WAS DOWN IN THE BASEMENT, A LARGE ROOM with walls the color of bile, containing two stainless-steel mortuary tables, an embalming station, two sinks and a trolley full of wicked-looking stainless-steel tools. Some mortuaries I've been in, you wouldn't want your cat being embalmed in, never mind your loved one. At least one mortuary I'd been in had doubled as a crack lab. Another was so filthy, the walls moved with living matter.

By comparison, Wills' mortuary room was spotless, every

surface gleaming, not a trace of anything on the floor. Barbara Keane's corpse, covered by a plastic sheet, was laid out on one of the two tables. On a tray next to her was a box containing various makeup products. Wills must've been working on her face when we interrupted him, having already fixed the damage done to her abdomen by Troy Turner. Staring at the box of cosmetics, I got the distinct feeling that the corpses weren't the only ones to benefit from a makeover. Wills seemed the type to use the stuff himself, and then prance around in front of a full-length mirror, maybe wearing one of his dead mother's old dresses. These are the kinds of thoughts that go through my mind, especially when I'm on the Mud.

"Ah, the smell of embalming fluid," Solomon said after breathing deeply and exhaling. "How I love it. It smells like—"

"Death?" Walker said.

"I was going to say possibility," Solomon said, his tall thin frame like a specter as he stalked around the table, having already removed the sheet covering Barbara Keane's corpse. He examined her from every angle with a look of delight on his face, itself corpse-like and deathly pale, with sunken eyes and a faint red gash for a mouth.

"I don't even want to know what that means," Walker said, making a face like she had a bad taste in her mouth.

"Alright, Solomon," I said as I lit a cigarette. "Time to do your thing."

"I'm not sure you can smoke in here."

"So it's okay to perform a necromantic ritual with a corpse, but I can't fucking smoke? Just get on with it."

"Very well," he said. "Once you begin to tell me about your father."

"What? I'm not talking about that."

"Then I don't do as you ask."

I took my cigarette out of my mouth and stared at him. "You're a twisted son of a bitch, Solomon. You always have been, even before all this necromancy shit. That's why they loved you at Blackstar because there's nothing you wouldn't do to complete your mission objective."

"Correction," he said. "That's why they loved both of us there. You were just as ruthless as I was, Ethan, if not more so."

Aware of Walker standing nearby, staring at me, I said, "This isn't Blackstar. We're trying to help here, not create profit for a few select individuals."

"I'm beyond simple morals these days." He ran his long fingers over Barbara Keane's face, caressing the cold, dead skin. "I walk a different path, my own path. I have needs that need satisfying, so please tell me about your father, and then I'll begin the ritual so you can commune with this woman here."

"There's not really much to tell," I said, somewhat uncomfortable talking about this in front of Walker. She'd be staring at me as I spoke, probably fascinated as she tried to work out what it all meant, as if doing so would bring her closer to understanding the human condition. "I never knew my father. He died when I was four."

"Who was he?" Solomon asked, his eyes now closed as he held his hands palm down over Barbara Keane's corpse. He then started to omit a kind of humming sound, as he was speaking so low that's what it sounded like, a constant hum as he uttered the words and syllables to the ritual.

"He was a heavy in the Irish mob," I said. "I've no idea how he got together with my mother, not that it lasted long. He came by on occasion to see me and give my mother money. That's what she told me one time anyway. His name was Jack O'Rourke."

"How did he die?" Solomon asked, his voice breathy, underlined with pleasure, but whether pleasure at hearing me talk or pleasure at doing the ritual and conversing with deathly energies, I wasn't sure. Probably both.

"He died right in front of me."

"How?" Walker asked as she stood to the side of me, her hands in her trouser pockets.

This whole sharing situation ran contrary to my belief that a man should keep his shit to himself. They did this at Blackstar, hitting recruits with a battery of questions that went on for days. No stone was left unturned, no dark recess of the mind left unexplored. They dragged it all out of you, and if you didn't give it up, they beat it out of you instead. Solomon eventually took part in these interviews as one of the questioners, which is probably where he learned to enjoy turning people's psyches inside out like he was doing to me now, with Walker helping from the sidelines. "A hitman for the Italian mob garroted him, nearly took his fucking head off."

"You remember this?" Walker asked.

I threw her a look as I took a drag on my cigarette, just to let her know I didn't appreciate her playing this game with Solomon. "I didn't until I had a mentalist pull it out of me at Blackstar."

"Yes," Solomon said in a hissy voice as wisps of dark energy began to form under his hands. "No stone unturned, isn't that right, Ethan?"

"I hate to fucking think about what they pulled out of you," I said. "It must've been like a fucking nightmare for the interviewers."

Solomon didn't so much laugh as hiss in response as the black energy under his palms swirled over the body of Barbara Keane. "It was…painful, but…enjoyable."

"That's terrible, Ethan," Walker said. "That you witnessed such a thing as a child."

"Terrible, yes," Solomon said, his eyes now open. "In the most delicious of ways."

"Yeah, tasty as fuck," I said, dropping my cigarette butt to the floor and squishing it with my boot, knowing it would annoy the shit out of Wills' OCD.

"The woman is coming. While we await her arrival, why don't you tell me, Ethan, how that memory makes you feel."

"How the fuck do you think it makes me feel?"

"Do you think that's where you derive your blood lust from, your love of violence?"

"Well, it didn't make me want to be fucking Gandhi, did it?"

"I'd wager it was the best thing that ever happened to you," Solomon said. "You made a friend of death that day, and of horror."

"Death is no fucking friend of mine," I growled.

"Why? Because it claimed your wife and daughter?"

"What do you think?"

"I know death well," he said. "And death always balances the scales. You got something in return for their sacrifices."

"Sacrifices? They were fucking murdered."

"Yes, taken so you could gain more strength, more power."

I shook my head at him. "What the fuck are you talking about? I didn't gain anything from their death's. Nothing. I lost…everything."

"You presume to know death's workings, when really, they are beyond you."

"Meaning?"

"Meaning," he said, but stopped when the temperature in the room went from moderate to freezing in the space of a few seconds. Then the cupboards and trays began to rattle, which was soon followed by a high-pitched wailing sound that I had to cover my ears against until it stopped a few seconds later.

When the wailing ceased and the room stopped shaking, the ghost of Barbara Keane appeared in front of me, a faintly glowing figure that wore the black dress she had been buried in, her long brown hair tucked into a neat bun, looking every inch the somewhat attractive school teacher she had been in life.

"I'm glad you summoned me, Detective," she said, her voice sounding like it was coming from down a tunnel. "For I need to talk to you and there's not much time left."

"Time left till what?" I asked.

"Until it all ends, Detective."

18

Barbara Keane hovered near the table her corpse lay on. Her expression was blank as she stared down at her former vessel. When she turned around, she floated down onto the floor and stood facing me. "How were you able to summon me like this?" she asked. "I've been trying so hard to break through here, but couldn't, not for long anyway."

"You have me to thank for that," Solomon said from behind her as he gently caressed one of her corpse's breasts.

Keane looked disgusted when she realized what Solomon was doing. "Please stop doing that," she said. "Have you no respect?"

"How would you feel," Solomon asked as if he was proposing a great idea, "if I fucked your corpse while you watched? Would that be a good experience for you? I know some who've enjoyed the experience so much they ask for seconds and even thirds. It's comforting to know that human depravity doesn't die with the body, isn't it?"

As I shook my head at Solomon, who was smiling to himself at this point, Keane floated across the room, moving herself as far away from Solomon as possible. "I've experienced more degradation in death than I ever did in life," she said, almost to herself. "I always thought the afterlife would be blissful, as the bible and all those preachers used to say, but it's all lies." She looked at me. "*It's all lies.* I can't even find my poor children. There's so much nothingness, so many lost souls…it's impossible to find anyone."

I thought of Angela and Callie as ghostly tears ran down Keane's cheeks. Is that were my angels were? Floating in nothingness, lost in the deep dark, all alone for eternity? It didn't bear thinking about.

"May I remind you that time is limited here?" Solomon said as he walked slowly around the mortuary table. "She will be pulled back to the Void soon."

"Tell me about this entity inside Troy Turner," I said to Keane. "What do you know about it?"

"I saw it," she said, her pale blue eyes focused on me now. "I was able to stay with my body for a while after it was snatched by those terrible kids. The things they did to me—" She shook her head, mashing her lips together to keep from crying. "Anyway, once the ritual was complete, the entity you speak of, it came, appearing over the top of my body. It was shaped like a human but seemed to consist entirely of light, a bluish light. Its blank face just stared at me, and I was able to connect with it on some level as if our two energies were mingling somehow. It was all very weird."

"Did it communicate with you?" Walker asked, coming to stand near me.

"Not directly," Keane said, her ghost form already starting to become translucent. "But I got images and feelings from it. The experience was intense and very frightening. I felt the being's pain and most of all, its rage. So much rage."

"Did it say what it was going to do here?" I asked. "When you appeared to me before, you said something about a key. What did you mean?"

"Yes," she said. "It needs to gather energy so it can create a doorway for others of its kind to come here."

"And do what?" Walker asked.

Keane's face turned grave. "Terrible things. The Litchghins want to kill everyone here and take the planet for themselves. They feel it's their right to take it as they were here first. Once the being inside of that fucking little shit Troy Turner gets enough energy from other supernatural beings, it will open a portal, and then there will be no stopping the annihilation they have planned. That's why I said to you, Detective, not to let him use the key. The Litchghin itself is the key, and you must stop it."

"Any idea how?" I asked her.

"That's your job, not mine."

"Fair enough."

"Is there anything else we should know, Mrs. Keane?" Walker asked.

"Yes, there is," Keane said as her body lost more of its density, to the point where you could see through her to the wall and sink behind her. "I need to tell you about that other detective. He's evil. He needs to be punished for what he's done."

"Who are you talking about?" I asked. "Detective Routman?"

Her face twisted up in rage at the mention of his name. "He set me up, framed me for the murder of my poor children. I didn't kill anyone. It was—" She stopped for a second to try to control her emotions. "It was my husband. He—he killed our children…and then he killed himself, that fucking —" She started sobbing then, her body fading away with each passing second.

"How?" I asked her. "How did he frame you?"

"Before my husband did what he did," she said. "He started suffering from paranoid delusions. He was sick, and I don't why. He often accused me of being a witch and said I wanted to sacrifice our two children to Satan, which was—" She shook her head. "Total nonsense, for I would never hurt my children and I certainly was not a witch. I was a Christian before I died, I paid my taxes, led a good clean life…more fool me, eh?" A bitter laugh left her mouth. "Anyway, it was my husband who poisoned our two kids and then himself that night, after he wrote that note accusing me of being evil, saying that I wanted to kill the kids, that letter they made such a big deal of at my court case. Detective Routman had become convinced of my guilt, but he knew the letter wasn't enough evidence to arrest me on, so he took residue from the bottle of sleeping pills used by my husband to kill himself and the kids. He took that residue and planted it on the infamous rubber gloves in my kitchen, implying that I used the gloves to handle the pills when removing them from the bottle so as not to leave my own fingerprints on the container. That false evidence, combined with my unsubstantiated alibi and the letter left by my husband—not to mention woeful representation at my trial—was enough to ensure a guilty verdict. Fourteen years I spent in a prison cell before I finally lost my life, and all because of that evil detective."

Keane's body was hardly visible anymore, her voice sounding so far away now it was barely audible, though I did hear her last words before she finally disappeared. "Get the man who framed me. Make him pay, Detective…"

Oh, I will. I will.

When we went back upstairs, Wills stood in the hallway surrounded by holy pictures on the walls, a worried look on his face, and the first thing he said was, "It wasn't me, I swear to God. They just turned up."

"Who just turned up?" I asked, knowing full well who he was talking about as I shoved past him and looked out through the peephole in the door. Outside, the street was swarming with cops, unmarked vehicles, and patrol cars blocking off the road as an entry team stood under the awning waiting to go in on someone's command.

Someone like Striker, who was standing by the entry team, gun in one hand, a loudspeaker in the other. "Come out, Drake," he said through the loudspeaker. "We know you're in there. It would be better if you just came quietly, otherwise we're coming in there to get you and your partner. We want her, as well, for aiding and abetting a wanted felon and perverting the course of justice."

"Fucking bald-headed son of a bitch," I snarled, moving away from the window and grabbing Wills by the lapels, who shrank in my grip. "This was you."

"No, it wasn't, I swear," he said. "They just turned up a minute ago. I didn't call them. Why would I call them when you told me not to? Plus, I had a deal with your friend there. I didn't call them, I—"

"Alright, shut the fuck up." I pushed him away.

"I'd wager it was the bystanders out in the street earlier before we came in," Solomon said.

"I fucking said you were causing a scene, didn't I?" I glared at him, and Walker as well, who dropped her eyes in shame.

"You can leave the back way," Wills suggested.

"They'll have that covered as well," I said, thinking there was no way I was going to let Striker take me into custody and throw me in a fucking cell.

"What are we going to do?" Walker asked.

"I could kill most of them," Solomon said. "I could cast a spell that would suck the life-force right out of them before they even knew what was happening."

"No," I said. "We're not killing anyone. Most of them out there are decent cops. They don't deserve to die. We'll have to think of something else."

"Last chance, Drake" Striker announced from outside. "Surrender or we're coming in. You have sixty seconds to comply."

"Motherfucker," I said, wishing I could run outside and break the cunt's neck, but that would have to wait for another time. For now, we just needed to escape.

"This is why you should've added magic to your skill-set at Blackstar while you had the chance, Ethan," Solomon said. "Instead of being so obsessed with weapons and technology. If you had, you might've been able to escape from here unnoticed, like I'm about to do."

"You're leaving, you son of a bitch?" I said to him.

"What? You think I'm going to hang around here to be manhandled by some dirty cop?" He shook his head. "No thank you. My job here is done. Good luck to you," he added with a smile, just before transforming himself into nothing but a shadow that slipped out under the front door and disappeared.

"Black-hearted cunt," I said under my breath.

"Pot kettle, Detective," Wills said, having found his courage again.

"Do you want me to punch you?" I said.

Wills looked away. "Just saying."

"Thirty seconds, Drake," Striker called from outside.

"I'd prefer it if my front door didn't get bashed in," Wills said. "Doors are expensive, plus I'd have to get a—" That's as far as he got until I shoved my arm out and grabbed him by the throat, slamming him up against the wall so hard that a picture of Jesus Christ fell off the wall, the glass shattering in the frame as it hit the tiled floor.

"I'm not sure, but I might have an idea," Walker said as I continued to hold Wills against the wall.

"It better be a good one," I said. "Because we're running out of time."

"Is there roof access here?" she asked Wills. Wills made a gurgling sound, but he was unable to form words because of my hand around his throat. "Maybe you should let him go."

I released Wills from my grip, and he slid down the wall, coughing and spluttering. "Answer her," I said.

"Stairs…" he gasped, pointing to the staircase. "Attic."

"What's your plan?" I asked Walker.

"I'm not even sure it will work."

I stared into her eyes for a second. "I trust you."

An involuntary smile spread across her face as she nodded.

"We're coming in, Drake," Striker shouted outside. "Be sure to resist now."

"We need to hold them off," I said.

"How?" Walker asked.

"With a little help from my friends."

It only took me a second to summon the Hellbastards, all six of whom appeared in the hallway, much to the surprise of Wills and Walker. Wills screamed as soon as he saw the demons, scrambling across the floor and broken glass to get away from them as Cracka snapped his jaws at him. "Dear God," Wills shouted, having found his voice again. "What the hell are those things?"

"Demons," Walker said. "Hellbastards. I remember Hell being full—"

"Yeah, yeah," I said, cutting her off. "Get up on to the roof so you can put whatever plan you have into action. And, Walker?"

"Yeah?"

"It better fucking work."

As Walker nodded and rushed off up the stairs, I addressed the Hellbastards. "Hold off anyone who comes through that door, but don't kill anybody, you hear me?"

All the Hellbastards groaned and pulled sad faces, disappointed that they couldn't indulge their murderous tendencies.

"But, boss," Scroteface whined, the legs of the tabby cat swinging under his chin.

"Just do as you're told," I said, already on the stairs and looking down at them. "Hold them off and then get gone, and try not to—"

I was going to say die, but there was a loud banging noise and the front door came flying off its hinges, almost landing on top of the Hellbastards, who jumped back out of the way just in time. The cops at the threshold froze when they caught sight of the demons, despite Striker shouting from behind them to move inside the house.

But before the entry team could do as Striker said, the Hellbastards sprang into action. Toast unleashed a fireball from his mouth that impacted the shield held by the entry team, creating a momentary wall of fire that the rest of the Hellbastards took advantage of straight away. Screeching and screaming like mad things, they launched themselves at the cops outside, all over them in seconds, clinging on as they punched, tore, clawed and bit in a violent frenzy that forced the cops back down the steps, not all of them on their feet. Before I rushed off up the stairs, I saw Striker standing near the bottom of the steps, his face a mask of rage as he realized I might get away from him.

Might being the operative word, because I had no idea what Walker was planning up on that roof. But I had no choice but to trust her, for there was no way I could've fought off so many cops without killing some of them. So now here I was, racing up the stairs and then up the steps into the large attic where Walker was already climbing up a ladder to make her way through a trapdoor that led out on to the roof.

From downstairs, I could hear lots of screaming and shouting, but one voice carried over all the others, that of Striker's.

"You won't get away, Drake," he shouted, sounding like he

was making his way up the stairs himself now, having somehow gotten past the Hellbastards. "Your little pets aren't enough to stop me."

Fuck you, Striker, I thought as I climbed up the ladder and out on to the roof to see Walker standing in the center of the rooftop, the rain falling down heavy around her, soaking her to the skin. I closed the trapdoor behind me, keeping my boot on it for the time being.

Three stories down, it sounded like the chaos was subsiding, though smoke was drifting up from the street thanks to Toast and his fireball antics. "Whatever you're going to do," I shouted to Walker. "Do it now."

Walker stood with her demon Visage looming large behind her, its eyes glowing in the failing light. As I watched, Walker dropped her head slightly and began to speak in some language that I suspected was Hellion, going by the number of consonants coming out of her mouth.

What the hell is she doing? I thought. *A spell of some sort?*

The more words she spoke, the deeper and more intense her voice became, growing louder until she sounded almost monstrous. The surrounding air became charged with energy, and from the blackening sky, a lightning bolt hit one of the TV antennas nearby, causing a huge burst of sparks to fly up.

Whatever she was doing, it seemed to be working, though it wasn't stopping Striker from trying to open the trapdoor I was standing on. He banged and pushed at it a few times, and when it didn't budge under my weight, the asshole fired a shot, the bullet exiting the trapdoor and whizzing up past my face. "Fuck," I said as I stepped back, drawing my own gun at the same time.

A second later, the trapdoor flew open and Striker emerged, keeping his gun trained on me as he climbed out onto the roof.

"Give it up, Detective," he said, showing no concern for

the fact that I had my gun pointed at him. "Drop your weapon and come quietly."

"Or what?" I said. "You'll shoot me? Your demon lord needs this body, remember?"

He knew I was right as he glanced around at Walker, who was still chanting in Hellion, wind, and rain swirling around her like a fledgling tornado, her Visage almost blending with the darkness surrounding her. "What is she doing?"

"No fucking idea," I said. "But I think we're about to find out."

At that point, another lightning bolt hit the rooftop near where Striker was standing, giving me the distraction I needed to move on him. As he jumped away from the lightning strike, I rushed toward him and elbowed him in the face before he could turn around. He cried out, and his gun went flying from his hand just as another bolt of lightning struck mere feet from him. As he staggered to maintain his balance, I kicked him in the chest, sending him flying back in Walker's direction, where he landed on his back on the wet roof, rainwater splashing up around him. "You'll never take me in," I said, advancing toward him. "And Astaroth will never take me either."

"You think you're invincible, Detective?" he shouted, impossibly raising himself up off the roof in one swift movement. Back on his feet, he shoved his hand out, and the next thing I knew, I was flying backward across the rooftop like someone who'd been hit by a truck.

Whatever power he had, it was potent, for I could hardly fucking breath as I lay there in the wet with the rain pounding my face. I no longer had my gun either, which I must've dropped when the energy blast hit. Fucking hellots. Always cheating.

"You're mine now," he said, coming toward me now. "And soon you will be Astaroth's."

His advance was interrupted, however, by a massive

cracking sound as if the very fabric of reality had split in two. Which indeed it had in a way, as Striker saw for himself when he turned around to see a huge beast standing there on the rooftop. Even my jaw dropped open as I sat up to look at the beast.

At first glance, it looked like a horse. It was the same shape as a horse, but bigger. A jagged length of bone maybe three feet in length protruded from its forehead, and steam blew out of its flared nostrils, its burning red eyes staring with malevolence at Striker. "What the actual fuck?" I said to myself, standing up, noticing now the jet-black hair on the beast which was broken up by the various wounds it had all over its body. Ribs were partially exposed, and there were gaping holes in its neck and head.

All in all, it looked like the most nightmarish unicorn I had ever seen. Not that I'd ever seen a real unicorn, but you know what I mean. It wasn't something you would want to paint on your little girl's bedroom wall, that's for sure.

Walker climbed up onto the beast's back and gripped its mane, the black wings of her demon Visage spread out behind her, making her look like some angel of death. When the beast reared up on its hind legs and made a thunderous neighing sound, its eyes cold and blazing, I figured it wasn't the friendliest of beasts.

Striker, for all his bravado, soon backtracked away from the beast, and as he did, he found my gun lying on the rooftop which he picked up and pointed at me. "I don't care if Astaroth wants your stinking body," he shouted. "I'll kill you before I let you off this roof."

"Will you now?" I said. "Look behind you."

Striker seemed unsure but afforded a quick glance over his shoulder, just in time to see Scroteface and Khullu launch themselves at him, Scroteface jumping with one of his short but powerful arms stretched out so that he ended up clotheslining Striker across the throat, pitching him back on to the rooftop. As soon as Striker fell, Khullu was on him, encircling one of his face tentacles around Strikers neck while Scroteface sat on the hellot's chest.

"Good job boys," I said, picking up my gun from next to Striker. "Hold him there." Striker was trying to speak, but he couldn't get the words out because Khullu was gripping him so tight. "Don't come after me, Striker, or next time I'll fucking kill you. Tell Astaroth the same."

A few feet away, the beast Walker sat atop was getting restless as it stomped its massive hooves down on the rooftop again and again. "Come on," she said.

"You expect me to get on that thing?" I said, holstering my gun.

"You see another way off this roof?"

"No."

"Come on then."

"Jesus," I said as I used a ledge to climb up onto the beast's back, where I then wrapped my arms around Walker's waist. "I can't believe I'm doing this. I can't believe *you* did this."

"Just hold on tight," she said.

"What do you even call this thing?"

"It's a Hellicorn. I rode one in Hell."

"Oh right, a Hell—" I never got to finish the sentence as the Hellicorn started charging across the rooftop at full speed, and the next words out of my mouth were, "Oh shiiiiiiii-itttt…" as the Hellicorn jumped off the edge of the three-story building, launching itself into thin air before dive-bombing toward the street below, which was still jammed with cars and cops everywhere. As my stomach flew up into my mouth, I gritted my teeth for a hard landing, and when it came, both Walker and I grunted as the energy from the impact traveled through our groins and up our spines.

The Hellicorn landed on the road next to a parked patrol car and then started sprinting down the street without hardly missing a beat, and considering how big the drop was, I was impressed by the beast's ability to maintain its balance, and also not to shatter its bones by performing such a death-defying stunt.

"Where to?" Walker gripped the beast's mane as she steered it down the street, swerving this way and that to avoid the oncoming traffic and anything else that got in the way.

"The scrapyard," I said as I noticed only a few faces on the crowded sidewalks were actually eyeballing us as we galloped past. The rest carried on walking as if they couldn't see us. "Who can see us, by the way?"

"Just the MURK's as you call them, and those in the know like yourself." She pulled on the Hellicorn's mane and made it do a sharp left turn as we headed in the direction of the scrapyard, in the main galloping down the middle of the road in between the cars, sometimes moving around them, and once, even over the top of one. I had to give it to Walker, she really knew how to handle this beast. "The mundane people can't see us as long as we are on the back of the Hellicorn."

"Invisibility. Nice."

With my arms still around her slim waist, I felt her muscles contract as she fought to steer the Hellicorn. Her firm buttocks kept pushing into my groin, and that plus the adrenaline resulted in me getting a semi-erection, though I didn't think she noticed. Her long, almost black hair kept swinging into my face, giving me whiffs of coconut-scented shampoo, that when mixed with the warmth and sweet smell of her neck, I found intoxicating, not to say arousing. Which surprised me, because I never looked at Walker in a sexual way before, maybe because I knew she was a demon. But she wasn't really a demon, was she? Before her fall to Hell, she was a celestial being, her full glory no doubt beautiful to behold. In that moment as we rode the Hellicorn through the streets, I felt a sense of freedom that I hadn't felt in a long time, and not just freedom, but connection. Connection with her, with Walker or with whatever being she happened to be on the inside. In any case, I didn't really care what she was. I was just glad she was here.

And with me.

Because then I didn't feel so alone anymore.

19

Walker brought the Hellicorn to a halt outside Cal's trailer, though there was no sign of Cal himself, and his battered Oldsmobile was gone, so I figured he was out and about somewhere, on a beer run knowing him. The dogs were there, though, but neither Ace nor Apollo was brave enough to go anywhere near the fearsome Hellicorn. Instead, they both maintained a safe distance among the scrap metal and growled their displeasure at having such a strange, demonic beast invade their territory. "It's alright, boys," I shouted over to them. "It won't hurt you." I looked at Walker. "Will it?"

The Hellicorn answered for her by snorting and moving its horned head up and down. "It shouldn't," she said. "As long as they don't annoy it."

Standing back, I stared at the great beast to get a better look. As magnificent as it was in its own dark way, it also looked like it had just risen from the grave. Parts of its body had rotted away, its bones showing through in many places, as well as muscles and tendons. The teeth on one side of its face were permanently on display, the flesh covering them having long decomposed, making the Hellicorn look like it was snarling all the time. The horn curving out of its forehead was a whitish-yellow color, stained with blood in places, pointed at the end with the underside tapered into a sharp edge that looked like it could shred flesh. I could only imagine how many demons and damned souls had been impaled by that horn in Hell. "So are Hellicorns a standard mode of transport in Hell?" I asked her as she came to stand beside me.

"There are all sorts of creatures used for transport in Hell," she replied. "The Hellicorn is just one, and a rare one at that."

"How the hell did you even get it here? Did you suddenly just find your power or something?"

She smiled. "It's amazing what you can do when you have to. I didn't even remember the Hellicorn until we were all standing in the hallway of Wills' house, and when I did, I thought—"

"Why not try to summon it."

"Yeah."

"But how come you could summon its body too? I thought only spirits could be summoned from Hell."

"So did I," Walker said. "Maybe it's different for the beasts."

"Does the beast have a name?"

Walker stared at the creature for a second. "I'm not sure if it had a name, or maybe I just can't remember it. Maybe you should name him."

"I'm not good at naming things. I called one of the Hell-bastards Toast, for fuck's sake."

"Fair enough. In the meantime, ride him whenever you want, as he's here to stay."

"You can't send him back?"

"Do you want me to send him back?"

I stared into the Hellicorn's red eyes and saw a soul in there, a living thing, even though it looked more like a dead thing. "No," I said. "He can stay."

"Good," she said. "Because here's a fun fact—that horn of his, I just remembered that it kills demons."

"Good to know." I nodded. "So do you think he wants an apple?"

"An apple?" Walker frowned.

"Horses eat apples, right? Maybe he's partial to them."

"Are you kidding? He eats human flesh, not apples."

"Human flesh, eh?" I couldn't help but smile at the thought. "Figures. It would be easier if he just ate hay or apples. It's a lot easier to grab an apple from the store than it is to source a pile of human flesh."

"He need not feed that often. Every few days should be fine."

"We have to feed him man-flesh every few days? What happens if he doesn't feed?"

"I can't remember," she said.

"It's bad, isn't it? You can tell me. Does he go nuts or something? Does he go on a killing spree?"

"Like I said, I can't remember."

"Let me know when you do. In the meantime, let's go to my trailer. We can hide him there."

"You have a trailer here?"

"I used to live here for a few years. Cal keeps the trailer here in case I ever need a place to crash or hide out."

"Cal? The owner of this place? Who is he to you?"

I laughed to myself before answering. "Cal is a lot of things to me, most of which I won't go into. He took me in when I needed guidance a long time ago."

"So, he's like a mentor or a father figure?"

"A father figure?" I laughed outright this time. "Please. Cal is the last person you want as a father figure."

"That bad, huh?"

"Let's just say, he's not a good role model and leave it at that. You'll get to know him yourself anyway if you stick around."

"Why wouldn't I?"

"You're a wanted felon now the same as me. I doubt your new life here is exactly going to plan."

"I didn't have a plan, I just wanted to live. And I'm doing that. With you," she added, somewhat coyly.

I looked away at the mountains of scrap rearing up in the darkness. "That's a decision you might come to regret."

"I haven't so far."

She's just naïve, I told myself. *She has no idea what she's getting into hanging with me. She's known me for barely a few weeks, and already she's a wanted felon. What's next? Prison? Death? Or worse, back to Hell?*

"Come on," I said. "Let's get Blackie here hidden away before Cal comes back and sees him."

"Blackie? That's what you're calling him?"

"What can I say? I state the obvious."

Walker smiled as she walked up to the Hellicorn without fear and said some sort of command to it that sounded like, "*Aahista*."

"Is that Hellion?"

"Yes, it means follow. There are other commands. I'll teach them to you if you like."

"Sure," I said as we headed toward the trailer, With Blackie's hooves crunching the gravel as he walked, Walker guided Blackie around the back and gave him another command in Hellion which I figured meant stay, for the Hellicorn stayed put as we headed around the front of the trailer and went inside.

It had been quite a while since I was inside the trailer. The last time was when Angela kicked me out of the house. I stayed here for a while until I found my current apartment in Bricktown. The trailer was narrow inside, with a small living area and a bedroom at the back. The place stank of booze and stale sweat and old cigarettes. Not the sort of place you would bring a woman, but where else were we going to go? "You want a drink?" I asked her, finding a half-full bottle of Jack Daniels in one of the cupboards, along with two dusty glasses.

"Sure," Walker said as she sat on the couch and looked around. "So this place is…cozy."

"That's one way to describe it. Shit hole might be another."

Walker laughed; a sound I was still getting used to hearing. Her laugh was throaty, sexy even. Every day, she seemed to become more human. I didn't know Hannah Walker well enough to know if the current Walker was like the old one, but I didn't care if she was or not. The current Hannah was good enough for me. "You haven't seen *my* apartment yet. It's in Little Tokyo. Barely enough room to swing a cat in it. Hannah was forced to downsize after her drug habit got out of control."

"How'd she end up a junkie?" I asked as I sat down beside her and handed her a glass of Jack. "Was it the job? I know she worked Vice. That can be tough on a person's mental state."

"Hannah was a junkie long before she became a cop, but she got clean. The job she could handle okay, but she had other things going on that eventually pushed her over the edge."

"Such as?"

Walker sighed and took her black leather jacket off as she settled back onto the couch. "It's a long story."

"Does it involve her Yakuza connections?"

"Yeah. It's what I've wanted to talk to you about."

"Well, we're here, and we're not going anywhere for a while," I said. "Fire away."

Walker nodded. "Okay, I'll give you the short version. Hannah's real name was Hannah Yagami. You probably know the surname."

"Yagami as in Kazuo Yagami, the oyabun of the Yakuza clan in this city?"

"Yep, the very same. Kazuo was—is—Hannah's father," Walker said. "Hannah's mother was one of Kazuo's mistresses, an American woman named Susan Walker. After Kazuo got her pregnant, he set her up in her own apartment and paid all her bills so she could raise Hannah. The only thing he demanded of her was her loyalty. But Kazuo is also a sadistic fuck, and he would often hand Susan over to his Yakuza friends, who liked a good white woman they could do whatever they wanted to, as long as they left her face untouched. One day, Susan had had enough and tried to leave. She was going to go to Europe, but she only got as far as the airport before Kazuo's men caught her and brought her back, along with Hannah. For her betrayal, Kazuo strangled Susan to death in front of Hannah, who was only five years old at the time."

"Jesus," I said, thinking Walker and I had more in common than I realized.

"Kazuo took Hannah in after that," she went on. "He groomed her to be a part of the family business and trained her to be an assassin. But things didn't go smoothly. Kazuo's wife hated Hannah, hated having to look at the result of her husband's infidelity every day. Kazuo's lieutenants didn't have much love for Hannah either since she wasn't full Japanese. They viewed her as a white girl with no business being anywhere near the Yakuza, even though she showed promise as an assassin. The real problems started when she went to private school as a teenager. That's when she got into drugs. And being a drug addict didn't help her training any, which didn't sit well with Kazuo or any of his lieutenants. Kazuo's wakagashira—his first lieutenant—was especially brutal. His name is Susumu Yagami. He's Kazuo's son."

"I know him," I said. "I questioned him one time about

the murder of a Triad boss. He's a cocky son of a bitch, thinks he's untouchable."

Walker nodded as she drank the Jack from her glass. "He's a real sociopath. He used to step in on Hannah's training just so he could beat the shit out of her. If it weren't for his father, he'd have slit Hannah's throat long ago. Susumu is also heavily into the occult. It's my belief that he cursed Hannah, turning her into a drug addict hoping she would destroy herself, which she almost did on several times. She was pretty much dead when I entered her body."

"I fucking hate gangsters." I got up to grab the Jack bottle from the tiny kitchen area, bringing it back to refill our glasses. "Every one of them are entitled fucks who think they're above the law and everything else."

Walker shrugged. "Most of them are. How many Yakuza do you know who've been arrested here? Or Italian mobsters? Or Triads?"

"Yeah, I get it." I got up again to turn on the small stereo that sat on a shelf opposite. A moment later, the trailer was filled with the bluesy tones of Mad Season as the first song on their only album came on. "How did Hannah end up a cop?"

"Well, unbeknownst to her, it had always been Kazuo's plan to have Hannah become a cop. He wanted a mole inside the department, and despite her various behavior problems and drug addiction, Kazuo got Hannah into the academy. He made sure she got clean before signing up."

"So Hannah was really a mole for the Yakuza?"

Walker nodded. "Yes, but she was also a dedicated police officer. She took the job seriously until…" She trailed off as she lapsed into silence.

"What?"

"Susumu made her kill another cop a couple years ago," she said. "A narcotics officer who was sniffing around the clan business a bit too much. This cop, he was gunning for Kazuo, so Kazuo ordered his assassination."

"Wait, are you talking about Brian Madden, the cop who was found with his throat slit in his apartment?"

Walker didn't answer as she stared down into her glass. Having Hannah's memories, she remembered the whole thing, and going by her face, the murder didn't sit too well with her. When she looked at me next, there were tears in her eyes. "Kazuo and his clan ruined Hannah's life. *My life.*" She pointed to herself.

"And let me guess," I said. "You want revenge."

"Fucking right I do, and I will get it."

"You're going to take on the whole Yakuza clan by yourself?"

"My powers grow stronger every day. They won't be able to stop me."

"You're a cop, not an assassin."

"I could say the same thing about you. How many have you killed? How many have you killed instead of arrested?"

I thought of the two hellots I shot dead recently. "Yeah, I suppose I'm not one to judge."

"Anyway," she said. "What's the chances of us keeping our badges after this shit storm we're in is over? You're wanted for two murders and I've been lumped in as your accomplice. We're both fucked."

"Maybe." I offered her a cigarette which she took. "Maybe not."

"What does that even mean?" she asked after I lit her cigarette for her.

"It means there's always a way. Believe me, I have no intention of winding up in a prison cell for the rest of my life."

"Me neither."

"So we put our heads together and figure something out."

"Like partners." She smiled.

"Like partners," I said, chinking her glass, our eyes meeting as we looked at each other. Her lips seemed soft and ripe as she slowly licked them. I stared at her for another few seconds and then found myself leaning my head toward her, about to kiss her when the door to the trailer was flung open and in walked Cal.

"Not interrupting anything, am I?" he said, standing there in his filthy jeans and leather half-cut, a knowing look on his face as his eyes went from me to Walker and back again.

"I'll be staying here a while," I said to him without missing a beat. "We both will."

"Uh-huh," he said. "So, you're the cause of that shit show at Wills' Undertakers, I take it? I drove past, saw the chaos, figured it was you."

"We went to talk to Barbara Keane," I said. "Then Striker showed up with the cavalry and it all went to shit. Walker here saved our asses."

Walker stood up and went to Cal, offering her hand. "You must be Cal," she said. "I'm Hannah Walker."

Cal just stared at her. "You're a fucking demon."

Walker's smile disappeared as she lowered her hand and turned away.

"Cal," I said. "Don't be an asshole."

"Does she know how many of her kind you've killed?"

"No, and I'm sure she doesn't want to know either."

"It's okay," Walker said. "I can go. I'll find somewhere else to stay."

"Maybe for the best," Cal said.

"No, you won't," I told her. "You're staying here. And, Cal?" I threw him a look. "Cut it fucking out."

"I don't like demons in my fucking yard," he said. "Or any other kind of monster. You should know that."

"I'm not a monster," Walker said defensively.

"No? What are you then? A fucking angel?" He laughed to himself. "You're all fucking monsters to me. You don't belong here. You should've stayed in Hell where you really belong."

Walker's face tensed up as her Visage grew in size behind

her. The demon in her was thinking of retaliating in a way that wouldn't end well for her. If she tried anything against Cal, he'd have his knife out and in her belly before she could say fucking boo. And going by his face, he was willing her to try, just so he could stick her.

"Alright," I said as I got up and stood between them. "Let's everybody take a breath here. Cal, I appreciate this is your place, but we don't plan on staying long. I'm asking you to do me this one favor. I never ask you for anything."

Cal glared at Walker for another few seconds before switching his gaze to me. "Just don't make a fucking asshole out of me, Ethan," he said.

"Hey, you're already a fucking asshole," I said. "So no chance of that."

"Fuck you. I mean it. I don't want no trouble here. I got a business to run. If people find out I'm harboring fucking demons here, that's it for me."

"I get it," I said.

"You better fucking had." He turned to leave, then stopped. "Why is there a fucking hell beast outside scaring my dogs?"

"That was our ride out of Dodge," I said.

"Don't think you're keeping it around here. You're lucky I didn't take a blade to its neck. Get it gone."

When he left, I turned to Walker, who was finishing the last of her cigarette. "So that was Cal," I said, smiling. "He's a pussy really."

"I see what you mean about him being the last person you'd want as a father figure," she said. "He really knows how to rile a person up."

"Word of advice, don't try to fuck with him. He'll kill you."

Walker nodded and went and sat back down again. "So what now?" she asked. "Do we just stay holed up here? For how long?"

"I'm gonna give it a few more hours for things to settle down. Then I'm going to my apartment to get a few things that will help us find Troy Turner, and hopefully stop the Litchghin he has inside him."

"So we have time to kill," she said, her eyes on me as she spread her legs slightly.

"Seems that way," I said, staring back at her as I finished my cigarette, stubbing the butt out in the glass ashtray by the stereo. When I was done, I looked down at her for another minute, saw the raw desire in her brown eyes, the rise and fall of her chest as her breathing quickened. Then I went over to her and pulled her up off the couch, lifting her until she wrapped her legs around my waist and threw her arms around my neck as we started kissing hard, her hand grabbing my hair as she pulled my head into her.

"I've…never done this before," she panted in between kissing me. "Hannah has…not me."

I leaned down and put her on the couch, unbuttoning her jeans, sliding them down over her smooth-skinned legs. At the same time, she tugged my trench off and started to unbutton my shirt and then my belt. By the time I slid her panties off, I was naked myself, and she was gazing almost confusedly at my ever-stiffening cock before her eyes shifted to the tattoos going up my arms and down my back. I hardly noticed her interest, however, for I was too busy gazing at *her* tattoos, pulling her up and turning her around so I could view her Yakuza ink. Her sinewy arms were covered, from the wrists up with a tattoo that wound its way to her chest and across her back, culminating, on her left shoulder, in the face of a Muromachi-era courtesan with one breast exposed and a knife clenched between her teeth. "Hannah hated the ink," she said.

"And you?" I asked her, still gazing at the greens, reds, and blacks of the design now faded somewhat over time.

"They just remind me of what I need to do."

After gazing at her for another minute, I pushed her back

down and dropped to my knees, pushing my head between her legs. She was tense for a moment, but then gasped and grabbed handfuls of my hair, spreading her legs wider as I pushed my tongue into her wetness, holding my head there until she came. Soon, she was on top of me, sliding herself over my waiting cock, her cunt warm and wet as she bucked on top of me, grinding down on me as I grabbed her small, firm breasts, taking one of her nipples into my mouth, her crying out when I bit down on her nipple, me gasping as she rode me harder, her hot juices spilling down over me as she came, my own juice spurting inside her as I came a few seconds later. Both of us gasping, breathing hard, she continued to ride me gently for another few minutes, making little moans of pleasure as she gripped my hair and pressed her soft lips against my neck. When she was finally done, she reared back a little to look at me, my cock still in her.

She looked like she didn't know whether to laugh or cry before she finally chose the former response, laughing gently almost to herself. "I always wondered what that would be like," she said. "As an Elohim, I used to watch the humans do this, always finding their carnal knowledge repulsive and dirty."

"And now?" I asked, still admiring her small but perfectly formed body.

"I could do this all night," she said in a husky voice, leaning forward to kiss me as she started grinding on me again.

"Well," I said, grabbing her hair with both hands, pushing up into her again. "We still have time to kill…"

20

A couple hours later, Walker took a shower while I went outside to get some air and smoke a cigarette.

The night was calm and still, the sky clear for a change, the stars out in force, the full moon beaming its silvery light down upon the mountains of scrap metal, giving the place an eerie glow that was nonetheless serene.

In the far distance, sirens blared, and closer by, scratching sounds as the yard's rat population scurried over the top of the scrap metal.

Lighting a cigarette as I stood wearing only dark jeans and boots, I stared up at the stars as my thoughts turned to Callie. I kept thinking about what Barbara Keane had said, that she had floated in a void with billions of other lost souls, surrounded by nothing but darkness. The thought of my beautiful little angel being trapped in the cold darkness for eternity was too unbearable to even contemplate, especially when I knew there was nothing I could do for her.

The only thing that stopped me from tumbling into grief was the hope Callie might be somewhere else, somewhere better, somewhere less cold and dark. Just because Keane found herself in the Void after death, didn't mean Callie or

Angela was there. When the voice in my head started questioning this assumption, I switched my thoughts to how I would deal with Striker instead.

The bastard had me by the short and curlies, there was no doubt about that. But that didn't mean I was totally screwed. I was already formulating a plan to clear my name—and Walker's—and hopefully take down Striker at the same time. Then I could get my badge back, no thanks to Lewellyn, who I felt let down by, to say the least. I had no doubt he would come back around, however, once it was safe for him to do so and his career was no longer in jeopardy. If he didn't, I would force him to do so.

But first things first. Troy Turner was still out there, a Litchghin inside him that had probably killed again since the last time. I didn't know how much energy the Litchghin needed to complete its plan, but I wasn't about to give it the time to find out.

About to head inside, I stopped when a gruff, masculine voice said, "Hey asshole," in an accent that may have been Spanish or Greek.

Frowning, I looked around for the source of the voice, but all I saw was the Hellicorn standing by the side of the trailer looking at me with its red eyes. "Did you…?"

"Yeah, I'm talking to you, big guy," the voice said again, clear as day, and this time I saw the Hellicorn's thick, rubbery lips move as if it was mouthing the words.

"Why am I not surprised?"

The Hellicorn ambled closer. "What did you think, that I was a fucking dummy or something? A pretty-pretty unicorn?" He shook his massive head. "Fuck you, buddy."

"Walker never mentioned you could talk."

"Who? Oh, you mean Xaglath."

"Not anymore."

The Hellicorn snorted. "Please, that bitch was a vicious fuck in Hell. Even the fucking Grand Dukes were afraid of her, and that's saying something. Just because she's now in the body of some human piece of filth, doesn't mean she isn't still Xaglath under all that stinking mortal flesh. Someday you'll see her in all her cunting glory."

"Uh-huh." I wondered now if maybe I'd taken too much Mud before I came out here.

"What's that dumb fucking look on your face for?" the Hellicorn asked. "You thought I was just a dull fucking animal, is that it, huh? Well, I'm not, asshole. Far from it. I'm smarter than you'll ever fucking be. I can speak languages you've never even heard of. I know things your tiny human mind couldn't begin to comprehend. Compared to me, you're just a silly little child. All you fucking asshole humans are. In Hell, you all just scream and whine like fucking babies. You know how many skulls I crushed in Hell, just to get those whining maggots to shut the fuck up?"

"How many?"

"Millions probably, and even then, they still didn't shut up. Their annoying screams still carried across the lakes of excrement, the ponds of cum and the mountains of toenail clippings."

"Toenail clippings?"

"Human filth filters down. All your disgusting bodily wastes end up in Hell. Every toenail clipping, every snot ball, every pubic hair, every load of cum that didn't go anywhere and every load that ran back out again, every shit you've ever had, every drop of stinking sweat you've excreted, it all ends up gathering in Hell."

"So, what you're saying is, you're glad to be away from the place?"

"I suppose so, though this fucking place ain't much better is it?" he said. "You know what I want? What I really fucking want?"

"No, but I'm sure you're gonna tell me."

"I want a nice green pasture that's full of horny mares I

can fuck whenever I want," he said. "Not like the fields of shit in Hell, or the rotting mares I had to make do with in that place. I want fresh fields and fresh pussy, you feel me, big guy?"

"So, you want to go to Heaven then?"

"Heaven?" He made a huge snorting sound before laughing with as much cynicism as I've heard from anyone, never mind a talking Hellicorn. "You humans are naïve motherfuckers, aren't you? There is no fucking Heaven anymore. Heaven's gone, *chaménos* …it's no fucking more."

I thought of Callie and Angela again, floating in the dark void. "And you know this for a fact, do you?"

"Says the human who lives in a fucking bubble called Earth." He stepped closer as he towered over me. "You fuckers think God is love. You think the soul is special. Let me tell you, God is a rotten cunt and your precious soul is nothing more than a noose around your fucking neck."

"Well," I said, a smile spreading across my face. "You're a real fucking sunflower, aren't you? I think we're gonna get along just fine."

"Don't go thinking we're pals just because I'm speaking to you," he said. "And for the love of fuck, don't ever call me fucking Blackie again, you got that? My name's not fucking *Blackie*."

"What is it then?" I lit another cigarette. "Snow Blossom? Moon Sparkle? Rainbow Dash?"

"No, you cheeky bastard," he retorted. "It's Haedemus."

"Haedemus? Is that Greek?"

"Before my soul was damned to Hell, I was ridden by a great Spartan warrior," he said, holding his head high as if he still felt the pride of such an accolade.

"I didn't think animals could go to Hell."

"That's because you're a know-nothing human. Any living thing can end up in Hell if it does something bad enough to get there."

"What did you do? Steal some hay or something?"

Haedemus turned his colossal head away and snorted. "Doesn't matter what I did."

"Tell me. How bad could it be?"

Glancing at me with his red eyes, he appeared to sigh. "I sodomized a human," he said quietly.

Laughing to myself, I shook my head. "Was horsey pussy not good enough for you or something?"

"I just wanted to see what it was like," he said. "Is that so wrong? Haven't you ever done anything you shouldn't have?"

"Yeah, lots of shit, though I've never fucked another *species*." *Oh, wait,* I thought. *I think I just did that.* "So you raped a human and went to Hell for it?"

"I didn't rape anyone. It was consensual and quite beautiful really—"

"You raped a human."

"Alright, fine. I raped the guy. So what?"

"It was a guy?"

"It was on the battlefield," he said. "I was riled up, I needed a release, you know how it is."

"Uh-huh."

"The man was there in front of me, lying on the blood-soaked earth as he struggled to keep his intestines from spilling out."

"So not only did you rape a human, you raped a human who was injured and about to die?"

"Stop judging me, human. I'm sure you've done worse."

"No actually, I don't think I have. How did that even work? I mean, you're a big fucker, aren't you?"

"I've changed since going to Hell," he said. "You think I looked like this back then? Fuck you. I was a magnificent specimen, beautiful by anyone's standards." He jerked his head then so his scraggy main flicked over as if to prove to himself or me that he still retained some of his former handsomeness. Although to be honest, with all his ravaged, decaying flesh, gruesome would be a better word to describe this snarky specimen. "But to answer your question, I simply lay down on my side and rolled him into me, holding him gently with my front legs, cuddling him you might say. Spooning, I think you humans call it. There was so much blood I slid right into him without any fuss, like it was meant to be. There was eye contact and everything. I think he came too, just before he died. It took his mind off his impending death, so it was a win-win in my book."

"A win-win with your massive cock jammed up his ass."

"It was poignant and beautiful. Stop it."

"God didn't think so if you went to Hell for it."

"What would that bigoted fuck know about anything?" he spat, steam flying out of his nostrils. "He sends crows to Hell for squawking at the wrong person, squirrels for stealing food from bird tables, dogs for barking at postmen, deer for causing car accidents, monkeys for throwing their own shit, insects for stinging people…the list goes on."

"I had no idea."

"As I already said, that's because you live here in this Earth bubble. Just you wait until it's your turn to die. You'll see then."

"Hell's gates are still open, are they?"

"You bet your ass they are, human. Don't ever let anyone tell you differently. Hell's gates never close."

"Good to know," I said, thinking, *Not really*. "I'm going in now. Maybe you'd like to give me a ride shortly."

Haedemus snorted and nodded his head. "What the fuck else am I gonna do? I can't go anywhere until Xaglath releases me from my servitude."

"Which I'm sure she will."

"She fucking better, the cranky bitch. I served her well in Hell, carried her into hundreds of battles, gored thousands of demons on her behalf."

"She says you can kill a demon. Is that true?"

"In so far as their rotten soul gets relegated to the Void, yes."

"Good to know, although that sounds like a release from prison to me."

"It's bad to worse is what it is. The Void is no place for any soul. It's nothingness for all eternity. Even Hell is better than that."

Back inside the trailer, Walker was out of the shower and dressed, tying her wet hair back as I walked in. "I was just out talking to your Hellicorn," I said. "Interesting guy. Has a few issues, I think."

Walker half smiled to herself as she sat on the couch and started putting her boots back on. "Yes, now I remember. Did he tell you his name is Haedemus?"

"He did." I found my shirt and put it on, recoiling at the sweaty smell of it. "He also mentioned you were a ruthless bitch in Hell."

She stopped tying her laces to throw me a look. "Everyone is ruthless there. You have to be."

"I'm not judging."

"I didn't say you were."

"Your face says otherwise."

Finished tying her boots, she stood up. "I spent millennia in that place. I just want to forget it now. Who I was there, it's not who I really am."

"So who are you really?"

She shrugged and gave me a mischievous sort of smile, and even though I knew she wasn't strictly human, I couldn't help finding her smile enchanting, sexy even. And since I hadn't found anything sexy or enchanting for a long while, I appreciated it. "That's what I'm here to find out."

~

Once we were ready, Walker and I headed outside to

Haedemus, where he stood idling by the side of the trailer, eyeing up the two dogs who watched him from afar. "I'm going to eat those two mutts if I don't get some food soon," he said, turning his head to look at us. "Getting dragged out of Hell is a stressful business, and now I'm hungry."

"I'm sure we'll find you something," Walker said, fully dressed now in her dark jeans and leather jacket, her long hair tied back in a ponytail. The smile on her face had barely wavered since we'd fucked inside the trailer, and she kept giving me little looks and glances as if we had just shared some deep and meaningful experience. I hadn't the heart to tell her it was just fucking, so I let it be. *Let her enjoy it before the inevitable complications set in.*

"Don't you mean some*one*?" Haedemus said. "I exist on human flesh, don't forget."

"You just said you would eat the dogs," I said.

"Yes," he said. "Animals will do in a pinch, but my delicate system is used to human flesh. Do you *want* to give me indigestion?"

"No, we wouldn't want that."

"We'll sort something out for you later," Walker said. "In the meantime, we need to go somewhere. Ethan's driving."

Haedemus glared at me with one huge eye. "Ethan, that's your name? You don't look like an Ethan. You look more like a Doug, or a Frank, or a—"

"Do you ever shut up?" I asked him.

The Hellicorn reared back as if in mock offense. "Well, the cheek on this one. And I thought Hell was the bad place."

"Jesus," I said, looking at Walker. "Can we just go now?"

"After you," Walker said, smiling at her pet's histrionics.

As I stood looking at the new ride, I realized I didn't know how to mount the thing. When I'd got on behind Walker on the roof that time, I recalled standing on a ledge of some sort that raised me up and made it easy for me to swing my leg over. With nothing to stand on now, there was no way I was going to be able to swing my leg up and over this time. "I, uh—"

"Fucking hell," Haedemus said. "He doesn't even know how to mount me."

"Maybe you should lay down like you did with your human lover," I said. "Make it easy for me."

Walker burst out laughing. "He told you about that?"

"Unfortunately," I said.

"Oh, here we go," Haedemus said. "Let's all laugh at Haedemus for having a tender five minutes with a dying man on the battlefield. I really cannot wait until you land in Hell, Ethan, and all your sins are laid bare for everyone to laugh at."

"Don't be so damn sensitive, Haedemus," Walker said before turning to me. "Just grab hold of his mane and swing yourself up. You'll soon get the hang of it."

"He's clearly too stupid to get the hang of anything but being stupid," Haedemus said.

"Fuck you." I grabbed his mane and attempting to swing myself up, managing to get one leg up before falling on my ass, much to Haedemus' amusement as he started laughing.

"Please," he said. "Try again so I can keep laughing at you."

Walker stood with her hand over her mouth to conceal her smile as I glared at the two of them. "It might be easier if I just took the Dodge."

"Oh, don't be a fucking pussy, Ethan," Haedemus barked. "Be a man and grab my mane. Swing that leg over, come on now."

"You're really enjoying this, aren't you?" I grabbed his mane again.

"Immensely so."

"Asshole." Once again, I tried to mount him, almost succeeding until he bucked slightly on purpose and knocked me off him, laughing his ass off as I hit the dirt.

"Haedemus," Walker scolded him, then said something in Hellion that made him stop laughing and drop his head in silence, his previous attitude now vanished as quickly as it came.

"Hey, Haedemus," I said after I got up off the ground. When the Hellicorn turned his head to look at me, I landed a punch on his decayed jawline that knocked out one of his teeth. "Don't fuck with me."

Quick as lightning, Haedemus turned his whole body and dropped his head so his razor-sharp horn was pointing at me. "I could have you in pieces in seconds," he snarled, his red eyes blazing. "How dare—"

Walker shouted the Hellicorn's name again, followed by another mouthful in Hellion, though her voice was much louder and more severe this time. Haedemus shrank back at the ferocity of it like a dog getting a telling off from its owner for misbehaving. "Now let him on this time," she finished. "Or you know the consequences."

"Yes, Mistress," Haedemus said. "Forgive my excitement at finally being free from Hell."

"We're good then?" I asked him.

"Yes," he replied, though it was hard to tell what the snarky bastard was thinking. When I grabbed his mane and swung my leg up onto him this time, however, he didn't budge. I was able to finally mount him.

"Good boy." I patted his neck.

"You don't have to be so condescending," he said.

Smiling, I grabbed Walker's hand and helped her up onto the Hellicorn so she could sit behind me with her arms around my waist, which I have to admit, I rather liked. "Onward, Jeeves," I said to Haedemus.

"Yes, Ethan. Of course. Your wish is my—"

"Haedemus," Walker growled.

"I know, I know…onward."

Haedemus took off at a gallop, forcing me to grip his

mane tight so I didn't fall off. No doubt the bastard knew what he was doing by going so fast on my first ride, but I wasn't going to give him the satisfaction of telling him to slow down. So as he sped through the yard in the black of night, I did my best to lean with him into the corners without overdoing it and sliding off. Soon, the front gates loomed up ahead, and I told him to slow down so I could get off and open them, but instead, he sped up, and before I knew what was happening, he was leaping into the air and we were jumping right over the top of the twelve-foot steel gates.

When we landed, Haedemus didn't miss a beat, taking off up the street like a bullet as I did my best to steer him in the direction we wanted to go in. Luckily for us all, traffic was sparse at this hour. If the streets were more congested, I'm sure I wouldn't have coped as well with the handling.

"Your city seems like a shit hole," Haedemus said, galloping through the neon-spiked darkness as downtown sought release for all the tension it built up during the day. Cabarets, nightclubs, and trendy bars operated at full capacity right next to fancy restaurants, theaters, cinemas, and the opera houses. Diners, coffee shops, and food stands lined the overcrowded plazas where live events took place. There was entertainment for everyone. Private parties with expensive drugs and high-class prostitutes were commonplace, but the backstage of the city's most flamboyant district had even darker, stranger pursuits to offer, which Haedemus had picked up on. "It wouldn't be out of place in Hell."

"Just keep your eyes on the road," I said.

"Why of course, Ethan."

21

When we reached my apartment building, I brought Haedemus to a halt in the middle of the street as I looked around for unmarked police cars, but saw none. I recognized most of the vehicles that were parked up along the side of the road, and all of them were empty.

Just to be sure, I rode Haedemus up the full length of the street as I checked the cars, before coming back down again and stopping outside my building once more. "I thought Striker would be having the place watched," I said.

"Maybe he thinks you wouldn't be stupid enough to come here," Walker said.

"He doesn't know me very well then." I dismounted the Hellicorn and stood looking around for a moment, half expecting a horde of armed cops to come streaming out of somewhere now that I was no longer concealed by Haedemus' invisibility, but no one came. The street was deserted. Even the dealers had gone home. The only other person present was Jed the homeless guy who was busy snoring among a pile of rags and old newspapers.

"I'll come up with you, just in case," Walker said as she got off the Hellicorn.

"You just want to check out my apartment."

She smiled. "Maybe."

"We won't be long," I said to Haedemus. "Shout if you see anything suspicious."

"Such as?" he said.

"Like cops. You know what cops are?"

He snorted. "Yes, I know what cops are. In Hell, I've heard every possible aspect of your human culture whined over, discussed, dissected, and by turns revered and denigrated to the nth degree by millions of damned souls over countless millennia. So much so I could write a fucking book about it all, fifty fucking books, a hundred fucking—"

"Okay, he gets it," Walker said.

"At least you aren't lumbered with all your memories and knowledge," he said, looking at Walker now. "Most of yours remained in Hell with your physical body. You didn't even have the good grace to just summon my spirit here, you had to drag me here in this decaying physical form that I've had to put up with for so very long now."

"It was your physical form I needed," she said. "Not your spirit."

"All I'm saying is, I could've possessed the body of some stunning steed somewhere by now, and then I'd be back to who I used to be."

"You're never going back to your past life, Haedemus," Walker said. "None of us are. We are what we are now in this new world."

"Suck it up, big guy," I said, a slight smile on my face. "The world is now your oyster."

"Fuck you, Ethan." Haedemus turned his head away. "Fuck you."

Leaving Haedemus to his bitter resignation, Walker and I went up to my apartment to find the Hellbastards crowded onto the couch, suspiciously quiet as they glumly watched a re-run of *The Muppet Show*. It was only when I got closer to the couch did I notice one of them was missing. "Where's Khullu?" I asked them.

They all stared at me with sad faces, or as sad as monstrous little demons can look. "He's dead," Scroteface said, causing Cracka to screech mournfully and burst into floods of tears, which to be honest, was more comical than sad.

"What happened?"

"The man on the roof killed him."

"Striker," I said, silently cursing his name.

"He strong," Scroteface said. "He uses his power to bang Khullu off wall over and over. I try to stop him but couldn't."

"Fuck's sake," I said, not knowing what else to say.

"We miss Khullu." Cracka wailed like a child who'd just lost his little brother in a tragic accident.

"I'm sorry, boys," I said.

"We want to kill Striker," Scroteface said.

"Rip him apart," Reggie said.

"Take head off," Toast said.

"And shit down his neck," Snot Skull added.

"He fucking dead!" Cracka screamed, the tears still spilling from his wide, bright green eyes. "He dead. He so fucking dead..."

"Alright," I said. "Calm down, boys. You'll get your revenge. Just gimme a little time."

They all looked at me like that wasn't good enough, but Scroteface said, "Okay, boss," which seemed to subdue them a little. They went back to watching the TV, barely acknowledging Walker's presence in the apartment. I opened the bedroom door and went inside with Walker, closing the door after her. "That was awkward," she said as she began to look around the room.

"Yeah," I said, annoyed if not fully upset Striker had killed one of my Hellbastards. I mean, they're just demons here to do my bidding, but you can't help but get attached to the little bastards. Khullu especially was one of the more well-behaved ones.

"I'm sorry about your Hellbastard. How long have you had them?"

"A while."

"They're a real annoyance in Hell. Like delinquent children."

"I've no doubt. They come in useful, though."

"They saved your ass on that roof."

"Like I said, they come in useful."

"You okay, Ethan?" she asked, looking at me now.

"Sure." I nodded. "Just thinking about Routman if you want the truth. It's not sitting well with me that he sent an innocent woman to her death just to close a case."

"What are you going to do about it?"

"I'm not sure yet. Let's contain the current crisis first before moving on to Routman."

"So why are we here then?" She took down glass containers from the shelves, smelling the contents, recoiling at most of them.

"I need a spirit bottle," I said as I began to rummage through a rack of freestanding shelves in the corner of the room. "To trap the Litchghin in."

"Then what?" she asked, her attention turned to the guns now, picking up an AR-15 to examine.

"Then it gets burned in Hell Fire, which will destroy it, I hope."

Soon, I found what I was looking for. A bottle not much bigger than a coke bottle, made from glass stained the color of blood and sealed with a cork. Inside, a dark red energy swirled. I acquired three of the bottles from a witch I took down years ago. The bottle in my hand was the last one I had left, having used the other two already. Putting the spirit bottle in my trench pocket, I crossed the room and took down the jar of Mud to refill the dropper bottle while Walker handled some of the blades I had lying around.

"Why do you use that stuff?" she asked as I filled the dropper bottle and she stood holding a wide blade made from scrap metal that resembled a machete, but with a jagged edge down one side.

"The Mud? I just do. It gets me through is all."

"Through what? Your grief?"

I nodded. "I guess."

"I'm sorry about your family." Walker put a hand on my shoulder that I didn't want there, so I shrugged it off and turned away from her.

"Let's go," I said, refusing to look at her face as I held the door open for her, locking it behind her as she stood in the living room waiting and looking over at the still subdued Hell-bastards, who I addressed before leaving. "Sit tight, boys. I may need you at some stage."

"To kill Striker?" Scroteface asked as they all looked at me with hope on their faces.

"We'll see," I said.

After leaving the apartment, I got as far as the stairs when my phone rang, which reminded me of the fact that I should've tossed it by now, as it was probably being tracked by the techies back at the precinct. Despite not recognizing the number, I answered anyway. "Yeah?" I said, half expecting Striker to be on the other end.

"Detective Drake?" a woman's voice said.

"Yeah? Who's this?" I said, glancing at Walker as I paused in the stairwell, my eyes going to the spot where I beat the shit out of Jarvis Heath. On the wall, I could see tiny flecks of blood still.

"It's Jacklyn Turner."

"Ms. Turner. Why are you calling?"

"You said to call if I heard from Troy. I just did." She sounded upset as if she'd spent the whole night crying. To be honest, I didn't know why she was calling me of all people. Didn't she know I was a wanted felon?

"Why aren't you calling the detectives in charge of the case?"

"I don't trust that Routman guy," she said. "Or any other cop. They all want my son dead."

She was right there. "And what makes you think I don't?"

"Do you?"

"No, of course not. Your son made a stupid mistake when he meddled with things he shouldn't have. We've all been there. He doesn't deserve to die for it."

She sighed with what sounded like relief. "I'm glad to hear you say that. I knew I could trust you. I knew Angela. She was a good woman, a good doctor." She paused. "Is it true what they're saying about you, Detective? That you're a murderer? That you killed that little girl?"

"Do you believe your son to be possessed, Ms. Turner?"

"Yes," she said after a pause. "There's no way he could do what they said he did otherwise. He's just a child."

"Well, you have your answer. I didn't kill any little girl."

"I'm finding all this hard to take in, but I just want my son back, so I'm willing to trust you. Can you bring him in alive?"

"I'll try my best," I said. "That's all I can promise you."

She sniffed back tears. "That'll have to do."

"Did you hear from him?"

"He just called me," she said. "He told me he subdued whatever creature was inside him, long enough to call me. He told me he was sorry, and that he loved me. Oh God, this is all my fault for leaving him alone too much, for treating my job as more important, for—"

"Calm down, Ms. Turner," I said, glancing at Walker, who stood staring at me. "Did Troy tell you where he is?"

"Yes," she said, getting control of herself again. "He said he's at a nightclub across the river on Bayside, near the docks. Some place called The Dripping Fang. I've never heard of it."

"I have."

"He said there would be a massacre if no one stops him. My son will kill again, Detective. You have to stop him before he does."

As soon as I hung up, I looked at the old school flip phone in my hand and then snapped it in half before dropping it to the floor and stamping on it, breaking it to pieces. It was probably too late anyway. They probably already had my location back at the precinct. "Come on," I said to Walker as I headed down the stairs. "We have a lead on Troy."

"Where is he?" she asked as she followed me down the stairs.

"At a vamp club in Bayside."

"A vampire club?"

"Makes sense. If the Litchghin needs an abundance of supernatural energy, a vamp club would be a good place to get it. We need to get over there and stop a massacre."

"I didn't think you cared what happened to a bunch of vampires."

"I don't, but we can't let the Litchghin get the energy it needs to open a portal so all of its friends can get through and destroy this place." We were in the downstairs hallway, and I opened the door to go back outside. "Besides, I told Troy's mother I would try to save him and—" I stopped dead when I got outside to the street.

"What?" Walker said as she came out behind me and then saw what I saw. "Oh."

It was Haedemus. He stood on the sidewalk over Jed the homeless guy, busy munching on a long length of intestine that he'd obviously just pulled out of Jed's belly. The Hellicorn stopped chewing for a second to look at us, then said, "What? I was hungry."

"Fucking hell." I walked over to see old Jed splayed out in his pile of rags and newspapers, which were now all covered in blood.

"I speared him through the chest," Haedemus said as he sucked up the remainder of the intestine like a long piece of spaghetti. "He died quick."

"Oh, well that's alright then." I shook my head as I stared down at Jed, thinking, *Poor bastard.*

"This man's flesh is absolutely pickled in alcohol," Haedemus said, just before he nuzzled his snout into Jed's open belly and pulled out what looked like a spleen, which he chewed a few times, blood squirting from his mouth before he swallowed the organ down. "It gives the meal a nice kick, I have to say."

As Haedemus used his long tongue to lick the blood from his decaying lips, I started to try to cover up Jed's body with what was lying around. I'd have to get the Hellbastards to dispose of it later. "You couldn't have waited?" I said as I placed a sheet of bloodstained newspaper over Jed's face.

"Hey," Haedemus said, not amused that I was covering up his meal. "I haven't finished yet. I was looking forward to eating his heart. It's always my favorite part. That and the brains."

"It might be easier if you just turn vegetarian," I told him. "Go back to eating grass like you used to."

"Believe me," Haedemus said. "I wish I could, but my physiology won't allow it. My indomitable spirit needs a new body to house it." He looked at Walker. "And since you brought me back here, I think you should try to arrange that for me. Mistress."

"I'll see what I can do," Walker said. "In the meantime, no more eating of random people please."

"Can I just have another little morsel?" he asked.

"No, you can't," I said. "We gotta go now, anyway."

Grabbing his mane, I pulled myself up on to him, and

then helped Walker up. "I don't care if your belly is full, ride like the fucking wind," I told him. "We have a massacre to stop."

"Oh, a massacre," Haedemus said. "Yummy."

"Just get moving," I said, and we headed off toward the docks.

22

The Dripping Fang is the biggest vampire club in the city, one of the only ones, in fact. Vampires have a presence here, but there aren't as many as you might think.

Since the influx of Fallen, the vamps have kept a low profile, mostly sticking with their own kind, running with whatever political faction they happen to belong to. The only time they all get together is at places like The Dripping Fang. A lot of humans hang out there as well. Feeders mostly—people who offer their blood to vamps in the hope that one day they too will become one of them.

Sometimes a body would turn up, washed ashore after being dumped in the ocean, the victim of a feeding gone too far. These deaths were investigated, but no one was ever held accountable for them. As far as the cops were concerned, these washed-up bodies were just another random murder victim. I knew different, of course, but even if I wanted to pursue the case, it was pointless.

Vampires were good at protecting their own, and even if you did find the one who did it, they wouldn't be in custody for very long before some fancy lawyer had them out, or failing that, vital evidence went mysteriously missing.

Such was the way of the supernatural fraternity in this city, and indeed, all over the world.

"Wow," Haedemus said when we finally reached Bayside. He had stopped dead on a hill that afforded a view of not only the sprawling docks but of the vast ocean beyond. "There's something I never thought I'd ever see again. Clear, blue ocean. The oceans in Hell only consist of shit, blood, piss, cum, sweat, menstrual fluid, spit, pus, aborted bab—"

"Yeah, we get it," I said. "It's all very lovely. Maybe later we can take a walk along the beach, what do you think?"

Haedemus craned his head back to look at me. "Can we? Don't tease me now."

"I think Ethan is being sarcastic," Walker said, her small hands resting on my thighs.

"I don't care," Haedemus said. "If there's a beach, I'm going to it. I bet they have pretty ponies there, do they? Donkeys perhaps? Those guys are funny. I remember once—"

"Jesus fuck," I said. "Didn't I say we have a fucking massacre to stop?" I banged my boots against his side. "Get going."

"Nope," he said. "Not until you promise me a trip to the beach."

Closing my eyes for a second, I tried to contain my frustration. "Okay, sure. You win, we'll all hit the beach later with a picnic and a good book. How's that?"

"You don't mean it," he said. "You're just humoring me. I can tell."

"Of course I fucking am. With everything going on, I don't foresee a trip to the beach in our immediate future. A trip to jail maybe, or the fucking graveyard, but not the beach."

"This world has been such a disappointment so far," he said. "A beach trip would really help matters. I'm just saying."

"Jesus," I said to Walker. "Help me out here, will ya?"

Walker leaned around me and said something in Hellion,

making Haedemus neigh in frustration. "I mean it," she added.

"Fine, Mistress, fine," he conceded. "Have it your way…as always."

"What was that?" Walker said.

"Nothing, Mistress. I thought since we aren't in Hell anymore, that things would change, that we might be equals now instead of—"

"Fuck, enough," I shouted. "Get moving, or I swear to god, I'll break your fucking horn off and shove it up your ass."

"I'd like to see you try…Ethan."

"Haedemus." Walker shouted in Hellion again. "Move it."

After huffing for another moment, Haedemus finally started moving again, galloping down the street as I steered him toward the nightclub we were heading to.

The club itself is a converted church nestled between empty row houses about half a mile from the shipyards. The area was once a bustling community until the vamps moved in, driving most people away over time, buying up the property in their wake, making sure no one else could move into the area, no one human anyway. As a result, the vamps had a few square miles of Bayside to themselves, which they used to house their various businesses. The Menesis Clan were most prominent in the Bayside, being the biggest vamp faction in the city, but there were other clans dotted around, albeit with smaller enclaves, with most being subservient to the Menesis Clan, who were also the oldest vamps in town.

Despite dawn being right around the corner, when we got to the club, there were vamps running out of the place in a panic, most of them scared shitless it seemed.

Which was saying something, because I've never known a vamp to fear anything but sunlight, and yet here they were, willing to expose themselves to it if it meant escaping the club and getting far away from the source of their terror.

A sixteen-year-old kid, laughably enough.

"I guess Troy is already in there," Walker said as I pulled Haedemus to a stop on the street outside the club. The vamps running around, being MURKs, could see Haedemus clearly, but few of them even acknowledged the fearsome beast as they ran around us to get to their blacked-out cars, which were parked up and down the length of the street. Just outside the huge wooden doors, I saw a few piles of ash on the ground, indicating that Troy—or the Litchghin inside him—had already sucked the energy from a few vamps. Not that the other's cared, who tramped through the ashes on their way out, scattering dust everywhere.

Jumping down off the Hellicorn, I grabbed hold of a young goth-looking vamp who was about to rush past me. "Is he in there?" I asked him.

"He's just a kid," the vamp said with fear and confusion on his deathly pale face. "I don't get it; he shouldn't be able to hurt us—"

"It's not just a kid," I said as if it mattered.

"What is he then?" the vamp asked as more of his kind swarmed around us.

"Your worst nightmare apparently," I said. "Now off you go before I kill you myself." The vamp gave me a look and ran off across the street. "I fucking hate bloodsuckers. I'd be happy enough to let this Litchghin kill them all."

"Then you'd be killing everybody," Walker said.

"I know," I said. "Maybe that's not a bad thing either."

"You don't mean that."

"So you think." I took the spirit bottle from my pocket and held it. "Come on. Let's go and get this thing."

"I'll just wait here, shall I?" Haedemus said. "Let me know if there's any food in there. I'm still hungry. I never got to finish my meal. Oh wait, you already know that because it's *your* fucking fault I didn't get to finish it."

Walking toward the front doors of the club with Walker, I said, "Was he this mouthy in Hell?"

"Pretty much," Walker said. "He carries a lot of resentment."

"Don't we all?"

Dark techno still blared as we walked inside the club, red and green laser lights cutting through the darkness of the arched interior, substantial stained-glass windows illuminated by under-lighting. A fog of dry ice was everywhere, to the point where you could hardly see a few feet in front of you. Whoever had been operating the machine must've just abandoned it and left it running on max output.

Despite the smoke, however, we could see that there were only a handful of vamps left inside the place, most of them standing around the edges of the large dance floor as they warily eyed Troy, who was standing in the middle of the floor surrounded by piles of ash, looking like he'd been rolling around in abattoir he had so much blood on him. By the looks of things, he had drained and killed maybe two dozen vamps so far, and his body was so full of energy he was giving off a bluish glow as if the Litchghin inside him was about to burst free.

"Troy," I shouted over the music, and he turned around slowly to stare at me, his eyes no longer human, but glowing intensely from all the energy he had inside him.

"I don't think that's Troy anymore," Walker said as the music continued to pound in the background, the fucking deejay having bolted as well, apparently.

"Be careful," I told her. "This thing feeds on MURKs, and you're one of them."

"Thanks for pointing that out."

Ignoring her, I started toward Troy. "I know what you are," I said, addressing the Litchghin. "And I know what you're doing here. Why don't you leave the kid's body and come out and talk to me?"

I didn't expect it, but the Litchghin did precisely that, bursting from Troy's body in a flash of light. As Troy fell to the floor—dead or unconscious, I couldn't tell—the Litchghin, electric blue and human in shape, floated about six feet into the air as it looked down on me.

Thatta boy, I thought. *That'll make it easier for me to trap you in the bottle.*

"Do you think you are going to stop me with that trinket in your hand?" the Litchghin said, its voice strangely calm and soothing considering its blatant antagonism.

"This thing?" I held up the spirit bottle. "I just brought this because I was thirsty." I raised the bottle to my lips and feigned drinking from it, even though the cork was still on it.

"You take me for a fool," the Litchghin said, its incorporeal form shuddering with emotion it seemed. "Compared to me, you are nothing but an insignificant insect. You call yourselves humans—children of God—but you have no inkling of what it means to be truly human and to have reached your full potential."

"And you do?" I edged closer to the Litchghin as it continued to hover in the air. "You've supposedly reached your full potential, but yet you still display the same selfish, antagonistic traits as all the chumps in this place. Plus, if you think you're so special, why did your precious God try to wipe your kind from existence?"

The Litchghin's body turned a darker shade of blue as if in an angry response, just an outline in the darkness now as the red and green laser lights cut through it at sharp angles.

"You know not of what you speak," it said. "God tried to wipe us out to spite Lucifer, our real Creator. God could not abide by the fact his second-in-command did a better job than He in creating us. Compared to us, the creatures of this world are nothing more than cast-offs. Even God Himself has abandoned you." The Litchghin floated down toward the floor, coming to rest a foot or so above it, its eyes glowing with blue fire. "This world belongs to us, the Litchghin. We are the true heirs of this great garden that you have so shamelessly wasted and poisoned, and we intend to make it great again."

"That's admirable," I said, edging forward another few inches, so there was only five or six feet of distance between us now. "If it weren't for the fact that you intend to kill everyone here first."

"Think of it as a mercy," it said. "A necessary cleansing. It's more than you wicked beings deserve."

"Think of this as a mercy as well then," I said, uncorking the bottle and releasing the luminous purple energy from inside, which shot toward the Litchghin like metal to a magnet, embedding itself within the Litchghin's body.

I then followed this up with the words, "*Et spiritum tuum captionem intra utrem*," which I repeated three times before placing the bottle on the floor in front of me.

The Litchghin let out a loud screech as the energy from the spirit bottle played havoc with its own alien make up, distending and pulling the Litchghin's form out of shape until bursts of energy began to fly from it in all directions, some of which hit the vamps who were still standing around, turning them to piles of ash before they could even scream their protest.

Before when I'd used a spirit bottle, the entity I'd been trying to trap had been sucked into the bottle almost immediately after I'd said the words of power.

The Litchghin, however, appeared to be stronger than those other entities, able to resist the pull of the spirit bottle long enough to get itself back inside Troy's body.

"Shit," I said as Troy stood, his eyes glowing with pure malevolence as he glared at me.

"It didn't work," Walker said from beside me.

"No shit, Sherlock."

The few vamps that were left inside the club used their supernatural speed to exit the place in seconds, so it was just me and Walker left behind.

"You'll pay for your foolishness," Troy—the Litchghin—shouted from across the dance floor. "You'll all pay."

"What now?" Walker asked me.

To be honest, I wasn't sure. It was hard to tell if the Litchghin had simply absorbed the energy from the spirit bottle—and thus neutralized it somehow—or if it was still fighting against the magic that threatened to pull it inside the waiting bottle.

When Troy's skinny body began to jerk and shudder in a grotesque way under the strobe lighting that had now come on, I guessed—I hoped—that the energy from the spirit bottle was still doing its job, despite the Litchghin fighting against it.

In fact, the struggle going on within was so great that his physical form simply couldn't take it anymore. It was too much power for a puny human body to contend with, and Troy literally came apart at the seams. His head detached itself from his neck with a tearing sound that was heard over the music. His arms and legs also got ripped from his torso as easily as a fly's pulled by human fingers. In the gaps between the bloody stumps of his limbs and the ragged holes of his torso burned the raging energy of the Litchghin, the only thing that was still holding Troy's body together now.

The Litchghin's face then stretched from out of Troy's face as if to peer out at us.

"Nothing is going to stop me from what I came here to do," the Litchghin bellowed, its voice distorted, louder even than the music. "My kind will rule again."

"What's it doing?" Walker asked as the Litchghin turned its head toward the ceiling, and with a cry, unleashed all the energy it had been collecting since possessing Troy's body. A torrent of raging blue light burst up through the ceiling of the club, punching a hole in it before shooting up into the dark sky outside.

"It's doing what it came here to do and opening a fucking portal," I said. "So the other Litchghins can breach."

"We have to stop it," Walker said, and before I could do anything, she rushed past me toward the raging pillar of energy that was the Litchghin.

"Walker, no!" I shouted, but she was already gone, picking up the spirit bottle, holding it out in front of her as she repeated the words of power I had spoken earlier.

"God damn it." Without thinking, I rushed forward as well, coming to stand next to her as we both now spoke the words of power, the Litchghin too preoccupied with unleashing its collected energy to even try to defend itself. "Put the bottle on the floor."

Walker put the bottle back down, and no more than a few seconds later, Troy's dismembered body hit the deck as the Litchghin's energy got sucked into the bottle, triumphant laughter echoing in its wake.

As soon as all the Litchghin's energy was inside the bottle, I jammed the cork in and sealed it, the Litchghin along with it. I was about to reprimand Walker for her foolish bravery when I heard the sound of slow clapping behind me, the club in silence now that the music had stopped playing.

Turning around, I was only half surprised to see Striker standing there on the edge of the dance floor, and he wasn't alone. Beside him hovered the wavering spirit of Astaroth.

"Well done, Detectives," Striker said, a smug smile on his face. "But it looks like you were a little too late. The portal is now open."

Turning around and looking up through the gaping hole in the ceiling, I saw that Striker was right. In the night sky, a swirling luminous portal had formed from the blue energy released by the Litchghin, creating a doorway to the Litchghin's dark, forgotten world. "Shit."

Before I knew it, Astaroth's smoky form was hovering in front of me, his burning yellow eyes on me.

"The Litchghins are on their way," he said. "I can feel them. Soon they will flood into this world and destroy everyone in it, or you humans at least. But I can stop them, Ethan. I can close the portal and save everyone from dying."

"Let me guess," I said. "All I have to do is submit to you and you'll close the portal."

"That's right," Astaroth said. "Submit to me now, give me your body, and I will save this world from destruction."

"Why should I?"

His spirit became motionless for a long second. "What?"

I stepped toward the demon. "What makes you think I give a shit about this world and the people in it? Maybe we all deserve what's coming. And besides," I said, taking another step closer until his shifting form was right in front of me, "you probably need this world more than I do. You have more to gain from it than I do. Me, I got fuck all left to gain."

"Don't be stupid," Striker said, coming to stand next to his Dark Lord now. "You would see this entire world destroyed just out of spite? What about all the good people here? You would see them die, all because of your foolish pride?"

I didn't need to see his self-satisfied smile to know that the bastard had me beat. He was right. As much as I hated this world sometimes, I wasn't about to allow everyone in it to die, making myself a bigger monster than either of the two evil fucks before me.

As I touched the locket in my pocket, I pictured Callie, her sweet smile and innocent eyes. There were millions of kids out there just like her, and every one of them would be killed as surely as Callie was. If I ever crossed paths with my angel again, she would never forgive me for not saving everyone when I had the chance.

Reaching into my pocket, I took out the bottle of Mud and emptied all of its contents into my mouth, tossing away the empty bottle when I was done. It wasn't like I was going to need it again anyway.

"Close the portal," I said to Astaroth. "And you can have my body."

"Ethan—" Walker said.

"Take the spirit bottle to Cal's," I told her. "Make sure it gets destroyed."

There were tears in her eyes as she started to shake her head. "But—"

"Just do it." I gave her a tight smile which I'm sure was cold comfort.

"Grant me permission," Astaroth said. "Open yourself up to me."

"I just said fucking yes," I said, a curious mix of anger and despair going through me now. I was going to miss being alive more than I thought, I realized. A lot more. "Take me. Fucking do it, you cunt."

There was a rush of wind as Astaroth's spirit entered my body, followed by an unbelievable cold that seeped into every inch of me.

For a few brief seconds, I was a part of the demon's consciousness. I felt his elation at finally having a physical body strong enough to contain him, and I felt his aeons of memories as they flooded into me, glimpses of the celestial Heavens and their utter beauty, glimpses of Hell and its absolute horror, all that he had seen and done since coming to Earth, and then—

Nothing.

23

When I came to, I did so into something akin to a dream state. I was still inside the nightclub, but I was now hovering a dozen feet above the ground as if I was made of nothing but air. When I looked at my hands, I saw they were translucent and ghost-like, and I soon realized that's what I was now.

A ghost. A dead person. A disembodied soul.

Already the pull of the Void was tugging on my intangible form, trying to pull me toward it so it could welcome me into its cold, dark embrace, just like it had done to all the other billions of souls that floated there.

Below me, I saw my own physical body, now possessed by Astaroth, who was standing tall and punching the air as if in victory. By the looks of things, he had closed the portal opened by the Litchghin.

At least this wasn't for nothing, I thought.

"This vessel is even more magnificent than I thought it would be," he said in my voice, which sounded like it was coming from far away. "Such strength and power for a mere human."

"Even more so now, Dark Lord." Striker was on his knees

in front of his master, a fawning smile on his face now that his Dark Lord was here with him in the flesh at last. "There will be no stopping us now."

"There will be no stopping *me*," Astaroth corrected him. "Know your place, Hellot."

"Yes, Dark Lord," Striker said, bowing his head in reverence, the slimy fuck. "My sincerest apologies."

Through all the smoke still hanging around the place, I saw no sign of Walker. She must've had the good sense to hightail it as soon as Astaroth possessed me. He would've killed her otherwise.

"So, what now, Dark Lord?" Striker asked, still on his knees.

"Now, I put my plans into action. Now we enslave the pathetic souls here and use their power to—" He stopped as a noise from behind him caught his attention.

I turned myself around and peered into the thick smoke surrounding everything. Both of the huge doors to the club had been flung open, and something was now moving through the dense smoke, something that appeared to be traveling at great speed.

So fast in fact that it sucked the smoke behind it as it moved.

To get a better look, I dropped down toward the floor behind Striker and Astaroth, who were both staring in the direction of the displaced smoke.

Now I could see a large black shape moving across the dance floor, and I soon realized it was Haedemus, his head down as he barreled toward Astaroth, who merely stood there as a look of shock and disbelief came over his face.

For it wasn't just Haedemus coming toward him, it was also an illuminated, celestial being of such magnificence, it was difficult to even look at it without becoming blinded by its sheer unadulterated beauty. It was a vision of radiant light coming from a perfectly proportioned androgynous human form, adorned with shining metal armor that radiated a light all of its own.

Spread out on the celestial being's back where two massive, feathered wings that shone so brightly I could hardly look at them.

Between the Hellicorn and the celestial being riding it, they represented the perfect marriage between Heaven and Hell, between Darkness and Light. If I could've cried, I probably would have, especially when I knew the celestial being riding atop Haedemus was none other than Walker, or rather, the angel she once was.

Adrielis.

How she had regained her former celestial glory, I had no idea.

Nor, it seemed, did Astaroth, who could only stand there frozen to the spot as he gazed upon the vision of darkness and light barreling toward him. Maybe Adrielis reminded Astaroth of the celestial being he once was himself; maybe that's why he appeared so stricken by the angel.

In any case, Astaroth never moved from the path of his oncoming death, despite Striker pulling at him. A second later, Haedemus' razor-sharp horn was driven through Astaroth's chest—through *my* chest—in a burst of blood, at which point Astaroth's spirit exploded from my body, letting loose a torturous howl before his smoky form dissipated into nothingness, leaving only heavy silence in his wake.

"NO…" Striker howled as he fell to his knees again, not in reverence this time, but in despair.

For not only was his Dark Lord no more—consigned to the endless Void with the billions of other souls—but so were the powers Astaroth had bestowed upon him.

Striker was now as vulnerable as any other human, a fact that made me smile with satisfaction, even though my physical body was now just dead meat hanging off the horn of a Hell beast like a carcass in a butcher's shop.

At my core, I felt the pull of the Void again, harder and more insistent this time. Soon an invisible cord began to pull me back through the air, taking me away from the scene on the ground.

It was truly over for me.

And there was no going back.

My soul belonged to the Void now.

There was no emotion involved in realizing this. It just was, and that was it.

Thanks, Walker, I thought, as I drifted further away from her angelic form and my own dead body.

Soon, the blackness began to close in around me…

And then there was nothing again.

24

A huge gasp left me as I sucked air into my lungs. I thought I'd arrived in the Void until I realized there wasn't darkness around me, but light. Then I felt the physical form of my body and the hardness of whatever I was lying on. Opening my eyes, I saw a figure leaning over me.

"Walker?" My voice cracked with dryness. Clearly dying had made me a little parched.

"It's me," Walker said smiling, tears glinting in her eyes. "You're alive."

"What the fuck is going on?" I sat up, realizing I was still inside the nightclub. Reaching into my trench pocket, I felt the locket still in there and almost sighed with relief. Then I took out my hip flask and swallowed what was left in it, feeling better once the alcohol hit my system. My blood-drenched shirt had been ripped open, exposing my chest. The hole made by Haedemus' horn wasn't there anymore. Not even a scar. "I don't understand—"

"There's not much to understand," a voice said, and out of the smoke, Haedemus appeared, his huge head hanging over me, my own blood still dripping from his jagged horn. "She saved you."

"I knew it was you," I said to Walker. "You rode in here like a fucking angelic badass and killed that motherfucker Astaroth." I managed a smile. "You continue to surprise me, Walker."

"Actually, that was *me*," Haedemus said, flushed with pride. "*She* just rode me. It was this boney bad boy on my noggin that did the damage. Mistress here thought her blindingly good looks would be enough to just bowl that dicky demon over. I mean, please," he scoffed. "Fucking angels need to leave the killing to the professionals, am I right?" He then turned to look at Walker. "I like you better as a demon. You're less…bright. If you'd warned me, I'd've brought my sunglasses."

"You did good, Haedemus," Walker said.

Haedemus stared, seemingly gob smacked for a change. "I think I'm going to cry…"

"Please don't," I said. "I'm not sure I could handle a crying Hellicorn right now." When Haedemus turned dramatically away, I looked at Walker. "How did you—?"

"I prayed," she said.

"Prayed?"

"Yes. I prayed to the Maker to restore me to my former glory as a celestial being so I could save you."

"And He…answered you?"

She smiled. "I was able to become who I once was and heal you. I guess He answered, in a way."

I nodded as if I understood. "So it wasn't really God, it was just you. You tapped your own power, that's all."

Walker shook her head as she held out her hand to help me up. "Always the cynic, even after your soul almost departed completely."

"You dug deep, Walker, that's all. Either way, I appreciate it." I looked around at the empty club. "Where's Striker?"

"He ran off."

Asshole.

"He's powerless now anyway," I said, knowing I would catch up to him soon. "Where's the spirit bottle?"

"In a safe place outside."

"We need to get it and destroy it."

"What about Troy?" she asked.

I looked over at Troy's dismembered body, still lying on the dance floor in pieces. Staring at him, all I could think about was his mother and the utter pain she would feel when she found out her only son was dead, especially after me telling her I would try to save him. "Can't you become Adrielis again and put him back together?"

Walker shook her head. "I don't think I can."

"Why not?"

"I don't even know where that power came from."

"So much for God then."

"Ethan, that's not what—"

"Let's get out of here," I said, cutting her off, probably saving her the discomfort of trying to explain something she knew she couldn't explain. "I'll call this in when we leave if someone hasn't already. Striker will no doubt try to pin Troy's death on me."

"How you gonna deal with him?"

I went to Haedemus and climbed up on to him, then held my hand out for her take, pulling her up behind me. "I have a plan to deal with Striker, don't worry." I tapped the Hellicorn's sides with my heels. "Onwards, Haedemus."

"Yes, Sir Lancelot," Haedemus said. "And perhaps, since we're not far away, we can hit the beach for a little while before—"

"No."

"Fine," Haedemus muttered. "Ungrateful bastard."

Upon leaving the nightclub, we rode hard through the

streets as the early morning light shone down over the city, making the streets seem gray and washed out. No doubt the vamps would be pissed about what happened at their club, and at all the casualties because of it, but I didn't give a shit about what the vamps thought. They could clean their shitty club and make more vamps, so fuck them.

Troy Turner was dead and Humpty Dumpty—Adrielis in this case—couldn't put him back together again. Despite her claiming God helped her, I believe her sudden celestial powers were nothing more than the result of digging deep in a crisis. People have more power than they know, even fallen angels like Walker. All it takes is a bit of desperation in a life or death situation to bring it out of them. I was just glad a disaster had been averted, and that was good enough for me, even if I did almost die.

It wasn't the first time I'd almost died, and I was sure it wouldn't be last either.

I dropped Walker off at the scrap yard and told her to give the spirit bottle with the Litchghin in it to Cal. He would know what to do with it.

"What are you going to do?" she asked outside the trailer as I prepared to head for the Dodge that was still parked up near the gates.

"I'm going to deal with Striker," I said. "And get my damn badge back."

"Ethan?" she said as I went to walk away.

"Yeah?"

"God wants you alive, no matter what you say."

I shook my head. "More fool Him then."

"Very true, Ethan," Haedemus called as I walked away. "More fool him indeed."

Raising my arm as I continued walking, I gave Haedemus the finger.

25

As soon as I left the scrapyard, I drove the Dodge to Bankhurst across the river to pay a visit to a couple guys I know. They're both coke-addicted Technomancers who've used their skills to amass a small fortune between them.

They lived in the penthouse of a luxury apartment block, where they sat at their computers and listened to heavy metal all day while doing lines of coke and taking the occasional break just to get a blowjob from some high-class hooker they'd called in.

They also rarely slept, so even though it was barely seven a.m. they were both up and at it, death metal blasting as I walked into their penthouse after one of them let me in.

"Detective Drake," Pan Demic said, wired to the moon on coke and god knows what else as usual. Pan Demic was in his late twenties, with hair that hung to the small of his back. He wore a pair of black leather trousers and a black Punisher T-shirt. "How's my favorite pig doing? I mean cop doing."

"Fuck off." I walked in, well used to his complete lack of respect for any kind of authority. "I need a favor."

"Who's that?" Artemis said from his station in the center of the room. Artemis had long blonde hair and sort of reminded me of that geeky, bespectacled guy from *Wayne's World*. Artemis had done so much partying over the years that his body had that wasted, emaciated look. If he lived past thirty—if either of them fucking did—I'd be surprised.

"It's the Drakester," Pan Demic replied as he went straight back to his workstation next to Artemis.

"Drakester." Artemis waved at me over his shoulder, still typing with the other hand. "How's it hanging?"

"Fine," I all but shouted over the pummeling death metal blasting from the ludicrously priced speakers in the corners of the room. The penthouse should've been a pristine, light-filled bastion of art déco decadence worthy of any movie star.

But the place was more like a dungeon from some tacky theme park. The walls were painted black, the large windows covered by thick, dark curtains, the only light coming from dozens of lit candles spread around the place, and the glow of the computer monitors in the center of the living room. In one corner there was a coffin with a life-sized vampire inside.

In another corner, there was a stuffed werewolf, a real one I might add, bought at an underground auction. In its clawed hands, someone had placed a BC Rich guitar, and a studded collar around the werewolf's thick neck.

Much of the furniture in the massive penthouse was fashioned from skulls and bones, or carved from dark wood, like the two huge thrones aligned along the back wall, one of which had a Union Jack flag draped over it. One wall was also completely plastered with posters from metal and porn magazines.

Everywhere I looked, empty bottles sat and ashtrays brimmed over with cigarette butts and half-smoked joints.

The two of them reminded me of a couple teenagers hanging in their rich parent's place while their parents were off on vacation, only instead of just partying, they gave the whole fucking place a total makeover in the most tasteless way possible.

Not that they gave a fuck about good taste, or anything else beyond partying constantly and manipulating the technological ether with their freaky, but no less useful, skills.

I crossed paths with the two of them several years ago when they got caught up in a murder case as witnesses. I saved both their asses when the murderer—a cyber-gang boss—tried to have both of them permanently deleted. I ended up deleting the boss instead, and both these guys have been in my debt ever since.

They have proper names but they insist on using their hacker names at all times.

"Carcass," Artemis said.

"What?" I asked as I came to stand behind them and the large bank of computer screens they were stationed in front of.

"Carcass," he said again. "That's who's playing right now. Britain's greatest death metal export, along with Bolt Thrower and Napalm Death of course." He turned to look at Pan Demic as he started growling along to the music. "*Snorting the stench of latent effluvium, and maturing damp fumes. This foul ménage forces tears to your eyes, As the corpse's gas are exhumed....*"

Pan Demic, his face saying he was feeling every word, then picked up, "*Intoxicated by foul body odors, And the nauseating tepid whiff, Pinching your nostrils as you irrigate flatus, From the emaciated stiff...*"

When the screeching guitar solo came on, they both broke into a crazy display of air guitar and headbanging, Artemis's glasses flying off he was going at it so hard. When they were both done, they each did a line of coke from off a small mirror, before Pan Demic held the mirror out to me. "Breakfast?"

"I just ate," I said, taking out my cigarettes and lighting one up instead.

"Suit yourself," Pan Demic said, putting the mirror down and going back to tapping on his keyboard.

"So, what do you need from us?" Artemis said. "Deep

background again? Who is it this time? Saw your video by the way. Great stuff. You really know how to go viral. Shooting a kid in the head? Fucking genius, man. You should see some of the comments online. Some people think you should have your own movie. You thought about how you're gonna capitalize on your fame yet? I have a few ideas if you want to hear them. Just say the word and I'll rhyme them off right now—"

"You need to lay off the fucking toot," I said. "I have no interest in capitalizing on my infamy. That's why I'm here, in fact, I want you to change the narrative."

"What were you thinking?" Artemis said. "More *John Wick*, less *Dirty Harry*?"

"Neither," I said. "I want you to put out that the video is a deep fake. People will believe it."

"I know they will," Artemis said. "People believe whatever the fuck we tell them, right man?" He grinned at Pan Demic and they both fist-bumped. "Gullible assholes."

"Here's something you won't believe," Pan Demic said. "But it's true. Ninety percent of kids' cereals contain traces of LSD. I shit you not."

"And," Artemis said. "Have you ever noticed that in any state you go to, the trailer trash is always the same? That's because they're all clones of the same twenty people, part of a secret CIA plot to populate other nations with self-destructive idiots. They haven't gotten the exact formula and training down yet, so whenever a trailer park grows too large for its own good, they use local weather generators to send a tornado to destroy it."

"Listen to him," Pam Demic said, his eyes like saucers. "He's preaching truth. And here's some more fucking Ctrl+Alt+Truth for you. Hummingbirds aren't birds." He paused, eyes wide, as if for dramatic effect. "They're feathered insects. The science community has gone to insane lengths to keep this a secret. I fucking shit you not," he added, leaning down to do another line.

"Jesus," I said. "You two seriously need to get out more."

"Out is overrated, Drakester" Artemis said. "In is where it's at."

"Deep, man, really." Pan Demic held his hand up and Artemis high-fived him while typing with the other hand.

"Can you do something else for me?" I asked them. "If you get time in between all this deep and meaningful conversation, that is."

"Sure, Drakester," Artemis said. "You know we're only here to serve you, right?"

He seemed totally serious, though you could never be sure with these two. "That's good to know. I need you to leave a trail to someone's door."

"Oh, a trail," Artemis said, rubbing his hands together. "Intriguing. I love leaving trails. Makes me feel like a really crafty slug."

"Dude," Pan Demic said. "I can't get that image outta my brain now."

Artemis chuckled to himself before returning his attention to me. "So tell us, Drakester, who's gonna get slimed?"

"Striker," I said. "Detective John Striker."

I ENDURED ARTEMIS AND PAN DEMIC AND THEIR BLARING metal music for another hour or so before saying goodbye and driving to my apartment building.

There, I knocked on Daisy's door and her mother answered, who was just the person I wanted to see.

With me, I had the five grand from the car, and I handed it to her, telling her she was no longer a witness against me, despite what Striker told her about losing Daisy if she refused to co-operate.

"There's no case anymore," I told her. "The money is just for any inconvenience caused."

"Inconvenience?" she said after snatching the money from my hand. "You killed my fucking boyfriend, you pig."

"I have no idea what you're talking about."

~

THE NEXT STOP I MADE WAS TO STRIKER'S PLACE, HAVING GOT his address from Artemis earlier. Striker lived in an apartment building in Oak Ridge, overlooking Hudson Park. When I knocked on his door, he opened it and tried to quickly close it again when he saw it was me, but before he could, I put my shoulder into the door and broke the security chain, letting myself into the hallway.

When I got to the living room, Striker was waiting with a gun trained on me. "What do you want?" he asked. "Don't come any closer or I'll shoot."

"Put the damn gun down, Striker," I said as I sat on his couch. The minimalist apartment was immaculate, as I expected from an anal-retentive asshole like him. "Mind if I smoke?"

"Yes, actually."

"Thanks." I lit up a cigarette and blew the first stream of smoke in his direction. "We need to talk, Striker."

"There's nothing to talk about," he said with the gun still raised. "Despite what happened at that vamp club, you're still a wanted felon, Drake."

"Not for long."

"What does that mean?"

"It means your plan to take me down has failed."

"Bullshit," he spat. "Last time I checked, you shot a child and killed a man with your bare hands. Those charges still stand."

"Like I said, not for long."

"You're full of shit."

"Am I? Check your computer."

He frowned. "What for?"

"Just do it. I'll wait."

Striker hesitated for a further moment, before finally opening up the laptop that was sitting on the black coffee table. He kept the gun trained on me as he stared at the screen, his frown deepening with each passing second. "What is all this?" he said. "What are all these files? They aren't mine."

"Yes, they are," I said, flicking my ash on his spotless wood floor. "Those files show how you faked a video of me shooting a child in order to frame me."

"This is bullshit. It'll never hold up."

"Oh, I think it will. The files exist on your work computer as well. Don't try to delete them. You can't."

"This is how you're going to get me to back down?" he said, and then laughed. "Drake, I thought you were smarter than this."

"Before long, everyone will believe the video was faked," I said. "Then the question will be, who faked the video and why? All the evidence will point to a disgruntled IAB detective who tried to frame a veteran Homicide detective over a personal grudge."

"Personal grudge?"

"Yes, this veteran detective knew the IAB detective's secret, you see."

"Secret? What are you talking about?"

"There's a video in one of those files. Hit play."

I watched Striker as he hit play on the video. Within seconds, the color had drained from his face as he looked like he was going to be sick. "This—this isn't me," he said. "This is all fake, not to mention—"

"Sick?" I said. "I'm sure everyone who sees it will think so."

Anger reddened Striker's face, and he slammed the laptop closed, standing once more to point his gun at me. "I should just fucking shoot you right now," he said. "You're a wanted felon who broke into my apartment to kill me. I was defending myself. No one will question it."

"Kill me, and that video gets released online," I said. Standing, I ground my cigarette butt on his floor. "So, which is it, Striker? Kill me and then have the world know what a sick cunt you are, in which case you'll go to jail for the rest of your miserable life, or drop the case against me and no one is any the wiser?"

Striker wrestled with his decision for a minute. I could tell he wanted to shoot me, but I also knew he wouldn't. He knew too well the consequences. He also knew I had him. "How do I know you won't release the video anyway?"

"You don't," I said. "Just stay out of my fucking way, Striker, if you know what's good for you."

26

It didn't take long for the narrative created by Pan Demic and Artemis to spread online. Backing up the new narrative were videos posted to social media showing how easy it was to fake a video of anything.

Pretty soon, people didn't know what to believe, which was good enough for me, and the charges of murder against me were dropped because of insufficient evidence.

The few people who witnessed me shooting Astaroth in that little girl's body, I tracked down and did a memory jam on them, ensuring they no longer knew what they saw that day, leaving them with no choice but to retract their statements.

Striker also did what he was told, knowing I had him beat. Without his demonic powers and the support of his now-deceased Dark Lord, his former arrogance was now shattered. The DNA evidence he had against me was deemed unreliable, and all charges against me were dropped, leaving him with no choice but to hand me my badge back.

Once I was in the clear, I got a call from Commissioner Lewellyn. He explained he may have been a little hasty in disbanding Unit X, and that if I was still willing, he'd like me to keep heading it up. Lucky for him, he called me first. I had dirt on him, and I was going to use it to blackmail him into starting up the unit again. After he fucked me the first time, I had Artemis and Pan Demic find me something on him. I didn't like doing it, but you do what you gotta do, right?

A few days later, I bumped into Routman inside the precinct. It was the first time I'd seen him since he took over the scene at the Turner house that night. "You're back then," he said as we stood in the hallway next to the vending machine. "Only you, Ethan."

"Yeah," I said. "Only me. Sorry about Stokes."

"He was an asshole, but he didn't deserve what he got."

I begged to differ but didn't say so. "Listen, Jim," I said, leaning closer to him. "I know what you did."

Routman's gray eyes stared at me for a second, his face saying it all. "I'm not sure what you mean."

"I think you do. Barbara Keane. You fucking framed her."

A smile spread across Routman's face. "That's far-fetched, even for you."

"Don't bullshit me. We both know you did it, and we both know it wasn't the first time either."

"Do you have any proof of this?" he asked, and when I said nothing, he said, "Didn't think so," before walking away.

"Watch yourself, Jim," I called after him, but he never turned around.

Later, as I sat in my apartment with the Hellbastards watching re-runs of *The Muppet Show*, I got a call from Carlito. Sighing, I answered after the third ring, knowing full well why he was calling. "Carlito," I said. "What's up?"

"What's up?" he said. "Is that a joke?"

"No."

"I fucking hope not. Where's my head on a platter, Ethan? You know, the head you promised me?"

"I've been a little tied up lately," I said.

"I'm a patient man, Ethan, but I have my limits." He paused. "I hear you got your badge back."

"Yeah."

"Well, don't think you being a cop again is going to stop me doing what I gotta do, Ethan. I mean, we're friends and everything, but you also owe me a substantial debt, which means I gotta treat you like every other person who owes me. So unless you wanna go to war with me, Ethan, either pay up or bring me my fucking head on a platter. You got two days, then I stop being so friendly."

"Trouble, boss?" Scroteface said after Carlito hung up on me.

"Trouble?" I said, going back to watching the TV. "I guess we'll see, won't we?"

~

DON'T FORGET! VIP'S get advance notice of all future releases and projects. AND A FREE ETHAN DRAKE NOVELLA! Click the image or join here: www.npmartin.com

Ethan Drake returns in book 2, Blood Summoned. Turn the page for an excerpt or GET THE BOOK ONLINE NOW.

MAKE A DIFFERENCE

For an indie author like myself, reviews are the most powerful tool I have to bring attention to my books. I don't have the financial muscle of the big traditional publishers, but I can build a group of committed and loyal readers...readers' just like you!

Honest reviews of my books help bring them to the attention of other readers.

If you've enjoyed this book, I would be very grateful if you could spend just five minutes leaving a review (which can be as short as you like) on my book's Amazon page by clicking below.

And if you're still not motivated to leave a review, please also bear in mind that this is how I feed my family. Without reviews, without sales, I don't get to support my wife and darling daughters.

So now that I've shamelessly tugged on your heart strings, here's the link to leave the review:

Review Infernal Justice

Thank you in advance.

TEASER: BLOOD SUMMONED (ETHAN DRAKE # 2)

The darkness in the forest was absolute. Dense, dark clouds covered the moon, allowing not a chink of light to penetrate. The wind rustling through the tall trees and the ever-present chorus of crickets and owls had been a constant for the last two days now.

That and the sound of Haedemus' voice, which hardly ceased, despite how many times I'd told him to put a fucking sock in it.

Didn't he ever go hunting in Hell? I asked him, to which he replied, of course he did, but added that it didn't matter about staying quiet because there was usually nowhere for the victim to run, and most prey in Hell didn't bother running anyway out of pure apathy.

"Though I must say, Ethan," Haedemus said as I rode him through the forest, weaving in and out of trees, his step assured on the sometimes steep and rocky slopes. "This little trip has been enjoyable so far. It's been a nice change of scenery from that dreary city you call home. Although, this place does remind me of the Suicide Forest in Hell, only without all the self-harmers everywhere and their sad faces. Fuck, how I hated those suicidal bastards and their pathetic attempts at killing themselves, feeble attempts that were always doomed to complete failure. I mean, as soon as they died they just came right back again, always with the same look of despair on their stupid human baby-faces."

"Like the look on my face," I said. "From having to listen to you this whole fucking time."

"Admit it," he said. "You enjoy my company, don't you? Why else would you take me along?"

"As I already told you, you're just a means of transportation. I thought it would be easier than walking."

Haedemus snorted. "Whatever, big guy. You can't hide your feelings from me. I can feel us getting closer with every step."

"Yeah, we're a real walking, talking buddy movie you and I."

"Your sarcasm is not lost on me, Ethan," he said. "And neither is your ironic use of the term 'buddy movie'. I know what a buddy movie is, you know."

"Do they have a cineplex in Hell? I never knew."

"No, but thanks to many, *many* damned souls and their continued obsession with pop culture, I was able to glean the finer plot points of many movies. They sound fun, I have to say. Maybe we could watch one when we get back from finding this person you're after out here."

"Sure," I said, keeping my focus on my surroundings. "I'll bring the popcorn."

"Fuck off, Ethan," he said, a sour tone to his voice. "You don't have to ridicule *everything* I say, you know."

"Why not?"

Haedemus snorted. "Your mother must be so proud of you, Ethan."

"My mother's dead."

"Lucky for her then she doesn't have to see what a bitter cunt her son has become."

Giving his mane a sharp tug, I said, "Watch it."

"Oh, hit a nerve have I? I enjoy hitting your nerves, Ethan. I get a special pleasure from—"

"Quiet," I hissed, pulling him to a stop.

"Don't try to silence me into submission. It won't—"

"I heard something, asshole. Shut it a minute."

Off to the left, I'd heard a cracking sound like a branch breaking underfoot. Blinking rapidly three times, I activated the infrared vision chip implanted in my cornea and began to scan the forest for signs of life. Small animals glowed bright red and orange in the distance, but nothing larger.

"It's those damn Faeries again," Haedemus said, his voice quieter. "They're just being nosey little bastards, as they are wont to do. I remember them from my mortal life. Most of them are harmless, if highly annoying. Thankfully, Hell's gates are barred to them."

I had to admit, I had little experience with Fae. Out of all the MURKs, the Fae kept to themselves the most, the more powerful of them choosing to remain in Faerie most of the time, where they had their own way of life and political system in the form of the Courts.

The Wyldefae—the little fuckers who'd been following us since entering the forest—spent most of their time here in the mortal world. As Haedemus said, most of them are harmless, but some of them grow to be large and powerful beasts who use their size and strength to feed their appetite for human prey.

It was these fuckers I was concerned about here in the depths of the forest, but as I continued to scan the area in infrared, I saw nothing larger than a deer in the far distance.

"Ride on," I told Haedemus after I'd finished scanning the area.

"Ride on, he says." Haedemus craned his neck to look at me. "Where to exactly? This woody nightmare is fucking never-ending."

"You said you were enjoying it a minute ago."

"I was until I realized I was hungry and horny. Now I'm miserable."

"Can't you munch on a squirrel for now? Maybe fuck a deer?"

"Fuck a deer, Ethan? Is that supposed to be funny? I don't fuck deer."

"I forgot you only fucked dying men."

"I'll fuck you in a minute, Ethan, if your cheek continues, you with your backpack full of provisions. You didn't even think to bring me a nice liver or kidney to snack on out here, did you?" He shook his head and whinnied. "No, you didn't, because Ethan is a selfish bastard who only cares about himself."

"You want a Snickers bar?"

"No, I don't want a fucking Snickers bar, Ethan. Shove your Snicker's bar up your—" He stopped talking as he raised his head, his jagged ears pricking.

"What is it?" I asked him.

"Magic, I think."

"Faerie magic?"

"No. Magic cast by a human."

I stared off into the dark woods as I considered the significance of Haedemus' discovery. If someone was casting magic this far in the forest, it had to be someone who lived here.

Someone like Scarlet Hood.

"Where's the magic centered?" I asked Haedemus.

"It's faint at this distance," he said. "Maybe a mile or two away."

"Any idea what kind of magic? Is it defensive?"

"Hard to tell at this distance. I'll know better when we get closer."

We rode farther into the dark forest, what little light there now was from the waning moon seeming to diminish as the trees grew closer together and the undergrowth got thicker.

"Take it slow," I said to Haedemus, my voice hushed. "We don't know what we're walking into."

"Maybe you should summon your Hellbastards to scout ahead, though I'd prefer it if you didn't." He veered right to get past a dense thicket of trees, taking us onto a slight slope that was dotted with large boulders. "I never told you this, but the smallest one—"

"Cracka."

"Yes, him, he kept asking me to show him my penis while I waited outside your building. He was vulgar. I don't know how you put up with them."

"You get used to them."

"I always hated Hellbastards. They're Hell's equivalent of annoying children, only worse. They try to fuck everything, and if they can't fuck it, they eat it instead."

"Sounds like someone else I know."

"Piss off, Ethan. You humans think you're so superior, when you are all just as bad as—"

"Wait."

"What?" He came to a stop at the brow of the slope. "Ah, I see."

At the bottom of the slope was a large clearing, and in the clearing was a small cottage with a thatched roof. The ground around the whitewashed cottage was flat and well-tended, covered with short grass and all kinds of wildflowers. Around the side of the dwelling, I could make out that the tilled ground and the shadowy outlines of the herbs and vegetables growing in it.

I got down off Haedemus and crouched on top of the hill, taking the high-powered rifle from around me and sighting through the infrared scope so I could get a better look at the cottage. There were no lights on, and no smoke coming from the chimney either. "Doesn't look like anyone's home."

"The whole place is warded with magic," Haedemus said. "I'm not sure I can go near it."

"I can."

"You're going down there?"

"What do you think we're doing here? I didn't just come to sightsee."

"She might be waiting for you. I'd be surprised if she didn't know you were here."

"If she's here at all."

I sighted through the scope again, checking out the small windows at the front of the cottage. Nothing moved behind the glass. "Can you sense anyone?"

"No," Haedemus said. "But that doesn't mean Miss Hood isn't here somewhere. She's probably watching us now from a distance. If she's as good as you say, she probably knew we were coming miles back."

"Then why aren't we dead?"

"I'm already dead."

"Why aren't I dead then?"

"Maybe she's just watching, waiting for you to enter her kill zone. Honestly, Ethan, if this woman is as dangerous as you say, I don't know why you're even here."

"I didn't know you cared," I said, still staring down at the cottage.

"I don't. I'm just saying. Anyone would think you had a death wish."

Placing the rifle on the ground, I stood and took out the SIG Sauer P226 pistol I had with me. "She's not here."

"How do you know?" Haedemus said.

"I'd probably be dead now if she was."

"Like I said, a death wish."

"Stay here. I'm going down for a look around."

"What for? You said she isn't here?"

"Just wait here. I'll be back."

"Don't expect me to follow you to Hell if you die," he called after me in a hushed voice. "Because I won't."

Ignoring him, I made my way down the slope to the clearing, staying low and keeping to cover as much as possible, finally crouching by a juniper bush as I stared over at the cottage.

There was a chance Scarlet Hood was inside, but I doubted it. Living in the forest as she did, I'd be surprised if she didn't have a deal going with the Faeries. They would've let her know about Haedemus and me long before now. That being the case, Hood probably would've ambushed us by now, if not killed us outright from a distance.

If I was right about her, though, she wouldn't kill without talking first. I didn't think she was the monster people made her out to be. She may have been a professional assassin, but she would want to know why I was here before she squeezed any trigger. She would want to know who sent me first. That's why I wasn't too worried about getting killed out here.

Besides, despite the deal I had with Carlito, I wasn't here to kill Scarlet Hood.

I was here to talk.

Making my way around the back of the cottage, I stopped to point my gun at one of half a dozen shadowy figures standing by the edge of the trees, realizing a second later that the figures were dummies carved from wood, put there for target practice I was sure.

There was a rope swing attached to an overhanging branch, which prompted a memory to flash through my mind. A memory of Callie on the tree-swing I made for her only last year, out the back of the house in Crown Point. For a moment, her smiling face was clear as day in my mind as she squealed her delight when I pushed her high into the air, Angela standing by the back door warning me not to push too high.

Sighing, I turned away from the rope-swing just as my Infernal Itch flared up without warning. "What the hell?" I muttered as the tattoos on my arms and back began to swirl madly under my skin, their extreme agitation signaling that danger was imminent.

Looking around, I thought perhaps that one of the bigger Faeries had followed me here and was preparing to ambush me, but after switching to infrared vision, I saw nothing in the surrounding forest.

It was only when I turned around again did I see the grassy earth a few feet away break up and get pushed out as if something was about to emerge from the ground.

"What the fuck is this?" I said, stepping back, my gun pointing at the broken earth, just as a massive hand burst out of the ground, clawed fingers stretching until most of an arm appeared. An arm covered in coarse hair by the looks of it.

"Uh, Ethan?" Haedemus called from the top of the slope. "You might want to come back up here."

Moving quickly around to the front of the cottage again, I got there just in time to see an enormous head burst from the earth, yellow eyes glaring at me as the monster peeled back its rotten lips to reveal a pair of huge incisors.

All around, monsters were bursting free from the earth, climbing out of their underground tombs with the express purpose of ripping me asunder.

The few that were free stood on thick hind legs and howled into the night, making me realize I was looking at werewolves.

Undead fucking werewolves.

~

Get your copy of BLOOD SUMMONED online now!

TEASER: BLOOD MAGIC (WIZARD'S CREED # 1)

When the magic hit, I was knocked to the floor like I'd taken a hard-right hook to the jaw. The spell was so powerful, it blew through my every defense. For all my wards and the good they did me, I might as well have been a Sleepwalker with no protection at all.

The faint smell of decayed flesh mixed with sulfur hung thick in the air, a sure sign that dark magic had just been used, which in my experience, was never good. Coming across dark magic is a bit like turning up at a children's party to find Beelzebub in attendance, a shit-eating grin on his face as he tied balloon animals for the terrified kids. It's highly disturbing.

I sat dazed on the floor, blinking around me for a moment. My mind was fuzzy and partially frozen, as though I'd awakened from a nightmare. I was inside an abandoned office space, the expansive rectangular room lined with grimy, broken windows that let cold air in to draw me out of my daze. Darkness coated the room, the only real light coming from the moon outside as it beamed its pale, silvery light through the smashed skylights.

I struggled back to my feet and blindly reached for the

pistol inside my dark green trench coat, frowning when I realized the gun wasn't there. Then I remembered it had gone flying out of my hand when the spell had hit. Looking around, I soon located the pistol lying on the floor several feet away, and I lurched over and grabbed it, slightly more secure now that the gun's reassuring weight was back in my hand.

There were disturbing holes in my memory. I recalled confronting someone after tracking them here. But who? I couldn't get a clear image. The person was no more than a shadow figure in my mind. I had no clue as to why I was following this person unknown in the first place. Obviously, they had done something to get on my radar. The question was what, though?

The answer came a few seconds later when my eyes fell upon the dark shape in the middle of the room, and a deep sense of dread filled me; a dread that was both familiar and sickening at the same time, for I knew what I was about to find. Swallowing, I stared hard through the gloom at the human shape lying lifelessly on the debris-covered floor. Over the sharp scent of rats piss and pigeon shit, the heavy, festering stench of blood hit my nostrils without mercy.

When I crossed to the center of the room, my initial fears were confirmed when I saw that it was a dead body lying on the floor. A young woman with her throat slit. Glyphs were carved into the naked flesh of her spread-eagled body, with ropes leading from her wrists and ankles to rusty metal spikes hammered into the floor. I marveled at the force required to drive the nails into the concrete, knowing full well that a hammer had nothing to do with it.

Along the circumference of a magic circle painted around the victim was what looked like blood-drawn glyphs. The sheer detail of them unnerved me as I observed in them a certain quality that could only have come from a well-practiced hand.

I breathed out as I reluctantly took in the callous butchery on display. The dead woman looked to be in her early thirties, though it was difficult to tell because both her eyes were missing; cut out with the knife used to slice her throat, no doubt. I shook my head as I looked around in a vain effort to locate the dead woman's eyeballs.

The woman looked underweight for her size. She was around the same height as me at six feet, but there was very little meat on her bones, as if she was a stranger to regular meals. I also noted the needle marks on her feet, and the bruises around her thighs. This, coupled with how she had been dressed—in a leather mini skirt and short top, both items discarded on the floor nearby—made me almost certain the woman had been a prostitute. A convenient, easy victim for whoever had killed her.

If the symbols carved into her pale flesh were anything to go by, it would seem the woman had been ritually sacrificed. At a guess, I would have said she was an offering to one of the Dimension Lords, which the glyphs seemed to point to. The glyphs themselves weren't only complex, but also carved with surgical precision. The clarity of the symbols against the woman's pale flesh made it possible for me to make out certain ones that I recognized as being signifiers to alternate dimensions, though which dimension exactly, I couldn't be sure, at least not until I had studied the glyphs further. Glyphs such as the ones I was looking at were always uniquely different in some way. No two people drew glyphs the same, with each person etching their own personality into every one, which can often make it hard to work out their precise meanings. One thing I could be certain of was that the glyphs carved into the woman's body resonated only evil intent; an intent so strong, I felt it in my gut, gnawing at me like a parasite seeking access to my insides, as if drawn to my magic power. Not a pleasant feeling, but I was used to it, having been exposed to enough dark magic in my time.

After taking in the scene, I soon came to the conclusion

that the woman wasn't the killer's first victim; not by a long stretch, given the precision and clear competency of the work on display.

"Son of a bitch," I said, annoyed. I couldn't recall any details about the case I had so obviously been working on. It was no coincidence that I had ended up where I was, a place that happened to reek of dark magic, and which housed a murder that had occult written all over it. I'd been on the hunt, and I had gotten close to the killer, which was the likeliest reason for the dark magic booby trap I happened to carelessly spring like some bloody rookie.

Whoever the killer was, they wielded powerful magic. A spell that managed to wipe all my memories of the person in question wouldn't have been an easy one to create. And given the depth of power to their magic, it also felt to me like they had channeled it from some other source, most likely from whatever Dimension Lord they were sacrificing people to.

Whatever the case, the killer's spell had worked. Getting back the memories they had stolen from me wouldn't be easy, and that's if I could get them back at all, which I feared might just be the case.

After shaking my head at how messed up the situation was, I froze upon hearing a commanding voice booming in the room like thunder.

"Don't move, motherfucker!"

~

Get your copy of BLOOD MAGIC online today!

~

TEASER: SERPENT SON (GODS AND MONSTERS TRILOGY BOOK 1)

They knew I was back, for someone had been tailing me for the last half hour. As I walked along Lower Ormond Quay with the River Liffey flowing to the right of me, I pretended not to notice my stalker. I'd only just arrived back in Dublin after a stay in London, and I was in no mood for confrontation.

I was picking up on goblin vibes, but I couldn't be sure until I laid eyes on the cretin. The wiry little bastards were sneaky and good at blending in unseen.

As I moved down a deserted side street, hoping my pursuer would follow me, I weighed my options. There were several spells I could use: I could create a doorway in one of the walls next to me and disappear into the building; or I could turn myself into vapor and disappear; or I could even levitate up to the roof of one of the nearby buildings and escape.

Truthfully though, I didn't like using magic in broad daylight, even if there was no one around. Hell, I hardly used magic at all, despite being gifted with a connection to the Void—the source of all magic—just like every other Touched being in the world.

Despite my abilities, though, I was no wizard. I was just a musician who preferred to make magic through playing the guitar; real magic that touched the soul of the listener. Not the often destructive magic generated by the Void.

Still, Void magic could come in handy sometimes, like now as I spun around suddenly and said the word, "*Impedio!*" I felt the power of the Void flow through me as I spoke. But looking down the street, there appeared to be no one there.

Only I knew there was.

I hurried back down the street and then stopped by a dumpster on the side of the road. Crouching behind the dumpster was a small, wiry individual with dark hair and pinched features. He appeared frozen as he glared up at me, thanks to the spell I had used to stop him in his tracks, preventing him from even moving a muscle until I released him.

"Let me guess," I said. "Iolas got wind I was coming back, so he sent you to what...follow me? Maybe kill me, like he had my mother killed?"

Anger threatened to rise in me as blue magic sparked across my hand. Eight words, that's all it would take to kill the frozen goblin in front of me, to shut down his life support system and render him dead in an instant. It would've been so easy to do, but I wasn't a killer...at least not yet.

The goblin strained against the spell I still held him in, hardly able to move a muscle. To an ordinary eye, the goblin appeared mundane, just a small, rakish man in his thirties with thinning hair and dark eyes that appeared to be too big for his face. To my Touched eye, however, I could see the goblin creature for what he was underneath the glamor he used to conceal his true form, which to be honest, wasn't that far away from the mundane form he presented to the world. His eyes were bigger and darker, his mouth wider and full of thin pointed teeth that jutted out at all angles, barely concealed by lips like two strips of thick rubber. His skin was also paler, and his ears large and pointed.

"I don't know what you're talking about," the goblin said when I released him from the spell. He stood up straight, his head barely level with my chest. "I'm just out for a stroll on this fine summer evening, or at least I was before you accosted me like you did..."

I shook my head in disgust. What did I expect anyway, a full rundown of his orders from Iolas? Of course he was going to play dumb because he *was* dumb. He knew nothing, except that he had to follow me and report on my whereabouts. Iolas being the paranoid wanker that he was, would want eyes on me the whole time now that I was back in town. Or at least until he could decide what to do with me.

"All right, asshole," I said as magic crackled in my hand, making the cocky goblin rather nervous, his huge eyes constantly flitting from my face to the magic in my hand. "Before you fuck off out of it, make sure Iolas gets this message, will you? Tell that stuck up elf...tell him..."

The goblin frowned, his dark eyes staring into me. "Go on, tell Iolas what?" He was goading me, the sneaky little shit. "That you're coming for him? That you will kill him for supposedly snuffing out your witch-bitch mother—"

Rage erupted in me, and before the goblin could say another filthy word, I conjured my magic, thrusting my light-filled hand toward him while shouting the words, "*Ignem exquiris!*"

In an instant, a fireball about the size of a baseball exploded from my hand and hit the goblin square in the chest, the force of it slamming him back against the wall, the flames setting his clothes alight.

"*Dholec maach*!" the goblin screamed as he frantically slapped at his clothes to put the flames out.

"What were you saying again?" I cocked my head mockingly at him as if waiting for an answer.

"*Dhon ogaach*!" The goblin tore off his burning jacket and tossed it to the ground, then put out the remaining flames still licking at his linen shirt. The smell of burned fabric and roasted goblin skin now permeated the balmy air surrounding us.

"Yeah? You go fuck yourself as well after you've apologized for insulting my mother."

The goblin snarled at me as he stood quivering with rage and shock. "You won't last a day here, wizard! Iolas will have you fed to the vamps!"

I shot forward and grabbed the goblin by the throat, thrusting him against the wall. "First, I'm a musician, not a wizard, and secondly—" I had to turn my head away for a second, my nostrils assaulted by the atrocious stench of burnt goblin flesh. "Second, I'm not afraid of your elfin boss, or his vamp mates."

Struggling to speak with my hand still around his throat, the goblin said in a strangled voice, "Is that why…you ran away…like a…little bitch?"

I glared at the goblin for another second and then let him go, taking a step back as he slid down the wall. His black eyes were still full of defiance, and I almost admired his tenacity.

"I've listened to enough of your shit, goblin," I said, forcing my anger down. "Turn on your heels and get the hell out of here, before I incinerate you altogether." I held my hand up to show him the flames that danced in my palm, eliciting a fearful look from him. "Go!"

The goblin didn't need to be told twice. He pushed off the wall and scurried down the street, stopping after ten yards to turn around.

"You've signed your own death warrant coming back here, Chance," he shouted. "Iolas will have your head mounted above his fireplace!" His lips peeled back as he formed a rictus grin, then he turned around and ran, disappearing around the corner a moment later.

"Son of a bitch," I muttered as I stood shaking my head.

Maybe it was a mistake coming back here, I thought.

I should've stayed in London, played gigs every night, maybe headed to Europe or the States, Japan even. Instead, I came back to Ireland to tear open old wounds…and unavoidably, to make new ones.

Shaking my head once more at the way things were going already, I grabbed my guitar and luggage bag and headed toward where I used to live before my life was turned upside down two months ago.

As I walked up the Quay alongside the turgid river, I took a moment to take in my surroundings. It was a balmy summer evening, and the city appeared to be in a laid-back mood as people walked around in their flimsy summer clothes, enjoying the weather, knowing it could revert to dull and overcast at any time, as the Irish weather is apt to do. Despite my earlier reservations, it felt good to be back. While I enjoyed London (as much as I could while mourning the death of my mother), Dublin was my home and always had been. I felt a connection to the land here that I felt nowhere else, and I'd been to plenty of other places around the world.

Still, I hadn't expected Iolas to be on me so soon. He had all but banished me from the city when I accused him of orchestrating my mother's murder. He was no doubt pissed when he heard I was coming back.

Fuck him, I thought as I neared my destination. *If he thinks I will allow him to get away with murder, he's mistaken.*

Just ahead of me was *Chance's Bookstore*—the shop my mother opened over three decades ago, and which now belonged to me, along with the apartment above it. It was a medium-sized store with dark green wood paneling and a quaint feel to it. It was also one of the oldest remaining independent bookstores in the city, and the only one that dealt with rare occult books. Because of this, the store attracted a lot of Untouched with an interest in all things occult and magical. It also attracted its fair share of Touched, who knew the store as a place to go acquire hard to find books on magic or some aspect of the occult. My mother, before she was killed, had formed contacts all over the world, and there was hardly a book she wasn't able to get her hands on if someone requested it, for a price, of course.

As I stood a moment in front of the shop, my mind awash with painful memories, I glanced at my reflection in the window, seeing a disheveled imposter standing there in need of a shave and a haircut, and probably also a change of clothes, my favorite dark jeans and waistcoat having hardly been off me in two months.

Looking away from my reflection, I opened the door to the shop and stepped inside, locking it behind me again. The smell of old paper and leather surrounded me immediately, soliciting more painful memories as images of my mother flashed through my mind. After closing my eyes for a second, I moved into the shop, every square inch of the place deeply familiar to me, connected to memories that threatened to come at me all at once.

Until they were interrupted that is, by a mass of swirling darkness near the back of the shop, out of which an equally dark figure emerged, two slightly glowing eyes glaring at me.

Then, before I could muster any magic or even say a word of surprise, the darkness surrounding the figure lashed out, hitting me so hard across the face I thought my jaw had broken, and I went reeling back, cursing the gods for having it in for me today.

Welcome home, Corvin, I thought as I stood seeing stars. *Welcome bloody home…*

~

Get your copy of SERPENT SON online today!

BOOKS BY N. P. MARTIN

Ethan Drake Series

INFERNAL JUSTICE
BLOOD SUMMONED
DEATH DEALERS

Gods And Monsters Trilogy

SERPENT SON
DARK SON
RISING SON

Wizard's Creed Series

CRIMSON CROW
BLOOD MAGIC
BLOOD DEBT
BLOOD CULT
BLOOD DEMON

Nephilim Rising Series

BOOKS BY N. P. MARTIN

HUNTER'S LEGACY
DEMON'S LEGACY
HELL'S LEGACY
DEVIL'S LEGACY

ABOUT THE AUTHOR

I'm Neal Martin and I'm a lover of dark fantasy and horror. Writing stories about magic, the occult, monsters and kickass characters has always been my idea of a dream job, and these days, I get to live that dream. I have tried many things in my life (professional martial arts instructor, bouncer, plasterer, salesman…to name a few), but only the writing hat seems to fit. When I'm not writing, I'm spending time with my wife and daughters at our home in Northern Ireland.

Be sure to sign up to my mailing list:
readerlinks.com/l/663790/nl
And say hi on social media…

Printed in Great Britain
by Amazon

41310668R00180